Totally Bound Publishing books by Jane Davitt:

Anthologies
Fabulous Brits: Bound Together
Master Me: Fresh Start

Totally Five Star
Life Under New Management

I0598559

Totally Five Star:
Vancouver

LIFE UNDER NEW
MANAGEMENT

JANE DAVITT

Life Under New Management
ISBN # 978-1-78430-509-3
©Copyright Jane Davitt 2015
Cover Art by Posh Gosh ©Copyright Month 2015
Interior text design by Claire Siemaszkiewicz
Totally Bound Publishing

Published in 2015 by Totally Bound Publishing, Newland House, The Point, Weaver Road, Lincoln, LN6 3QN, United Kingdom.

Totally Bound Publishing is a subsidiary of Totally Entwined Group Limited.

LIFE UNDER NEW MANAGEMENT

Dedication

To Amy, as always, for being a truly supportive friend
and constant inspiration.

Chapter One

And if he chance to speak, be ready straight,
And with a low submissive reverence
Say, 'What is it your honour will command?'
– The Taming of the Shrew, Shakespeare

"Tell me why you think I should hire you, Mr. Naylor."

Andy directed another winning smile at the man behind the desk. Ethan Mason hadn't responded to the last three, but maybe they were chipping away at the ice – ice that had formed when he'd told Ethan to call him Andy then solidified after the confession that most of his experience of bars had been as a customer.

"I'm a hard worker." If he was doing something interesting. "Reliable." Up to a point. "Good with people." True. "I invented a cocktail once." Then drank so many of them, he'd forgotten the ingredients. Puked up around three in the morning. It had been a nasty mess.

Ethan pushed back his heavy wooden chair – no padding for this guy – and stood. Not an overly tall man, no obvious muscles bulging underneath the dark gray suit, but Andy guessed Ethan could break up a bar fight if needed without ruffling his smooth, dark hair. Cool guy. Ice-cool. And now 'ice, ice, baby' was stuck in his head in a retro hip-hop loop-de-loop, and shit, he *needed* this job. His rent was due. His place was a crappy dump, but this was Vancouver and even shoebox-sized rooms without a view of the water or the mountains—which took some doing—weren't cheap. He hadn't heard back about the dog food commercial yet, but something told him he hadn't gotten the part—the something being his main competition emerging from the final interview with lips barely dry from giving a blow job. No jizz streaking his chin, but that smug, used look was unmistakable. Andy had seen it in a mirror often enough, but he sucked cocks for pleasure, not to get a job. When he got his first major role—and he would, anytime soon—it would be down to his acting talent and nothing else.

His determination was wearing thin after a few years of bit parts that went nowhere, but he patched it when needed.

"Show me," Ethan said and left his office without looking back.

Andy chewed the inside of his cheek—a bad habit he had to stop—and followed him. They walked along a hallway with doors opening off it—storeroom, break room, cleaning supplies, the paintwork clean, the black and white floor tiles freshly mopped. Even behind the scenes, the Totally Five Star Hotel lived up to its name. The corridor led to a swinging door with a narrow glass panel set in it, allowing safe passage in either direction.

Behind the door was a bar, although not the main one for the hotel. Andy had seen that on the way in, impressed by the muted elegance of the place, all gleaming brass and dark green carpet, the swoop of the counter drawing attention to the glitter of glasses and bottles behind it. This was a smaller lounge— clean, severe lines, a black granite surface shimmering in the overhead lights as if it was liquid instead of solid enough to resist the blade of a knife, the walls painted bronze. Upmarket but still welcoming. At eight-thirty in the morning, it was empty.

Ethan kept going, opening a gate to give him access to the room. He took a seat on a stool with a curved back. Did that make it a chair or did they need four legs? Andy wasn't about to ask.

Ethan tapped the bar. "Make me your cocktail. And without getting tacky—we don't twirl bottles here— give me something to look at."

"Huh?" Andy's tie made his blue eyes a shade darker, but it had clearly developed a new ability of tightening at crucial moments, throttling the wearer. He couldn't breathe. He was a performer, for God's sake. What was wrong with him? He'd always excelled at improv sessions, even when the audience was hostile or unreceptive, and Ethan was neither of those. More like a teacher with a disappointing student, waiting for the correct answer and sure it wouldn't be forthcoming.

"I'm a customer in a classy cocktail bar. I'm about to pay fifteen dollars for a fancy drink with an improbable name from an attractive young man." Ethan's mouth twitched. Not a smile. More of a pained grimace. "Give me my money's worth, Mr. Naylor. Charm me, so the tip I leave is a generous one."

Andy eased the knot on the tie and gave Ethan smile number four—or five. He'd lost count. "Sure thing."

Ethan's gray eyes hardened and he raised an eyebrow. "Excuse me?"

"Yes, sir?" Andy hazarded.

"Better."

If he got the job—and it wasn't looking likely—he hoped this guy stayed in his office and delegated. Working under that chilled-steel glare was going to rack up the breakages. His hands sweating, he turned to survey the bottles. They weren't in any order he could see, not at first, and his gaze darted from bottle to shakers, swizzle sticks to frankly scary implements whose purpose he could only guess at. He'd never realized how much stuff there was back here.

"You said on your application you'd worked behind a bar before."

"Yes, true, I did, I—" For ten minutes. As a favor to his friend, Paula, who'd been called away to sign for a delivery with no one else around to take over. He'd flirted for six of the ten minutes and mixed a vodka and coke that was supposed to be a double but had been a quadruple by the time he'd worked out how to get the upside down bottle to release a full measure.

Ethan stood, hand slashing through the air, a dismissive gesture that stung like an actual blow. "You're wasting my time."

"I'm not! Look, let me—" Andy snatched up a martini glass. He turned, setting it down, then lifting it again and grabbing a cocktail napkin to go under it, emblazoned with the hotel's logo. "You look like a man in the mood for something smooth and sophisticated."

"Is that so?" A flat growl, but Ethan sat again then crossed one leg over the other, the impeccably pressed trousers he wore pulling taut across his thigh.

Cocktail shaker. Take off the lid. Scoop up some ice. *God, the metal of the shaker got cold fast.* Andy threw a grin over his shoulder, toning down his inner slut before he added a wiggle of his ass. "Trust me, sir. It's my job to know what my customers need."

Calling Ethan sir felt wickedly good, as if he was getting away with something, flirting without anyone knowing. Where the fuck had that come from? He was used to examining his motivations when he was playing a role, not so much when it came to himself. Andy shoved the question aside to think about later or better yet, forget. Now what the hell had he put in that drink? Vodka. Yeah. A cheap Polish one had been on sale at the liquor store and he'd bought two bottles for the party.

He picked up a bottle of Grey Goose and sloshed some into the shaker, shielding what he did from Ethan's view because he was probably supposed to measure it. What else? Cointreau had been involved, the screw top sticky with crystalized sugar, hard to open since no one had used it in months. The bottle behind this bar opened smoothly, the neck clean. He added a slug of the liqueur and a quick shot of club soda from the gun then put the top on the shaker.

Turning back to Ethan, he began a brisk shake, the rattle and swoosh of the ice sounding reassuringly professional. He had the common sense to hold the top. Showering his prospective boss with freezing liquid would leave him without a job and probably barred from the hotel for life. When condensation clouded the outside of the shaker, he removed the top with a flourish, poured the drink into the glass then looked around for a garnish.

"The fruit for the drinks is sliced shortly before opening," Ethan said, reading his intention but with luck, not his mind. "What would you have used?"

"Orange," Andy said promptly. "No sense trying to fight the Cointreau."

"Hmm."

Ethan raised the glass to the light, studying it. The clear liquid held a silvery glow. It wasn't fancy, but something told him Ethan wasn't a fan of complicated. "What do you call it?"

Since 'damned if I know' wasn't going to cut it, Andy shortened his late grandmother's favorite saying about necessity being the mother of invention to one word.

"It's a Necessity."

Ethan took a sip, then another, before pushing the glass away. "Make it again, this time using lemonade. The real stuff. There's some in the fridge over there."

"Yes, sir." It slipped out naturally this time, drawn from him by the note of authority in Ethan's voice.

Ethan tasted the new version, rolling the liquid around like mouthwash, though he didn't spit it out. After swallowing, he pursed his lips. "Okay, it's basic but it's not bad."

"I've got the job?"

Ethan snorted. "No. You got a compliment you barely deserved on a drink that's halfway to being a real cocktail. You never stood a chance with the job, not once the lies on your application outnumbered my thumbs. I would've let you get away with shining up your experience, but you can't polish thin air. You've wasted my time. The door's over there, eh?"

"Wait!" Andy's hands were cold now, disappointment and nerves shredding his optimism. "I *need* this job."

"Were you telling the truth about the acting degree from UBC?"

"Yes!" His indignation made the word echo off the walls. He took out his wallet. "My student card's in here somewhere." He needed to clear out his wallet. Along with his single credit card, close to maxed out, were expired vouchers for free coffee, receipts and cinema tickets.

"Don't bother. I can tell when you're lying and that sounded true. So you're a wannabe actor looking for a job until he gets offered a starring role?"

Yes, but admitting it would guarantee he was shown the door. Time to test Ethan's lie detector skills with a half-truth. "Three years ago, yes. Now I'm a guy who's been to more auditions than there are bottles in this bar and I know it's not going to happen. I need to pay my rent and I'm not fussy about how I do it."

"Even if it's bar work?" Ethan asked.

Had his eyelid drooped in a wink?

"We both know that a trained monkey can mix drinks, smile and make change, right?"

Andy laughed, relaxing with Ethan as if their moods were magically linked. "I guess."

Ethan slapped the bar, a flat, uncompromising smack, making Andy jump like a hooked fish. "Wrong. And with an attitude like that, good luck getting any job. Bartending's not rocket science, but people take courses in it. Get trained. For a place with a reputation to uphold, it's mandatory. You're not good enough to work here. Aside from a pretty face, name one skill you have that would interest me."

Ethan thought he was pretty? Well, he was—no doubt about it—but straight guys didn't notice shit like that. Not proof Ethan was gay, but a definite pointer. It didn't matter to Andy, of course. Ethan probably had a sophisticated boyfriend waiting for him when he got home. He was too tightly wound to be Andy's type anyway. Though de-icing the guy would be a fun challenge. Hmm. What was underneath the stern disapproval? A molten center or a lake of beige?

Time to get on his knees, metaphorically at least.

"I can learn." The words poured out—pleading, begging words. "I can learn fast. Show me once and it's all I need."

For a moment, he saw something in Ethan's eyes. Interest, heat, as if his words had pushed a big red button inside Ethan's head where dark fantasies lurked. And that was what getting up early did to you. Hallucinations. Random acts of insanity. He blinked and Ethan looked indifferent again.

"Save the theatrics. Though if that's the best you can do, I can see why you're looking for a job."

Ouch. And fuck you, *sir*.

"I want staff I don't need to train," Ethan continued. "This is a hotel, not a college."

Speaking quickly before Ethan walked away, Andy said, "You told me the job's open in two weeks when someone starts her maternity leave."

"Amanda in ten days. So?"

"In ten days—no, in one week—I can learn everything I need. I'll hit the library and get a friend who works the bar at a club to coach me. See me again in a week and I'll prove I'm worth taking a chance on."

Ethan studied him. "You *are* desperate."

Andy ran his hand through his shaggy hair, back to its natural dirty blond after highlighting had wrecked its condition. "Yeah, eviction and impending starvation do that to a guy."

"And you've got quite the mouth on you."

"So my dates tell me," Andy retorted with the recklessness of pure despair. Shit, he'd shaved, removed all his piercings and combed his hair into something resembling tidiness, though the wind had undone his efforts there. He'd made an *effort*, not to mention getting up at the ass crack of dawn to be here at eight. He deserved more than a flat rejection and a few insults.

"I think you'll find my standards are more exacting than theirs."

A rush of arousal swept through him, the source startling him. Andy lived in a perpetual state of horniness. He liked sex—liked it a lot. A week without anything except his hand and the vibrating butt plug he'd got for his birthday as a gag gift, and he was whimpering. Not that a week between encounters happened often. Shit, turned on by a block of ice and a sneer, though? Something wrong there. Ethan wasn't like his usual hookups. Older. Most definitely not a party animal. Strict. Andy went for men his age and they passed into his life then out with a smile and a wave. He preferred it that way. Ethan didn't seem the one-night stand kind of guy. And yet he was making Andy's libido break into a tango even with the implication that Andy wasn't good enough for him.

Or because of it.

"I want this position filled today." Ethan tapped his finger against the bar slowly, a rhythmic drumming.

Outside the room, the hotel was busy, people checking out or ordering breakfast in the huge dining room. The night before, Andy had looked up the hotel online. The food on offer throughout the day sounded delicious. If he stayed here—not that he could afford it—he'd splash out on the breakfast buffet, even if it did cost thirty-five bucks. Mimosas, eggs Benedict, omelets, smoothies blended to order...sure beat the chopped up melon and stale pastries most places offered for the same price.

"I leave for a conference at noon and I won't get back in time to do any more interviews before Amanda leaves. You're the last applicant I've seen and in some ways the least qualified, but..."

"Yeah?" Andy prompted when Ethan drifted off, mouth screwed up in thought, forehead furrowed. "But?"

Ethan's attention snapped back to him and there it was again, that slow, relentless wash of need, leaving Andy's cock pressed uncomfortably between his stomach and the too-tight trousers of a suit he'd last worn at graduation. Auditions called for something more casual, mostly.

"Two of the applicants were overqualified." Ethan smiled thinly. "They were looking to replace me in time, I could tell, and that's not going to happen. I like it here." He glanced around, expression softening as if every sparkling glass, every square inch of spotless carpet, was down to him. "Another was arrogant—argumentative, even. Not the sort to take direction well."

"He was? I mean, he wasn't?" Arguing with Ethan? Now that took balls. And when it came to Ethan, Andy found himself prepared to follow all sorts of directions. Like 'get on your knees and rock my world, Andy'. It wouldn't be breaking his rules. Blowing Ethan would be pure pleasure. He was sure of it, though it was unlikely he'd ever verify his theory. Well, that was what jerk-off fantasies were for.

"She—and yes. The last one was barely able to speak above a whisper."

"You *are* kind of intimidating." Ethan had to know that already, but he couldn't help defending his fellow interviewee.

Ethan snorted. "You don't seem to think so. But you're useless. I'd sooner limp along short-staffed than fill the position with someone I'd end up firing by the end of the week."

"You wouldn't!" Andy spread his hands helplessly. "What can I do to make you give me a chance?"

Too late, he realized he'd stepped back far enough that if Ethan glanced down, he'd see Andy's erection, making his heartfelt plea look like offering sex for a job—and he wasn't. Wouldn't. Ever. Oh God, with Ethan sitting on the high stool, he'd have to kneel up to reach his cock, arch his neck to take Ethan deep, swallow carefully so not a drop fell on the expensive trousers, the crisp shirt. He coughed, breaking free of the fantasy.

Ethan's gaze stayed above Andy's waist. That was a good thing. Not a disappointment. "You said you could learn all you needed in a week."

Andy nodded, the vigorous up and down bob making his head ache. He'd drunk too much the night before, celebrating, sure he could charm his way into the job. He'd gotten the interview, but the job was frustratingly out of reach, with the wages that went along with it. "I've got a good memory. Give me a script and I'll have it down after—"

"You've got an hour." Ethan stood. "Stay in here and learn the layout. Then come to my office. I have a few books you can read. At the end of the hour, I'll test you. Pass, and you've got the job on a week's trial.

Fail and—well, I think we both know what happens then, right?"

"You kick my ass out the door."

Ethan wrinkled his nose as if the idea stank of skunk. "You walk out," he corrected. "Your ass is safe from me."

"But you're gay, right? Like me?" Andy asked. When would he stop blurting out what was in his head? It had cost him an audition once, and earned him a split lip another time.

Showing more mercy than Andy deserved, Ethan ignored that, pressing buttons on his watch until it beeped obediently. "One hour."

"You're *timing* me?" *Jesus, what a control freak.*

"Yes. When I say an hour, I mean sixty minutes." Ethan walked around to Andy's side of the bar and paused, speaking directly into Andy's ear—warm breath, not frosty at all. A faint whiff of expensive cologne, citrus-based, fresh and sharp, made Andy's mouth water. "You're wasting your time now. And if you think coming on to me will get you the job, you're *really* wasting your time."

Might as well dig the hole deeper and find out for sure. "Not gay?"

"Not interested."

Left alone, Andy exhaled and ran his hands through his hair again. He'd done everything wrong. Everything. And yet somehow he'd received a second chance.

Tick-freaking-tock.

He turned and surveyed the bottles. Time to memorize the order, then he could prowl around and see what went where. Ethan had made this a challenge and Andy had a competitive streak.

After ten minutes, he went back to Ethan's office, tapping on the door and getting flashbacks to unpleasant visits to the principal's office.

"In," Ethan called.

A man of few words.

Ethan wasn't alone. A petite woman, her stomach bulging to the point where giving birth seemed imminent, stood beside him. Amanda, had to be. She looked surprisingly relaxed around Ethan, her hand on the back of his chair, leaning over as much as her belly allowed.

"Over there." Ethan jerked his head at a chair in the corner of the room with two books, a notepad and a pencil on it. The chair had been in front of the desk for the interview. He checked his watch. "Forty-seven minutes."

"And how many seconds?" Andy asked, trying to sound politely curious, not sarcastic.

"None or I would've said. Forty-six minutes, fifty seconds now."

"Humor him." Amanda straightened. She rubbed the small of her back with both hands and groaned. "God, it's twins. I know it is."

"Not according to the scan," Ethan said. "I can handle the time sheets before I leave. Why don't you check on the kitchen? Beth wants someone to try an appetizer she's dreamed up and she says I'm useless."

"Why?" Andy asked, clearing the chair so he could sit. It wasn't comfortable but he could take it for forty-whatever minutes.

Ethan and Amanda exchanged glances, then Ethan gave a tiny shrug. "I don't think he's got an off switch. Or any concept of a private conversation."

"Hey!" Affronted, Andy dragged a small table closer with his foot then dumped everything onto it. "I get curious. I ask questions. It's not a crime."

"Depends on who you ask." Amanda caressed her baby bump, a gesture Andy guessed was routine by now, done as unthinkingly as breathing. "Kitchen. Food. On it, boss." She gave Andy a stern look. It didn't have the chilling effect of Ethan's, but Ethan didn't have a froth of red hair, green eyes and freckles to up his cuteness factor to eleven. "If you do get the job—"

"Doubtful," Ethan said, picking up a printout.

"You'd better not break my record."

Andy found himself glancing at Ethan for help.

"Most glasses smashed in her first week," Ethan told him. "If I remember correctly, a full tray, a swinging door and you talking on your cell phone were involved?"

"Good times. Did I mention I adore you for not firing me?" Amanda pointed at the books in front of Andy. "They won't help you with customers six-deep and dying of thirst. There's more to bar work than that."

"No, but my smile will." Andy bared his teeth at her and growled. "See?"

Ethan laughed, and, after rolling her eyes, Amanda left the room, waddling rather than walking. The laughter was probably an aural hallucination to go along with the visual one. When Andy got home, he was taking a nap.

"Cute." No traces of amusement showed now. "Want another time check or are you going to impress me by actually cracking open a book?"

"Book," Andy muttered. He grabbed the top one, discovering from the title that it promised to teach him the basics of cocktail mixing. Oh joy. He could find out how many mistakes he'd made mixing his drink for Ethan. The other was a small ring binder, looking like a handout from a course. When he abandoned the cocktail recipes and picked it up, that was exactly what it was. The binder presented information on setting up and running a bar logically and concisely, with sections covering everything from hygiene to stocktaking. Andy concentrated on what seemed to apply to him and skimmed through, blessing his ability to read fast and retain what he read. It had saved his ass often over the years.

Ethan worked quietly at his desk, paying no attention to Andy, but not in a marked way — more as if he'd forgotten Andy existed or knew he was there in the same way a man knew his dog or cat was in the room.

Andy peeked at Ethan, taking a break from an enthralling section on the care and maintenance of glassware. Short, dark hair, cut with military precision, high cheekbones, in a thin face... A quotation from a Shakespeare play popped into his head and he murmured it to himself, shaping the words without sound. "'Yond Cassius has a lean and hungry look.'"

Hungry for what?

"Time," Ethan announced, a fraction of a second before his watch beeped. "Time to impress me, that is."

"Uh, I'll try."

"Self-doubt and indecision. You're off to a good start." Ethan turned his chair so he faced Andy who sat tucked away in the corner. "Come here. Bring the chair."

Somewhat hesitantly, Andy set the chair down as directed. It put him close to Ethan. Not close enough their knees touched, but it wouldn't take much movement forward to make that happen. He danced at clubs surrounded by sweaty bodies, strangers crushed against him as intimately as lovers, so why sitting face to face with Ethan disturbed him, he didn't know. His face burned and his tongue became dry and thick.

Ethan studied him, taking in everything Andy couldn't hide, judging by the twitch of his mouth. "What did you think of the way the bottles are arranged?"

"Uh, it's good." Floundering already? Shit. Andy wet his lips, acutely conscious he was fidgeting, small, pointless shifts in position. "You've got the fancy stuff high up on the top shelf where people can see it and be tempted, but it's expensive, so it's safely out of the way. Then you have the basic ones handy in the...um...the speed rail. So that's—"

"How do they run, left to right?"

Andy closed his eyes for a moment, conjuring an image. "Tequila, scotch, bourbon, gin, vodka, rum."

"The sexiest bartenders get very rich."

Startled into laughing by the mnemonic, Andy relaxed, forgetting what had happened the last time he'd done that around Ethan. "Good one."

"I didn't invent it, so stop kissing my ass. What's muddling?"

And they were off again. The questions rained down on him, Ethan asking the next while Andy was still stammering out an answer to the previous one. He got his second wind and began to enjoy the verbal tussle, invigorated by the satisfaction lighting up Ethan's face when he got an answer right. If it had been the other way around and Ethan was gloating over his mistakes—and he made plenty—it wouldn't have been any fun.

"Okay." Ethan raised his hand, silencing Andy's explanation about why a good bartender never scooped ice with a glass. "You've convinced me you're a quick learner, but I'm still not sure you're up to it."

"Well, what does she do?"

"Who?"

Andy gestured at the door. "Amanda. Tell me what she does and I'll tell you if I can do it."

"You think you're replacing her?" Ethan shook his head slowly, clearly pitying Andy's abysmal ignorance. "Amanda's my assistant. She could run this place if she had to. You're starting at the bottom— collecting glasses, washing them, prepping the bar, keeping it supplied and running errands. You won't be serving or drink mixing for a while."

"Oh." Andy processed that. "So I'm everyone's butt monkey."

Ethan stared directly into his eyes, demanding Andy's attention, and yeah, there it was again, that zing of heat flashing between them—or was it one-way and he was reading too much into every word, every look? Andy couldn't tell for sure and it intrigued him.

"No. You're *my* butt monkey. Anyone else gives you trouble, you tell me. I give you trouble, you suck it up." Ethan spread his hands. "I'm a nice guy. Friendly. Approachable. Reasonable—unless someone breaks the rule. Do your job right and you won't get to see what I'm like when I lose my temper."

Friendly? Approachable? Ethan had a sense of humor, at least. "Rules?"

"You're on time—early is better—and you're presentable when you're likely to be seen by guests. Black suit, white shirt, black shoes and tie. Real shoes, not running shoes. You don't lie, steal or cause trouble. You're polite and helpful to the guests. You show me and anyone else over you the respect we are due. That's about it."

Ethan stood and Andy tipped his head back to meet Ethan's gaze before he did something stupid like checking if Ethan dressed left or right. The interview was over and he'd gotten the job. He should be on his feet and out the door before Ethan reconsidered, but his fascination with Ethan made him reluctant to leave.

Rules. They were part of life. House rules, school rules and the self-applied ones he stuck to for the most part, like never fucking without protection and always drinking a glass of water before bed when he'd been clubbing, to stave off a hangover. Okay, that wasn't a rule, just common sense.

Ethan's rules were reasonable, expected even, but they split Andy in two. Obey and get the warm glow of Ethan's approval or bend them a little and discover the promised consequences? Both options appealed.

"Was there something else you wanted to say?" Ethan asked, his polite words holding an impatient edge.

Swallowing back half a dozen inappropriate responses, Andy shook his head and got to his feet. Head rush. He swayed, grabbing the edge of the desk until the dizziness passed.

"Got up too fast," he explained to an unmoving, unsympathetic Ethan. "Well, thanks."

"For what, exactly?"

He'd answered so many of Ethan's questions that one more didn't bother him. "For giving me the job. For giving me a chance to prove I can do it. For believing…" He shut up. *Shit, start the violin music to go with the soap opera moment, why don't you?*

"I'll ask you at the end of your first week if you're still grateful," Ethan said.

He put out his hand and Andy touched him for the first time, not even trying to win the battle of the squeeze. Ethan gripped Andy's hand with enough pressure to leave it tingling. It was an impersonal act, traditional enough to carry no weight of intent, but it grounded Andy, clearing away the fog of anxiety that had surrounded him the last few weeks.

He had a job.

"I will be," he said.

In that moment, he meant it.

Chapter Two

"Make up your mind." Henry pushed his glasses up with two stabs of his finger, a habit of his that drove Andy nuts. "Is he hot or not?"

The roommate before Henry had disappeared in the middle of the night, owing a month's rent to the landlord and about three hundred dollars to Andy. The six-pack of beer he'd left in the fridge had seemed like a wordless apology—until Andy realized the full bottle of vodka in the freezer belonging to him had gone along with Seth.

Henry was the anti-Seth. Named after Prince Harry by his mother, who adored the royal family, he was reliable, trustworthy and totally, utterly incomprehensible to Andy. Henry flossed then brushed his teeth for a timed two minutes. Paid his half of a food bill to the cent—until the government phased out the penny—then he rounded up or down with a pained grimace. When he'd shown up at the door, dressed in a brown and cream plaid shirt and cheap jeans that were both stiff and baggy, Andy had taken a step back in case dork syndrome was contagious. He didn't buy into the stereotype that gay men were innately stylish, but Henry's clunky hiking boots screamed straight.

Henry wasn't. Henry—mild brown eyes, big nose and a scattering of zits—was, as he informed Andy solemnly, homosexual since birth and celibate by choice. Andy had accepted the first, not the second. Henry was nineteen. Celibacy and nineteen didn't go together. He didn't want to hurt Henry's feelings by suggesting a makeover—or shock him by taking him to a club—but getting Henry laid was on his to-do list.

"Hard to say. He's nice one minute, giving me a chance to read up on stuff, then the next, he's freezing my balls off and telling me I'm useless."

"Being unpredictable isn't relevant to his hotness."

"Yes, it is," Andy said irritably. "Attitude counts as much as looks. I'm not even sure he's gay. On top of that, he's my boss. I can't start something with him. It would be awkward. Do I even want to? See? I'm back where I started—not knowing if he's hot."

He was mimicking a goldfish going round in circles, deciding to put Ethan in the 'want to fuck' or 'don't want to fuck' column. There was a third option of 'maybe', but Ethan affected him too strongly to fit in that slot.

Henry picked up his favorite mug—a thrift store purchase, chocolate brown outside, decorated with a complex swirl of black, a rich cream inside. The mug proved Henry had a glimmering of style in him somewhere. He took a tidy sip of herbal tea—spiced apple, by the smell of it—though all teas tasted like hot water in Andy's opinion. Coffee was Andy's choice when it came to caffeine.

"You're assuming a lot," Henry told him.

"Such as?"

Henry set down his mug. Ticking off his points on his fingers, he said, "One, if he's gay that he's interested in you."

"He said I was a pretty boy." Was that offhanded and casual enough? Remembering it made Andy wish he could show Ethan he had more than a cute face. His ass rocked too.

"That's not a compliment, even if you think it is. Two, if he's attractive and employed, he's probably got someone in his life."

"Maybe." Probably. Almost certainly. Andy hated whoever it was.

"Three, you're off-limits."

"Technically, the hotel's my employer, not him," Andy pointed out. "It's not as if we're cops working together or he's my commanding officer. Businessmen screw their secretaries all the time."

"You report to him, and if he fired you after an argument, you could sue for wrongful dismissal. He wouldn't want that complication."

Andy made a wordless sound of frustration. "Why am I doing this? So he got me hard. So what? The barista in the coffee shop does that when he smiles at me and I see his tongue stud. So does the blond in that toothpaste commercial wearing a towel that's about to slip. I'm a slut and I know it."

Henry didn't blush, but he ducked his head and took a noisy slurp of tea, betraying his discomfort. Did he jerk off with his eyes closed or not jerk off at all? Andy wasn't sure, but asking was out of the question. Henry would clam up, vanish into his room and avoid Andy for several days. He'd done that twice now and Andy had gotten the message. Henry's sex life wasn't up for discussion, though he didn't seem to mind participating vicariously in Andy's, up to a point.

"You could look him up online," Henry said. "I'd like to see him."

"You would?" And why hadn't he thought of cyberstalking?

Henry nodded, eyes bright with interest, head cocked like a bird studying a juicy worm. "I'm curious."

That was one personality trait they shared, at least. Henry's laptop was close by, as always, and he tapped away, hands barely moving, his long fingers finding the keys unerringly though his gaze never left the screen. Andy used his middle fingers and had to look at what they were doing.

"He's gay," Henry reported. He swung the laptop around so Andy could see it. "It says so in this interview."

"Someone interviewed him? Why?"

"Local paper did an article on hotel bars." Henry didn't offer any more information than that. A man of few words. Like Ethan. "Is it a good photo of him?"

Andy stared at the image. Ethan stared back at him in a pale green shirt, sleeves rolled up, unbuttoned at the throat, meeting the probing eye of the camera with a direct challenge, the smallest of smiles curving his lips.

"Yeah." Blood thrummed in his ears. "That's him."

Henry grunted. He hadn't shaved, probably avoiding the three zits on his chin, but there was nothing designer about his stubble. "He's thirty-four."

"Yeah."

"It doesn't say if he's single or not."

"No."

"And he's your boss."

Andy sighed.

"Hot, then," Henry said with the air of a man glad to reach a definite conclusion. He opened a new tab to check the weather, the way he did every morning, as if looking out of the window was too much effort. And in late February, odds were good it was raining and misty. This was Vancouver, after all. An umbrella came in handy most months. "Glad I could help."

A text came in from a friend asking how the interview had gone. Composing a reply to Gary without giving away how close he'd come to blowing it took some thought, but organizing a night out to celebrate was easy enough. Andy's life was a mess in general, but his social life was thriving. He sent a final text to his parents, knowing they'd be too tactful to contact him in case the news was bad, then he retreated to his room to think.

It was an uninspiring setting. The small house had a two-bedroom flat on each floor with shared laundry and storage in the basement. He and Henry had the top floor, reached by an outside stairway opening into the main living area. A small kitchen off to the left and two bedrooms with a bathroom between them occupied the rest of the space. At the time of the renovations, it had probably looked fresh and light, but that was twenty years ago and now the oatmeal carpet and off-white walls were grubby and marked. The landlord's attitude was that any improvements would cost money, meaning an increase in the rent, so his apathy did them a favor.

Andy had covered the bedroom walls with posters and the floor with rugs. It made the room appear smaller, but it brightened it up. It was still a dump. He had plans to tidy it but when he wasn't working, he was too depressed to bother and when he was, he didn't have time. Clothing—some used, some clean—

lay in heaps, and old scripts littered every flat surface, competing for space with dirty mugs and plates. Henry, like Seth before him, didn't seem to care about the dismal surroundings, though he'd gone to take his first bath and had spent forty-five minutes scrubbing the bathroom down before running it.

It was a roof over his head and that was all it needed to be. Andy had dreams of living somewhere close to the water, a few classy clubs nearby and a coffee shop filled with attractive men who bought him lattes thick with cream and got narrow-eyed and intense when he sucked his straw. Dreams with no possibility of turning them into reality.

The room was big enough to take a queen-size bed, at least. Andy took off his interview clothes and hung them in the closet. Naked, apart from socks and scarlet briefs, he shivered in the cool air and got into bed, huddled beneath a thick comforter and sheets in need of washing. It was eleven in the morning, but jerking off would calm his post-interview jitters and residual lust.

He didn't hesitate in making Ethan the focus of his thoughts when his hands got busy. The more he thought about it, the more he was convinced Ethan had been flirting with him. Was that the same interview experience a straight guy or a woman would've had? Not a chance in hell. He squeezed hard flesh then relaxed his grip. No rush. He was in the mood for a slow tease. So he stroked the underside of his shaft with his fingertips, tormenting himself with the light touch. In his head, Ethan was asking questions again, but this time they were more personal, demanding to know Andy's fantasies and kinks, how often he beat off and where, how far he could shoot and his opinion about a creative scale of punishments for breaking those rules of his.

Eyes closed, his thumb and first finger a narrow, tight circle under the head of his cock, he settled into a rhythm. How many times had he done this? Did he want to know? Sometimes he preferred it to sex. Well, it was sex. Solo sex. And he knew what to do to make it feel better than good, which was more than he could say for most of his partners.

Sure, a blow job always hit the spot, but he liked some variety in the approach. Most men seemed to think taking his dick in deep was all they needed to do and a vicious scrape from their teeth not worth apologizing for. Same with fucking. If he didn't count the prep work involved, he could bottom and be wiping his ass clean of lube after two minutes. If he topped, he tried to make it interesting, but he'd had more than one guy tell him to stop fucking around.

Ethan came across as a man who knew what he was doing. Instinct told Andy that Ethan would make a memorable partner, the kind who asked questions. God, those questions earlier under Ethan's searching gaze had been a turn-on.

He came with his mind a tangle of confused images and echoing words, leaving his balls empty and his restlessness unabated. He wanted something new — something different. Ethan was both, but as Andy mopped the streaks off his stomach and hand, he knew he was making a lot of soup from one oyster. How much did the real Ethan resemble the fantasy one he'd created from a short encounter? Maybe it was for the best he couldn't make a move without risking his job, because Ethan would never measure up.

Not much in life did. Even his dick was an inch short of what he claimed when the subject came up.

Chapter Three

First days were hell — new school, new job, same deal. Andy got up early after not sleeping well, eyes gritty and bloodshot. He beat Henry to the bathroom and took pains over shaving and showering, ignoring Henry's threats of reprisal from outside the door. Henry was the only student at his community college who showed up on time — or at all — for an eight o'clock class on Monday and the teacher would cut him some slack if he was late — which he wouldn't be.

Henry wasn't late for anything. He built in time to allow for emergencies, then he added another ten minutes to be on the safe side. He'd made coffee while he'd waited, so when Andy emerged, damp, fragrant and smooth in all the right places after stealing some of Henry's toothpaste, there was a mug waiting for him.

Henry had locked the bathroom door by the time Andy had discovered it had two spoons of sugar in it and the pot was empty. Shuddering at every sweet, revengeful mouthful, he drank it anyway. He needed the boost and a stop at the coffeehouse on the corner was out of the question. That always led to maple crème donuts and with his luck, the creamy filling would ooze out and splat down on his ironed shirt.

Okay, not technically ironed, but the wrinkle-release cycle on the dryer did the same job.

He'd been like this before on audition days—same sense of being half a second out of sync with the rest of the world, so objects he picked up slipped through his fingers and conversations were a morass of apologies for speaking over people or leaving too long a gap. Same lurch in the stomach rehearsing his entrance and running through his lines.

This was a job, not a part, so it didn't matter, but he'd see Ethan again after two weeks, and by now the man was seven-foot tall with a whip in one hand and a collar in the other. Disappointment inevitable in three, two, one…

He didn't see Ethan when he arrived. The day was a confusing rush interspersed with hours of being bored. The people he worked with were friendly enough and willing to point him in the right direction if he got lost, but their attention wasn't fully on him. Apparently, the hotel chain's head office in London had arranged a surprise visit from the Quality Assurance Director. Gabriel Sosa had swept in with a smile, Spanish accent to the fore, and the staff had gone on red alert.

"Ethan's in a meeting with him," Joel said, slicing lemons with a knife so sharp it looked capable of drawing blood from air. He'd taken Andy into the small prep room assigned to the two ground floor bars to show him how to do garnishes. "He's been interviewing all the managers."

"So on a scale of one to ten, how important is this Sosa guy?"

Joel chuckled, pausing for a moment, the blade of his knife glistening with juice. "You're totally clueless, aren't you?"

"First day," Andy reminded him. Joel was a year younger than Andy but he'd been at the hotel working under Ethan for three years. It showed. Joel was competent, capable of working at speed with accuracy. Watching him exhausted Andy and copying him seemed impossible. He went through the motions, painfully aware Joel was doing his new job and training Andy to take over his old one at the same time without visible effort.

"Yes, but didn't you read the welcome package?"

Andy had scanned the glossy brochure that had arrived in the mail looking for a photograph of Ethan, found one, and decided it didn't do him justice. He'd tossed the brochure in a box he planned to go through one day when he had time. "Kind of."

"The chain's owned by Mr. Conroy. Mr. Sosa reports directly to him. Work out how important he is from that."

"So Eth—everyone's kissing his ass, scared he'll give them a bad report?" Andy shook his head. "Man, that has to suck."

Joel gave a noncommittal grunt, impossible to interpret as agreement. Andy knew the drill and didn't take offense. Moaning to a fellow employee was an allowable form of venting and even built morale, but it was disloyal if the employee was brand spanking new like him. He'd seen actors go from scathing comments about a rundown theatre to gushing praise of its charm, depending on their audience.

"Okay, your turn," Joel said. "Thin, even slices. No less than an eighth of an inch, no more than a quarter. Get that right and we'll move onto wedges."

"Don't spoil me."

He sounded as bitter as the fruit.

Joel straightened from his slouch and stabbed his finger at Andy. "Ethan's going to want to know how you did. I can tell him your attitude sucked and you'll get his lecture on positive energy or you can lose the snarl and I'll tell him you tried. Your choice."

The lecture would mean he got to see Ethan, but at what cost? Andy pasted on a repentant smile, holding up his hands in surrender. "Hey, I'm sorry, okay? First day nerves. You're being great and I appreciate it. Seriously."

"Okay, you've sucked up enough," Joel said dryly. "Show me your knife skills."

The bowl of lemons, washed and inspected for blemishes, stood beside a wooden cutting board. It was Andy's job to keep the boards clean and oiled. He chose a particularly yellow fruit and set it on the board then took the knife from Joel.

"I cut off the ends..." Jesus, the knife was sharp. "Until all the white stuff—"

"The pith."

"The pith, yeah. Until that's all gone. Then I slice it and cut a line from the center out so I can stick it on the rim of the glass."

"If it's up to standard, yeah."

Sneaking a peek at the size of the slices Joel had done, Andy did his best to make his match. The first two were ragged, thick at one end, wafer thin at the other. The next two were better. A bit better, anyway. Then he ran out of lemon.

"One lemon and you got two usable slices out of it," Joel reported with disgust when Andy had finished. "Lemons—"

"Don't grow on trees?"

Joel studied him in silence for a moment. "I can't decide if you think you're funny or you're nervous and overcompensating."

"Can't it be both?"

"Practice," Joel said. "I'll be back to see how you're doing in a while. If you think you have the hang of slices, try wedges. And no seeds allowed, but take them out tidily."

Andy had never given the garnish on his drink much thought. He'd plucked it off, dunked it in his glass, stabbed at it with his straw to make it sink— anything apart from grading it on uniform thickness and lack of seeds. He didn't see that changing in the future.

After hacking away at a few more lemons—and for the hell of it, a lime—he caught sight of the clock. Ten minutes after his shift officially ended. He was out of here. Gone.

Washing the sticky off his hands took thirty seconds, retrieving his jacket a minute. He could've walked out into the ever-present drizzle and headed home, but why not explore? He worked here, so no one would give him any grief and if he walked purposefully, he'd slide by unnoticed. He'd read that in a spy thriller once.

The hotel was a straightforward column but it was the two floors at the top where things got interesting. The top floor, divided into four luxury suites, was accessible by a private elevator for the guests and a separate one for the staff. Not any staff. A special crew, security vetted and experienced, dealt with the room service and housekeeping for the penthouse suites. Andy's temporary pass during his probationary week wouldn't get him onto that floor and neither would his permanent one if he made the grade.

The floor below it was accessible, though. That was a function room, with a three hundred and sixty degree view, used as a restaurant most nights of the week unless it'd been booked for a private function. The list of celebs who'd spun on the dance floor of the Acadia Room was long.

And below that floor was one that didn't exist for the guests. It housed the kitchen for the Acadia Room and the four suites above it—administration offices, laundry, storage, a security center and, in a separate wing, rooms for the staff and a small gym.

"The managers get solo rooms. We get dorms," Joel had explained. "They're not for living in, so don't get any ideas. If you pull a double shift and need a shower or an hour's nap, you ask if you can use one of the beds. If there's a big function on, the managers sometimes sleep here, so they're on call if there's an emergency."

Andy wanted to see them. And he definitely wanted to see the penthouse suites—named the Elements—but he guessed that wasn't going to happen. The brochure had devoted a double spread to them, catching his eye even on his hunt for a photograph of Ethan. Earth, air, fire and water were the themes the interior designer had gone with, one for each set of rooms, and whoever it was had gone all out. The suites made Andy's place seem on a par with a cardboard box in an alley.

He wandered around the lobby, breathing in the scent of rich people, perfume trails from the women hanging in the air. It was an incredible space, the vaulted ceiling high lit by chandeliers. Balconies ran around three sides of the floor above and the carpet was a midnight blue with a subtle pattern so not every crumb dropped showed up. Off the lobby was a row of shops offering everything from designer purses and shoes to local art and old-fashioned candy and ice cream. A coffee shop, a café and a restaurant gave the guests options when it came to food. There were areas set aside for them to read by a huge fireplace, use laptops at desks fitted with power outlets or have a drink at a small bar tucked away behind a six-foot wall made of translucent black glass bricks streaked with gold and silver.

Andy wasn't sure he had permission to use the bar, even off duty, so after seeing everything the lobby had to offer, he took the elevator to the level with the main pool and fitness area. His card let him enter, but the questioning glance he got from the female instructor showing a middle-aged man how to use the weights machine had him backing out again.

He didn't belong here. Well, of course not. He was an actor, not a hotel worker. This was a stopgap on the way to doing what he loved and being paid for it. It didn't get much better than that. He took an elevator up, deciding to scope out the view then head home. It was full when he got on, jammed with a family hauling everything they owned by the look of it. He squeezed into a space next to a little girl clutching a My Little Pony suitcase on wheels, ignored by the family, but it was the indifference of exhaustion. He bet they'd check in and collapse. Apart from the little girl, who looked hopped up on sugar bribes and ready to party.

She ran the wheels of her suitcase over his foot when she left, but he remembered the courtesy to guests rule and turned his whimper to a smile when her mother apologized.

The elevator had mirrored walls and once alone, he checked himself out. He'd picked up some splashes of juice on his white shirt and an ancient stain on the lapel of his jacket drew his eye, but not bad — not bad at all.

The fiftieth floor was quiet, long stretches of hallway empty of people, the closed doors blank and forbidding. He found himself tiptoeing through the hush, jumping at a blast of sound from a room when someone turned their television on with the sound cranked way high. They muted it and he exhaled. Okay. Someone else was alive up here. He could forget the horror movies he'd watched. At the end of the hallway was a huge window. He jogged over to it, the soft thud of his shoes against the carpet breaking the silence, only for it to seep back when he reached his destination.

He gazed out at Vancouver Harbor. Across from him, lost in the gathering night and the lowering rainclouds, were the mountains, snowcapped and remote, their lower reaches thickly forested. If he turned to the right, he saw the city lights, the vast sprawl of humanity cradled by stone and water. To the left was Stanley Park, recovering now from the huge storm of 2006 that had toppled trees and caused ten million dollars' worth of damage. Andy had been a teenager, self-absorbed as most kids that age were, but he'd joined the volunteers who had helped with the replanting on three or four weekends until a sprained ankle had left him hobbling.

He'd grown up in Mount Pleasant in a heritage home—comfortable, eclectic, reflecting his parents' taste more than his. His parents sold the house when they moved to New Zealand, following Andy's older sister, Louise, and her family.

He'd been left behind and it had hurt. "You don't need us here hovering," his mother had said, cupping his face with warm hands smelling of cucumber and green tea lotion. "You're too independent. Louise does and we want to be part of the twins' lives as they grow up, not distant strangers who send them birthday presents."

He'd understood—of course he had—but their move had left him homeless. Finding a place off the haven of Davie Street, Vancouver's best known 'gayborhood', had helped with the feelings of being isolated and abandoned, but every Skype conversation he had rubbed in the fact that he was here and the rest of his family was about as far away as it was possible to get and still be on the same planet.

After turning away from the window, he headed back to the elevator. Time to go home, regale Henry with an account of his day and eat whatever glop Henry had created out of the contents of the fridge. They took turns cooking, but mostly Andy bought pizza or Chinese.

As he waited, he heard voices from around the corner. Two men. Oh God, one was Ethan. Heart hammering, he pressed the button again, not wanting to meet Ethan like this. Rescue didn't arrive. The men rounded the corner and caught him.

He gave them a weak smile and a small wave. "Uh, hi."

The man with Ethan—good-looking, dark, around Andy's height of five-ten—raised his eyebrows, smiling back with a question in his eyes, but Ethan sighed.

"Mr. Sosa, meet our newest employee. Mr. Naylor's on probation as a bartender. He started work this morning."

"Ah." Gabriel Sosa glanced around him. "I see no bar here. Is it possible our young friend is lost?"

"It's possible, but not likely." Ethan pinned Andy with a hard stare. "Are you?"

"I was exploring," Andy said. "My shift's over and I thought it would be a good idea to uh…know my way around."

"Very enterprising." Gabriel nodded. "It shows initiative. But a word of advice on your first day?"

Andy tried to look receptive and eager.

"We prefer our staff presentable. If anyone asks, please don't tell them you work here."

Andy was dead. Deceased. Terminated. Someone needed to bury his ashes because Ethan's glare had incinerated him.

"Here it is," Sosa said to Ethan, still smiling when the doors slid open. "I believe I'll take that swim I've been looking forward to, and our dinner tonight, of course. I'll see you later, Ethan." He nodded at Andy and walked away, whistling under his breath, his room key in his hand, the slim piece of plastic that gave him access to everywhere in the place.

"Are you going down?" Andy asked. "I can take the next one if you're checking out the restaurant upstairs or something."

"That's very kind of you."

Clearly, no one had told Ethan sarcasm was the lowest form of wit. The doors began to close and Andy reached out to punch the button. Ethan clasped his wrist. "Don't bother. I always like to chat with a new employee at the end of their first day, so why don't we take care of that now?"

If anyone else had grabbed him, Andy's instinct would've been to struggle, even lash out if the situation called for it. With Ethan holding him, forbidding him from moving, he found himself slipping into obedience without effort, though not without reacting to that light grip. His breathing shallow, rapid, his gaze fixed on the hand cuffing his, he waited for what came next.

Ethan released him and the world juddered back to normal. Swallowing hard, Andy stood in place. Ethan took out his phone. "Ethan here. Hi, Rashid. Tell me, what rooms are unoccupied on fifty? Uh-huh, yeah. No, that one's fine. I need it for five minutes. Thanks."

He shoved his phone back in his jacket pocket and walked away, raising his hand to shoulder height and beckoning for Andy to follow him.

Ethan was taking him into a room with a bed and a lockable door? Andy wasn't sure where this was going, but he wasn't inclined to protest or point out most people interviewed staff in an office, not a bedroom.

The room lay in darkness but Ethan hit the wall switch without looking at it, illuminating a large room with a king-size bed and the usual en suite bathroom. A glassy, smooth expanse of bronze quilt covered the bed, dazzling white sheets folded down over it, the pillows plump and firm.

It was one hell of an inviting sight in Andy's opinion, but Ethan ignored it and walked over to the dark wooden desk by the window then pulled out the chair beside it, angling it to face the room.

"Sit."

Ethan made it an order, not a request, and that made it simple to obey. Andy sat, locking his hands together in his lap to keep them steady.

Ethan took up a casual pose, leaning against the desk. "So how did it go today?"

He'd been expecting a blast, not a gentle breeze. "It was okay, I guess. Joel was nice. Showed me around. He—"

"Joel's an excellent employee. I'm glad you appreciate him. Why don't we see if the feeling's mutual." Ethan took out his phone and tapped the screen a few times, then he set it on the desk. "Hi, Joel. It's Ethan."

On speakerphone, Joel's reply was audible to Andy. "Hi, boss."

"I know you're headed off but give me your impression of Andy Naylor before you leave."

Joel sighed. "Not a good time to ask when I'm in the prep room looking at the mess he left me to deal with. He disappeared when his shift ended, so I guess he went home without signing out. Not sure he'll be back tomorrow. I got the feeling he's not invested in the job."

Andy opened his mouth to refute that, but Ethan shot out his hand. He didn't touch Andy's mouth, but his finger was a bare inch away from it, silencing Andy as surely as a gag.

He could've kissed it, licked it, drawn it between his lips to suck, but frozen by Ethan's unspoken command, he did nothing. A moment later, Ethan withdrew his finger.

"No good points to make?"

"He's friendly," Joel said. "The customers would appreciate him. And he did try at first, but when he screwed up, he gave up. He was slicing lemons, for God's sake, not defusing a bomb."

"I'll deal with the mess. Go home."

"Are you sure?"

"Don't make me repeat myself."

Joel's grin came through in his words. "Yes, boss. Thanks."

Ethan ended the call. "So. Pretty but a quitter. That's what I thought when I interviewed you, but I took a chance on you surprising me. You've disappointed me on both counts."

Astonishing how it hurt to hear that and know he'd failed to impress Ethan. "No, listen. Let me explain—"

"Explain what?" Ethan gestured him to his feet. "Look at you. Is this your idea of suitable clothing for working here at one of the top hotels in the city?"

"I'm chopping fruit and moving boxes!"

"And when you're doing that, there's protective clothing available, but when you're wandering around the hotel, in view of the guests, you'd better look presentable or you're letting the hotel down. You're letting *me* down."

Aware he'd rejected the offer of an apron and overalls, Andy hung his head.

"Your suit needs dry-cleaning. Your shirt will never be white again, no matter how much you wash it, but you could at least have ironed it. Your shoes need polishing, one of the laces is broken and knotted and you should be wearing a tie."

"I tried."

"Not hard enough." Ethan got close enough that Andy couldn't see past him. "If I stripped off everything you're wearing that wasn't up to my standards, you'd be naked. I'm betting your socks have holes and your underwear's trashy."

And with that, Andy hit a wall. His temper flared, extinguishing his guilt over his poor performance and his arousal. He kicked off his shoes, sending them flying, then flung himself onto the bed, raising his feet one at a time, shoving them at Ethan. "No holes. See? And I'm not going to flash you my briefs but they're plain red, clean and the only hole in them is the one I stick my dick through when I want to piss."

Ethan twisted his lips in an approximation of a smile. "Thank you for sharing. Now get your ass off the bed and out of my hotel."

At points in the day, walking out would've been a welcome escape from tedium, but that would've been his choice. Being kicked out was unendurable. "Did I get you in trouble with the guy from head office? You weren't this much of an asshole the first time we met."

"I don't think he was pleased but I'm not the one in trouble." Ethan nudged Andy's shoes, kicking them closer to the bed. "Put them on."

"Tell me something I can do to make this better." And he was back to begging, this time for real, his flash of rebellion fizzling out in the face of no job and no more Ethan. Though his chances of getting anywhere with Ethan were close to zero, he wasn't ready to give up on two weeks of fantasies. "Joel was wrong. I didn't leave. And I planned to clean up before I left."

Ethan raised his eyebrows, his skepticism plain. "I doubt the second and the first isn't a point in your favor. We don't pay you to wander around places you've no business being."

"I haven't done enough to get fired. And I was getting the hang of the lemon slicing. Joel's like…super fussy."

To his shock, Ethan laughed—a dry chuckle, anyway. "I trained him and trust me, if you think he's fussy, you'll need a new word for me. I'm a perfectionist, Andrew, even when it comes to lemon slicing. It's a trivial task but that doesn't mean it doesn't matter."

No one had called him Andrew in years. He'd learned to associate it with being in trouble, but said by Ethan, even when he *was* in deep shit, it resonated with him the same way calling Ethan 'sir' had.

"Show me." Andy stood, though an inner voice urged him to go to his knees and appeal to Ethan that way. "Show me how you want it done and I'll try. If I fuck up, I'll clean the room and go and that's it—over. But if you're firing me, I want you judging me too. Not Joel. You."

And there it was again. That flash of heat in Ethan's eyes telling him he'd struck a chord. He wasn't playing Ethan exactly, but he was learning where Ethan's buttons were and how to press them. It seemed fair given the way Ethan reduced him to naked lust with a look.

Ethan checked his watch. "I suppose I have time. Once I've shown you, you get one shot at it. One."

"Understood and thank—"

"Don't," Ethan said. "Just don't."

Ethan didn't seem in the mood for small talk on the ride down or the walk to the prep room and Andy's ready flow of chatter stuck in his throat in the face of Ethan's silence.

Ethan gave the prep room a sweeping glance and turned his gaze on Andy. "Before I pick up a knife, I want every board and knife you used cleaned, every surface wiped." He struck his hands together, the sharp, flat sound making Andy jump. "Hop to it."

Working under Ethan's unwavering stare wasn't easy. Clumsiness slowed him down and nerves made the clumsiness worse. Eventually he placed a clean board on a clean surface, a sharp knife beside it, and handed Ethan a lemon.

Ethan tossed it, caught it then placed it on the board. The knife flickered and the lemon split neatly, leaving Ethan with two ends for the trash and five identical slices. He notched them, scooped them up then deposited them in a bowl inside one of the refrigerators, never looking at Andy.

"You did that fast."

"Not really."

He meant it, Andy realized. Ethan hadn't been showing off, simply performing a routine task with trained efficiency. He probably didn't know how to do it any slower.

"Your turn," Ethan said.

The knife held no heat from Ethan's grip, but Andy pretended it did to steady him. He placed a fresh lemon on the board and trimmed the ends off, using confident slashes of the knife but no flourishes. It wasn't a magic trick and Joel was right. Neither was it rocket science.

He set the blade against the peel and prepared to make his first cut. Ethan made a small sound, a warning, a hint and Andy hesitated. Too thick? Too narrow? What? It looked fine to him. With an impatient shake of his head, he carried on, refusing to look up and check Ethan's expression.

"How did I do?" he asked when he'd finished. "Good enough to use?"

Ethan nodded at the fridge. "You know where they go."

"I did it? I passed?" Delight fizzed up in him and he beamed at Ethan. "Can I thank you now?"

"No. You get to come back tomorrow. If your suit and shirt are still filthy, you go home again. If you can't keep yourself clean until the end of the day, bring a change or use an apron. You report to me when you arrive and whenever I tell you to. I'll be on your ass every single fucking minute and if you screw up, you'll wish I had fired you tonight, because I *will* make you pay for every mistake. Now prep another dozen lemons for tonight, clean up and find a dry cleaners."

"Yes, sir."

Ethan's nostrils flared as if he'd scented blood. "My team usually calls me boss."

Yeah, well that didn't get his cock juiced up the way sir did and he was entitled to some fun at work. "Yes, sir."

"Oh, Andrew," Ethan said, soft and dangerous. "You have no idea how big a mistake it is to push me."

Andy knew he had the perfect reply, but Ethan turned on his heel and left before he voiced it.

Chapter Four

Thank God for sensible parents who marked his birthdays and Christmases with money transfers. Dipping into the fund marked 'only for emergencies and not even then' enabled him to pay cash for a new suit, two blindingly white shirts and still have enough to leave his old suit at the cleaners. He went into work the next morning looking good enough to man the front desk—hell, even sitting in Ethan's chair.

Feeling pleased with himself, he rapped on Ethan's door then posed for a moment after opening it, giving Ethan time to appreciate the wonder that was Andy Naylor.

Ethan glanced up and studied him. "Hmm."

Andy walked over to the desk, crestfallen but determined not to let it show. "You don't like it? It's new!"

"I'm pleased you made an effort and the suit will do, I suppose."

"I'll be living on ramen until I get paid, so that's good news."

Was that a wince, as if Ethan hadn't thought through what upgrading Andy's wardrobe would cost?

"I told you to clean your old suit, not buy a new one."

Andy drew in a breath then launched into a spirited defense. He'd learned early on in life that if he talked fast and loud, he could get away with more than being meekly apologetic. "By the time I'd gone home, got changed and found a cleaners that doesn't hold onto stuff for a week before handing it over—"

"There's a laundry service here in the hotel," Ethan pointed out. "Employees get a discount and if you'd explained the circumstances, they would've had it waiting for you this morning and loaned you something from the lost and found box to wear home."

Deep breath. Be Zen about it. "Why the fuck didn't you tell me?"

"I value initiative and quick thinking. You demonstrated neither by panicking and rushing out to buy the first suit you tried on." Ethan stood and walked around to Andy's side of the desk. "It doesn't fit. Too loose in the shoulders." He pinched the fabric. "Cheap. It'll look like crap in six months." He moved behind Andy and tugged at the hem of the jacket. "Too short."

Ethan's hands were an inch from his ass. Sweet Lord have mercy. His cock stiffened with a rush of arousal, eager for a touch.

"You should never buy hemmed pants. Get them measured and turned up. It's worth the cost."

"I can hem pants." Being stage-struck involved costumes and his mom didn't know which end of a needle to thread. Andy had learned to sew in grade three and could handle most alterations.

Ethan wasn't moving, his words drifting past Andy's ear, a solid presence behind him. He yearned to lean back, make Ethan hold him if only for long enough to shove him away. "It's a two-person job. You can't pin them up while you're in them."

Andy stared forward, somehow locked into a game with a single rule forbidding him to turn around. God, how weird was this, playing statues, talking to empty air? "My roommate could help me out, but it's too late now. I've worn these. I can't take them back."

"You live with someone?"

It was the first personal question Ethan had asked, and the implications weren't lost on Andy. How did he phrase his answer without declaring his availability? Ethan had to know Andy was attracted to him, but Andy had some pride.

"Two-bedroom rental. I can't afford to rent both and I like the company. Henry's quiet. Doesn't date, doesn't drink, still a virgin. He's the anti-me." He winced. "TMI?"

"It's hardly a shock that you like to party." Ethan went back to his desk. "Well, you can take the suit off now."

Elation and panic squeezed his chest. Would it be an easy seduction? Had a show of obedience and a willingness to adapt to Ethan's requirements bought him a few minutes on his knees, Ethan's cock jammed down his throat? "Excuse me?"

"There's a double delivery due. Alcohol and food. It'll be chaotic at the loading bay if we don't empty the trucks fast. Joel showed you the overalls we provide, so grab a pair and change into them. Then you're with him again, and do a better of job of listening today. Which reminds me…" Ethan took out his phone when someone knocked on the door. Ethan grinned when Joel walked in. "Saved me a call."

"I live to anticipate your every need, boss," Joel joked.

It didn't prevent a sick surge of envy welling up inside Andy. Joel glanced over but didn't greet him.

"Andy's going to help with the unloading, but he's got something to say to you first."

He did? It took him a moment to realize Ethan wanted him to apologize to Joel. What was he, six? This was humiliating and yet his dick, which had retreated to a less demanding state, perked up again. It was a test and he wasn't going to fail.

"Joel, man, I'm sorry I bailed last night. I took a wander around the hotel, getting my bearings, you know? I cleaned up the prep room and I've gotten the hang of the lemon slicing — and quartering — so thanks for showing me how to do that. Really am sorry."

He smiled, tentative, abashed. Yeah, it was an act but despite the failed auditions, he was good at playing a part and from what he'd seen of him, Joel was essentially a nice guy, too sweet-natured to hold a grudge.

"If you disappear on me again, you will be." Joel sounded stern, but he clapped Andy's shoulder forgivingly. "Are you done with him, boss?"

Ethan gave Andy a measuring look, head to toe, seemingly checking off points on a list. If he noticed the way Andy's cock ruined the line of his pants, he didn't give anything away. "Completely. Get out, the two of you. Some of us have work to do."

"Like humping boxes isn't work?" Joel asked while they walked. "Managers, huh?"

"I hear you," Andy agreed. "Listen, about yesterday—"

"Save it." Joel nudged him with an elbow. "You groveled enough back there."

"Yeah, I kinda did." Andy rubbed his nose. "He brings it out in me. Guess you think I'm a wimp, huh?"

Joel gave a hoot of laughter. "Don't beat yourself up. He scares the crap out of most people at first—and it's not an act. He's a stone-cold asshole at times, and totally OCD about stuff, but he's fair. He won't put up with crap but he's not like some of the managers here who let you get away with something when they're in a good mood, then come down on you for it when they're not. You know where you stand with him at least."

It matched his impression of Ethan. With no excuse to prolong the conversation, Andy changed and started work. Time to improve on yesterday's screw-ups.

* * * *

"First paycheck that isn't spent before I got it." Andy waved it in front of Henry's nose. "See?"

Through some complicated system he didn't understand, he'd had to work two weeks before getting paid for his first week, then weekly after that. After a month at the hotel, he'd repaid Henry and had gotten the landlord off his back. Now he had enough spare cash to make a guilt-free night out possible— and he wanted one. He'd been crawling into bed exhausted and stressed. Time to crawl into someone else's bed.

His shallow crush on Ethan had dissolved like sugar in hot water, replaced by a steady thrum of need as much a part of him as his hands. Futile, pointless, deeply stupid, yes, but he couldn't help it. The man was impossible to please, riding Andy's ass every time their paths crossed. It should've been annoying, but Ethan got this intense, determined look in his eye when he rebuked Andy for a fuck-up that left Andy weak-kneed with confusion and desire. Ethan hadn't touched him or critiqued his dress sense again, but he was always there when Andy slipped up or decided to take a shortcut to complete a task faster.

Ethan didn't believe in shortcuts. If there was an optimum way to do something, he'd figured it out. Any deviation compromised the accurate completion of said task, making it a Very Bad Thing to do.

What*ever*. Edgy with lust, half-resentful and half turned on by Ethan's strict rules, Andy veered from pursuing perfection dutifully or rebelling for the hell of it in small ways Ethan couldn't fire him for.

He needed alcohol—lots of it—and a warm body to grind against and fuck. If Ethan wasn't interested—and clearly he wasn't—it was time to move on and end this interminable dry spell. He'd received some interested looks at work, particularly from one guy, Niall, but he'd kept his distance.

It made sense to cut his losses, so why a vague sense of dissatisfaction hung over him like a cloud, he wasn't sure.

Henry blinked at the pay slip from behind his glasses. "Money. Well done. I had a bet on you being fired before a month, so I guess I lose."

"A bet? Who with?" Andy demanded, more than a little insulted. He wasn't that much of a flake he couldn't hold down a job for a few weeks.

"Myself." Henry picked at a zit on his chin. "Well, I suppose I was betting with you, but you didn't know it."

"Can you do that?" Andy tucked the piece of paper into the back pocket of his pants. He'd file it later. By which he meant he would shove it into the top drawer of the desk in his bedroom where he kept anything official. "Never mind. What do I win?"

"Win?"

"You can't bet without a stake."

"I suppose not." Henry tapped the edge of his laptop, brow furrowed in thought. "How about I teach you how to set up a spreadsheet so you can keep track of your expenses?"

"That would work if I'd *lost*."

Henry sniffed as if Andy's rejection had cut him to the quick. "Fine. I'll buy you a drink to celebrate. Ten dollars should be enough. If it isn't, you're out of luck. It's all I have."

"Much better, but there's one condition." Before Henry asked what it was, Andy told him. "You come out to a club with me and buy me that drink in person. I'll pay for the rest of the night, but I want you out of this fucking dump and into the real world before you sprout mold or something."

"That's not—"

"Jesus, Henry, I'll take care of you!"

Henry blushed a discordant red, his zits glowing. "I would. I mean, I don't want to, but I would. The thing is, I have a date tonight."

World. Rocked. Henry had a date? "With a real person? Involving you and this person making actual physical contact with each other tonight?"

"Yes and yes." The blush faded and Henry stood. "This is why I didn't tell you. I knew you'd be like this."

"Like what?"

"You'd laugh." Henry folded his arms across his chest, hugging himself. "I always said I didn't want to date and I never thought you believed me—"

"I didn't."

"And now that I've met someone, you'll say you told me so, then start fussing over me trying to make me look like you."

'In your dreams' would've been rude and hurtful, but Andy couldn't help saying it inside his head, safe from being overheard.

"So I left it until it was too late for you to do anything." Henry walked to the door, hurrying, and grabbed his coat off the wobbly stand that fell over at least once a week. The coat was thick brown corduroy lined with matted fleece and it made Henry look like a bear with bedhead. "Don't wait up."

Andy moved fast when he wanted to and he put his back against the door before Henry could open it. "You don't leave this house without telling me where you're going, young man!"

"Even my mother doesn't sound like that."

Katie Braden was a small woman, shrunk by illness and ongoing pain from multiple sclerosis but undefeated by her debilitating condition. Andy adored her and he'd only met her on Skype. She'd left Vancouver to live with her sister in Kelowna, refusing to let Henry give up his dreams of college to take care of her. The two women—both widows—got on well, but Andy knew how much Katie missed her son. Henry didn't drive, turning the four-hour trip to Kelowna in a car into a three hundred dollar or more airfare neither he nor his mom could afford. Andy did drive, but didn't own a car or know anyone willing to lend him one, or he would've taken Henry there himself.

"If she knew her baby boy was headed out to meet a total stranger without letting anyone know where he was going, she would."

Henry tried to push Andy out of the way, but he wasn't budging. "Spill, Henry."

With an impatient huff, Henry stepped back. "Fine. He's in my class, so he's not a stranger. His name's Mahito. His parents went back to Tokyo last year but he was born here and didn't want to leave. They weren't happy when he came out to them, so they didn't mind leaving him behind and he didn't mind them going. He's twenty. He lives down by the water, and—"

"Whoa. I didn't ask for his life story. Telling me he's not a serial killer would've done."

Ignoring him, Henry finished, "And we're meeting at the Pumpjack."

Safe enough, though it wasn't somewhere Andy went often. Last time he'd walked in, he'd found it packed with leather-wearing bears, the music quiet enough he heard every comment made about his ass. Picturing Henry in there stretched his imagination to snapping point.

"Try again. There's no way in hell you'd go there. Leather's not your thing."

"How do you know?" Henry countered, but he shifted his gaze and yeah, he was a pants-on-fire liar.

"Tell me where you're going."

"You never tell *me* where *you're* going."

"I would if you ever asked. Tonight, for instance, I'm going with you to meet this Mahito guy. After that, I'm working my way along Davie until I hook up with someone I know can show me a good time without getting weird about it."

"You're not coming—" Henry threw up his hands, the most dramatic gesture Andy had seen from him. "Fine! We're meeting for a pizza then coming back here. He's helping me with a project."

"*He's* helping *you*?" And things kept getting stranger.

"Yes! What, do you think he's using me to get a better grade or something? You are so full of shit." Henry's mild eyes blazed with hurt and anger. "Not everyone looks at me and sees a loser the way you do. And he's loaded, so you can cross being after my money off the list too."

"Hey!" Aghast, cursing himself for not making himself clear, Andy shook his head. "I didn't mean it that way. I didn't, okay? But you're so freaking good at everything, what do you need the help *for*?" He snorted. "It was a compliment, you touchy diva, you."

"Oh." Henry bit his full lower lip. "Right. Yeah."

"Sentences, Henry. Use your words."

"Asshole," Henry said, but without the seething rage, thank God. "I don't need much help. More of a second opinion."

"Ah. It's a cunning plan to get him into your lair and pounce. Got it." Andy held up his hand for a high five. "Way to go."

"It's not like that!" Henry screwed up his face, absently patting Andy's hand to return the high five. "Maybe a bit. But I'm not planning to pounce and if he did, I'd freak. He's shy. I'm clueless."

"But you like him?"

Henry gulped, the bob of his Adam's apple eloquent enough before his nod.

"Then it'll work out." Andy looked Henry over. "I'll make you a deal. I won't chaperone you if you at least change your shirt. That one has jam on it."

Henry blinked at him, eyes wide. "Mahito knows I'm clueless about fashion. I don't want him to think I'm trying to impress him."

Fashion? Try wearing clothes that fit before you aim for style. Baby steps, dude. "Why not? Everyone likes to think someone's made an effort for them." Andy paused. It was true. And he'd made one hell of an effort with Ethan. If he kept on dripping, he'd wear away that particular stone eventually.

"I guess." Henry rubbed at his nose, hard enough to redden it. "Okay, I'll do that, but I'm not wearing anything fancy."

"God forbid if you look nice." Andy tousled Henry's hair, which he'd at least washed. "So do you want me to crash with one of the Crew and give you some privacy?"

The Crew was their name for the group of friends Andy hung out with, so called because Henry claimed he couldn't remember their names. The members changed, but there was a core of three Andy had known for years. Any of them would provide a couch for the night. Not a bed. They were friends, not fuck-buddies. Gary was straight, Lee in a serious relationship and Simon and he had a no-sex-ever agreement dating back years.

"Love you like a brother," Simon had said once, drunk and chatty, "which is why I never want to know what you sound like with my dick in your ass."

"Would I even notice something that small?" Andy had asked and the discussion had gone nowhere after that, which had suited them both.

"No need." Henry squirmed like a toddler who needed to pee. "I told you we're hanging out."

"If it changes, text me. Keep it simple. Something like, got lucky, fuck off."

"Yeah, that sounds like me." Henry gestured at his bedroom. "If it'll get you off my back, I'll go change."

Watching him walk away, Andy thought he already had. A date. Henry. He repressed the urge to text everyone who knew Henry to tell them the news. Simon was convinced Henry was an alien.

"He doesn't drink—not even coffee—his clothes scare me and he's a virgin. Add it up and you get alien."

Simon always did suck at math.

Chapter Five

The first two bars Andy went to were good places to start a buzz, but empty of anyone hot and available. He texted his friends with depressing results. Gary was working a late shift, Simon wasn't answering—which meant he'd already scored—and Lee was visiting his boyfriend's twin sister, Carole, on the island. Andy pointed out he was only a ferry ride away, but got a terse message back from Carole telling him they were eating a meal she'd spent three hours making and she'd confiscated Lee's phone and her brother's, so would he kindly piss off.

Downing his second raspberry sorbet vodka, Andy left, headed for the Junction. If he didn't have anyone to talk to, he'd dance instead. The music there would be too loud to make conversation possible, which suited him. If he woke up with a sore throat on Saturday morning, it should be from giving a great blow job, not from yelling himself hoarse the night before.

People crowded the sidewalks, but every face belonged to a stranger. Andy was usually part of a crowd, raucous, uninhibited and confident in their hotness. Going clubbing by himself was a humbling experience, placing him in the desperate and friendless category. It didn't help that the thought of going into work on Sunday depressed him. Being new meant getting stuck with a crappy schedule and filling in for people when needed. A six-day work week took some getting used to and when tourists flooded the city in the summer, it would be even worse. Pointing out he was supposed to have two days off a week hadn't gone down well with anyone in the break room.

The club didn't help lift his mood—which was a first—and after an hour and three more drinks, he gave up. Too noisy. Too full of people enjoying themselves the way he'd planned to do and apparently couldn't when he was flying solo.

He pushed through the packed bodies on the dance floor, T-shirt sticking to him with sweat. His ass got pinched and someone caressed his junk three steps later. Irritated, he put his head down and aimed for the coat check. He didn't know where he was going but he wasn't staying.

Outside, he stood, unsure of which direction to take. His stomach growled. It had been doing that for a while, the sound lost in the insistent beat of the music. He patted it. Pizza. Yeah. Henry had put the idea in his head, so why not?

He went into the first pizza place he passed and ordered a veggie, hold the olives. He wasn't a vegetarian but he didn't like meat on his pizza. The guy behind the counter was cute but distracted, ready to flirt, but too busy to put much effort into it. Andy sat at one of the small plastic tables and ate two slices before conceding defeat. Pizza and raspberries didn't go together and the harsh lighting made his head ache. He was drunker than he'd realized. Those last two drinks…single or doubles? Oh God, of course they were doubles. He'd forgotten the two-for-one promo the club did early on in the evening, when he usually arrived much later.

Some bartender he was, not noticing that. No wonder Ethan was always on his case, nagging, finding fault, pushing at him to do everything better, everything perfect—the Ethan way.

With self-pity gathering steam, he closed the pizza box and wiped his greasy fingers on a paper napkin that shredded after use. The ones at the hotel were thick and soft. Everything in the hotel was expensive. He'd taken to wearing the trashiest underwear he had as a silent rebellion against so much class. Even a sequined thong one day, though he'd taken it off on his first break. The sequins itched and he wasn't prepared to suffer pointlessly. Going commando and bumping into Ethan had been a mistake. He'd received a searching appraisal and rolled eyes, though Ethan hadn't come out and called him on it. Maybe there were lines even Ethan wouldn't cross when it came to monitoring his staff.

On the street again, the pizza box warm against his hands, he focused on walking in a straight line, thoughts muddled, balance an issue. Avoiding a couple holding hands took him close to the edge of the road and he almost trod on a huddled shape, using a trashcan to lean against.

Andy had lived in the city all his life and was used to seeing homeless people sleeping in doorways. He moved from faint pity to a stronger relief it wasn't him, followed by a stab of guilt at his mopiness. Compared to this guy, he had everything he needed.

He glanced down, seeing a lot of dark, greasy hair and a beard covering the man's lower face.

As if sensing Andy's gaze, the man looked up, mumbling a few words, his hand outstretched, but Andy kept walking. He didn't buy into the idea any money he handed over would go on drugs or alcohol—and if it did, he couldn't blame people for buying a slice of oblivion—but he'd pass five or six more homeless people on his route and giving them all something was impractical.

Justifying his lack of charity, he was about to turn a corner when the words the man had muttered surfaced in his head.

'Spare some food?'

Not cash. Food. He'd misheard and he'd walked past a hungry man with a pizza he'd end up tossing out in a day or two because he never remembered he had leftovers in the fridge.

Shit.

Andy spun around fast enough to make him stumble even when he wasn't drunk, and ran back to the man, cursing his lack of basic human kindness. How hard would it have been to listen? Where did he get off treating the man like garbage with a pulse?

The man was still there, slumped listlessly, clutching a blanket to his chest with grimy hands. The hotel provided blankets in case anyone experienced a momentary shiver in the climate-controlled rooms. They were thick and soft, lying folded across the beds, a splash of color in some rooms, muted beige in others. Thousands of blankets and none of them were ripped and filthy like this one.

If the guy recognized Andy, it didn't show on his blank face.

"I'm so fucking sorry," Andy said, breathless from the short run. "I didn't hear you. Here. Pizza. Take it."

He opened the lid of the box so the smell wafted out as an appetizer and squatted down to hand it over.

The man took the box and shot him a bewildered, questioning look when he saw there were six slices left.

"Take it," Andy said again and stood, then he backed away, still gripped by the horror of realizing how close he'd come to failing Humanity 101. His face burned with embarrassment but the mist cooled it on the way home.

No sock on the door, no text heating up his phone, but when Andy entered, he wished he hadn't. Henry and his date were naked on the couch, the room lit by a lamp in the corner with an inadequate sixty-watt bulb. The dim light didn't hide enough.

Andy had walked in on Seth fucking a few times, but that was different. No one had cared. Hell, Seth's partner had invited him to join them once. Andy had turned him down with a shudder. Henry's first time should've been private and special. The guy deserved that much at least.

Henry saw him, took his hand off Mahito's cock—and if he'd been wearing his glasses, he would've pushed them up. Andy was sure of it—then put his hand back, using it to shield Mahito from Andy's view. Henry had a protective streak a mile wide—and a surprisingly muscular body under all the layers of shapeless clothing he wore. Mahito yelped and hid his face in a cushion like a kid defeating a monster by diving under the covers. He was, from the glimpse Andy had got, totally out of Henry's league when it came to looks, his hair dyed silver streaked with purple, with high cheekbones and a pouting mouth, lush and kissable. Cute as hell.

It was a dramatic entrance, but Andy wished the stage directions had called for him to back out unseen. This was awkward for everyone. With an apologetic grimace, he jerked his thumb back at the door. "Leaving right now. I'll be back in the morning. Nice to meet you, Mahito. Love the hair."

Henry sighed and banged his head rhythmically against the arm of the couch, prompting Mahito to straighten and grab him, murmuring a reassurance Andy didn't catch as he backed away fast.

Once he'd closed the door behind him, he clattered down the stairway to the alley between their house and the one next door. He didn't have a destination in mind, but he'd sort something out. He could use all his wages and get a room at the hotel. See what it was like being a guest there. As grand gestures went, it had promise, but checking in with no luggage or recognized as a staff member might lead to another awkward situation.

He sat on the first bench he came to, soaking the seat of his jeans with rain in the process, and called Gary, shunted to voicemail a moment later. Crap.

Maybe he could sweet-talk his way into one of the employee dorm rooms, though his chances weren't good. Joel had stressed they were for work-related emergencies only. Andy suspected the rule would be flexible for a long-term employee, rigid as steel for a new employee like him.

And now he had an image of Henry's dick in his head and that was all kinds of wrong.

He could always go back to the club and stay there until it closed at three, then find a coffee shop if he hadn't scored. It wouldn't be the first time he'd skipped sleep to party. It threw his body clock out of whack, but he could spend Saturday sleeping, after a suitable amount of time lecturing Henry for screwing around on the communal couch. Considering Henry's reaction to a tiny spill of soy sauce, he had no business getting bodily fluids on the cushions. Shit, did Henry have condoms and lube? Should he text Henry and tell him to help himself to the stash in Andy's bedroom?

He took out his phone then reconsidered. Interrupting them once had been their fault. Doing it twice would look like revenge. He contemplated the growing puddle at his feet. Mist had turned to drizzle and he was dressed for clubbing, not warmth. Time to move, but the necessary energy eluded him. Easier to sit and get wet, thoughts drifting, the alcohol in his system insulating him from the physical discomfort of a damp ass.

A man walked by the bench and paused then tapped Andy's foot with his to get his attention.

What the hell? "Hey, asshole, walk on, will you—Oh!"

Ethan. Staring down at him with exasperation darkening his eyes. "Would you like to try that again?"

Recklessness had made Andy do a lot of stupid shit in his life, accounting for a broken toe, six stitches on his shoulder blade and a one-week suspension from school at the age of ten. Age had brought wisdom. He swallowed a retort and said, "Hi, sir. Out slumming?"

Okay, he needed a few more birthdays under his belt. And a few less slugs of vodka.

"We're not at work. You don't need to call me sir." Ethan's hair lay sleek with rain, but the long coat he wore protected what was undoubtedly a suit. Ethan didn't wear anything else. "In fact, you don't need to use it at work, but you seem to enjoy being different."

"What?" Andy shook his head, strands of hair clinging to his cheeks. "That's not why I do it."

"Then why?"

What a surreal conversation on a rainy night. Andy let the vodka do the talking, disassociating himself from the words and any fallout—not him speaking, spilling out a confession. Not him locking his hands together to stop himself from reaching out to touch Ethan.

"It turns me on and so do you. Big time."

"Ah. I don't play those games."

Andy looked up, made bold by the certainty this was the only chance he'd have to lay it out for Ethan. "I don't see you in leather with a whip, but when I call you that, you like it. So why don't you do something about it? I want you to. Ever since that first day. It's driving me crazy. Can't figure you out, but I know I want you to fuck me."

"You're drunk." For a man in charge of several bars, Ethan sounded disapproving. "And rambling. Go home."

"Can't." Andy went back to staring at the puddle. Rejection on top of a crappy Friday night. He never got rejected—ever. He was cute, like Mahito, and getting someone to sleep with him had never involved more than asking. Usually, it was them doing the asking and he was the one picking and choosing.

"Why?"

God, Ethan had the persistence of a thirsty mosquito. "Room-mate's getting laid for the first time. I cleared out to give him some space. I'd crash at a friend's but I can't get hold of anyone." Andy risked a peek up through his lashes. "I don't suppose I could use one of the staff rooms at the hotel?"

"For once, you're totally correct."

"I knew you'd say that." Andy sniffed, trying to make it pitiful not gross. "You're an asshole, *sir*."

"Possibly, but I'm an asshole who's fond of his job and doesn't want to lose it." Ethan sighed. "You've got nowhere to go?"

"I've got options. Always do. Club, then coffee shop. Or I might stay here." Andy patted the bench. "It's a nice bench. Hard. I like sitting on hard things."

"Spare me your attempt at humor. Sober or drunk, it doesn't amuse me." Ethan crooked his finger and the night grew warmer. Tropical even. "Fine. You're coming home with me."

The unexpected invitation took a moment to register. "I am?"

"Yes," Ethan said flatly. "I'm not continuing this conversation in public and I need you healthy—and sober—for your shift on Sunday."

"It's a fallacy getting chilly and wet gives you a cold." Andy frowned. "I read that somewhere, but I can't remember why. What's a fallacy anyway? It sounds kinda dirty, but you didn't yell at me, so I guess it can't be." He stood, wet jeans clinging to his ass and thighs like clammy hands he couldn't shake off. "Your place? Sure. Why not? I can't wait to get out of these jeans."

"You can take everything off, if you want, but we won't be having sex." Ethan arched his eyebrows. "Does that change your answer?"

"No."

Andy supposed Ethan had to say that, but one look at him naked and that would change, Andy was sure of it. Mentally, he was doing a victory dance with fist pumps and pompoms. Okay, ditch the pompoms.

"You think I'll change my mind." Ethan shook his head slowly, erasing the possibility. "I'm a man of my word, Andrew, but I'll let you discover that yourself."

"'Andrew?'" Andy protested, falling in beside Ethan when he strode away.

"I could always make it boy in retaliation for the sir."

"No one calls me Andrew. Ever. Only you."

"Good."

Ethan had said it so quietly Andy wasn't sure he'd heard correctly, but the implications kept him silent until they reached the car.

* * * *

Ethan lived in a split-level loft on Beach Avenue with a view of Granville Island and one—count them—one bedroom. It was spacious enough, but the complete lack of clutter would've made even a smaller place seem large.

Andy stood on the main floor beside a dark green leather couch. He tilted his head back and looked up at the master bedroom, open to view, a balcony in light wood, the color of maple syrup, flowing into a handrail for the stairs. The floor was the same wood with the exception of the kitchen. Tiles in a richly shimmering mix of green and brown covered that area. The appliances were copper, not the standard stainless steel. This wasn't a place for visitors. It was Ethan's shell, perfectly formed to fit around him. Bedraggled and drunk, Andy was as out of place as a dirty plate would've been.

Glass doors led onto a balcony, an outside light showing an all-season table and two chairs. Evergreens in stone pots added life, and planters filled with branches of willow and dogwood waited for the addition of spring flowers to provide more color. Andy pictured Ethan out there in warm weather, sipping a coffee and reading a book. He added himself to the image. There. Across from Ethan in the other chair, watching the boats sail by in the harbor or the clouds scudding across the sky. Or maybe kneeling at his feet, waiting for a touch of his hand, a quietly spoken order.

Though the patio floor *was* concrete. Not good for kneeling on. And though he kinda got off on that dynamic in porn if it wasn't too out there, he wasn't sure that translated to enjoying it when he was the one collared and chained, waiting for a whipping. He'd be screaming his safe word before the first blow landed.

"Wow." Inadequate, but it was all he had.

Ethan eyed him thoughtfully. "Do you like it or is that what you think I want to hear?"

"Not bullshitting you. It's different. It's like you. It's also so freaking tidy I'm scared to move. How do you do that?"

"Everything has a place and when I'm finished with it, I put it back."

"That simple," Andy marveled. "Wow. Again."

"Stop saying that. And take off your socks, please. You're leaving marks on the floor."

Andy had taken off his shoes and jacket when he'd arrived, Ethan tidying them away into a closet, out of sight. He lifted up his right foot, and yeah, his damp socks were killing the dull sheen on the wooden floor. He peeled them off and stood clutching them.

"If you were serious about letting me stay, can I get changed and throw all this in the dryer?"

"Changed into what?"

With anyone else, that might've been the lead to a joke, but he couldn't read Ethan well enough to know how to respond. At least he'd discovered Ethan owned something other than suits. Under the long coat, Ethan wore a formfitting dark gray sweater over casual black trousers, the sweater scooped at the neck to show a hint of skin.

Andy shivered. The loft was toasty warm but his wet clothing meant he was cold to the bone.

"A sweatshirt? Maybe a pair of shorts or something? I don't know. Anything you have. I usually sleep naked, but..."

"Not on my couch, you don't. I'll dig out something for you to borrow." Ethan nodded at the stairs. "Bathroom's up there. Shower and leave your clothes outside the door. I'll take care of them."

A fuzzy layer coated his brain by the time he reached the bathroom. Pink, raspberry-flavored fuzz. Shower. So he needed to undress. Yeah.

He'd forgotten to close the door and Ethan walked by, presumably on his way to hunt up some clothes, as Andy skinned his T-shirt over his head. Ethan paused and Andy tossed the balled-up garment in the general direction of the door before he could stop himself. His impulse control sucked.

The soft clump of damp cotton hit Ethan in the face, before falling to the floor.

"Sorry." Andy giggled. "Getting undressed."

Ethan raised his eyebrows. "Don't let me stop you."

Sober, Andy might've looked for a way out. Drunk, he took the implicit dare and added a twist.

It wasn't a bump-and-grind striptease. Andy had done them in the past for a laugh, but this wasn't a tease or even an invitation. This was showing Ethan he didn't intimidate easily. Everything he took off, he threw, missing Ethan because he wasn't suicidal, but still tossing them at him.

Meeting Ethan's cool, blank gaze, he stood naked, arms by his sides, showing Ethan he wasn't hard and didn't mind an audience. Except, even as he thought that, the spark of defiance quelling his shivers, Ethan passed his tongue over his lips and Andy's cock hardened, a helpless surge of lust stiffening it. He wanted to push it down, slap it soft, punish it for revealing his interest, but what was it telling Ethan that Andy hadn't already shared?

So he ignored it and walked toward the shower, concentrating on making each step a dignified pace, not part of a helter-skelter scramble for an enclosed space.

Hand on the shower door, he turned and caught Ethan staring at his ass in the moment before Ethan closed the door. Jesus, why had he thought Ethan didn't care if he was naked? The guy looked hungry and Andy had put himself on the menu.

He looked around before getting into the shower. Nice bathroom. Towels so fluffy and white they looked like pieces cut from a cartoon cloud. Towels could look like that, Andy knew, but his were thin, ratty and limp, clean enough, but uninviting. He wanted to spread these towels on the floor and roll around on them.

Ethan apparently had magic toothpaste, designed not to ooze out and crust around the lid. White fixtures in here, and the tiles, also white at first glance, were iridescent, subtle lighting bringing out a dozen different colors, faint and watery.

The white bathmat was fluff-free and yet fluffy. It would be easy to mock so much attention to detail, but this was Ethan's way of living and the orderliness and neat freak cleanliness was restful in a way. Everything was where it should be, ready for use. Ethan would never be late because he couldn't find a clean shirt or go to work with stubble, after forgetting to buy razors. Ethan would never fall out of bed an hour after the alarm should've gone off because the batteries in his SpongeBob clock had been dead for a week. And Ethan wouldn't still own a clock from his tenth birthday.

Andy pushed the bottle of hand soap an inch to the left. It looked wrong. He edged it back and it still didn't look right. Ethan must've positioned it using a ruler. Or one of those gadgets that sent out a beam of light, making picture hanging a breeze.

He gave up and stepped into the shower, a huge one next to a deep soaker tub. A skylight and a window beside it that came down level with the edge of the bath ensured plenty of natural light. Soaking on a sunny day would feel like swimming with that water view to look at. A blind covered the window now, making the space intimate, safe.

The hot water streamed down from a waterfall showerhead, soft and heavy, soaking him in seconds and bringing warmth to his chilled skin. He washed with Ethan's gel, leaving his skin smelling of cucumber and mint, according to the bottle, and dried off with one of the clouds masquerading as a towel.

His erection had subsided. Being ignored was a huge turn-off for Andy and his dick agreed. Jerking off in the shower was one of Andy's favorite places for that activity— private, discreet, no clean up needed— but in Ethan's shower? The man would know—Andy was sure of it—and he wouldn't be pleased.

He'd forgotten to flick the switch for the fan and condensation fogged the mirror. On impulse, he drew a heart in the fog, followed by a smiley face, then flipped the switch and watched the misted surface clear.

He wrapped a dry towel around his waist and carried the damp one with his clothes into the small laundry room next to the bathroom. Ethan hadn't dealt with them nor left out dry clothes, which Andy guessed was payback. Kind of petty but it didn't bother him. He spread the clothes out instead of starting the dryer. The clothes would dry by themselves overnight and he was warm enough not to mind being dressed in nothing but a towel.

He heard Ethan talking on the phone and without exactly eavesdropping, Andy caught a few sentences here and there. Boyfriend? Parent? No, Ethan was telling someone called Cathy what the book club was reading that month. Ethan in a book club kinda fit the picture he had of the man, but it was disappointingly mundane. Of course, it could be an erotic book club. That idea held promise.

Grinning, he padded downstairs and found Ethan, call ended, sitting in an armchair by a wall-mounted plasma fireplace, flames licking up from a crystal ember bed. The rug in front of the fire had a pile deep enough to lose change in, a complex swirl of earth tones slashed with thin black lines. Andy wanted to curl up on it and let the firelight paint his skin red.

"Towels belong in the bathroom or the laundry room." Ethan took a sip from a glass of what could've been anything from brandy to tequila. There was no bottle out and no second glass in sight. Ethan wasn't the ideal host. Andy's mom offered visitors a drink and food before they'd got through the door.

"It's okay. It's dry." Andy tucked it in more securely and sat on the couch.

Ethan snapped his fingers, looking a little pinched around the mouth, and pointed at the stairs. "If it's dry, put it back in the bathroom, please. Fold it the way the others are."

"Excuse me?"

"You're not good at following instructions, are you? I've noticed that." Ethan's words seemed directed more at himself than Andy. "Never mind."

"Did you find anything for me to wear?"

"Do you have a principle you follow in life?"

"Don't get caught," Andy said promptly, if only to break the cycle of questions answered with more questions.

Ethan curled his lip. "Illuminating. I believe actions have consequences, unavoidable and if it's down to me, equitable."

"Break it down smaller. The vodka's still in my system."

"You tossed your clothes at me and pissed me off with your attitude. Consequence being, I took back the offer to lend you something. Get back into your wet clothes or sit naked. Your choice. But the towel goes back in the bathroom."

"Huh? What happened to no naked Andy on your furniture?"

"You're clean and dry. You won't hurt the couch."

Good to know. Andy went for a different approach. "Why do you want me naked if we're not having sex?"

"Payback. How drunk *are* you?"

Andy surged to his feet, and stepped closer to Ethan, outrage rising. "I'm not your fucking puppet! What kind of game are you playing?"

"I'm not, but if I was, it would be my game, my rules." Ethan sipped his drink again, outwardly unmoved by Andy looming over him. "You throw tantrums a lot, Andrew?"

"No!"

"Then why do you act like a spoiled kid around me so often?"

"Is that how you see me?" Andrew demanded. "I'm no kid and I'm not spoiled, either. See me living in a million-dollar loft with a view? No, you fucking don't."

"It cost half that amount and the mortgage payments eat up most of my wages." Ethan pasted on a faux-penitent look. "Sorry. I interrupted you and you were building up a nice head of steam on your rant. Carry on."

Baffled by Ethan's refusal to join the fight, Andy asked, "Why does it matter I'm wearing the towel outside the bathroom?"

"I prefer my belongings in their proper places and in good condition. You won't find a chipped mug or a dog-eared book lying around. You've worked for me for long enough to know I have my little quirks. Do you think I lose them when I come home? I don't. Ask anyone I've dated."

"You're making zero sense, you know that? Zero. But I'm not sitting around in wet jeans. You want me naked but don't have the balls to say so? Fine. You got it." He tore off the towel. "Happy now?"

Ethan's gaze went to the staircase, then the towel in Andy's hand. He didn't say anything. He didn't need to. Andy huffed out a sharp exhalation and stomped his way upstairs. White towel back where it came from, folded and draped over a rod. Check. Naked Andy going back downstairs to talk to the crazy man... Yeah, he was doing that too. Ethan had promised him a conversation. If it ended with him struggling back into his damp clothes and leaving, he was no worse off than he'd been an hour ago.

Unless he counted losing the chance to get to know Ethan better. Somehow, even after everything that had happened, that would hurt.

Chapter Six

The approval in Ethan's eyes when Andy returned to the couch naked was plain to see. It soothed Andy's irritation a little. He'd thought pleasing Ethan was beyond him and it was nice to be wrong. There was a quilt draped over the couch now, a tacit opportunity for him to cover up if he wanted. To prove he didn't mind flashing Ethan, Andy sat on the quilt instead of crawling under it.

"See?" Ethan asked. "Not so difficult, was it? I don't ask the impossible."

"I need to know what's going on." Andy stifled a yawn. God, he was tired. Long shifts with plenty of hard physical work coupled with a disruption of his sleep pattern—stay up late, sleep in later—were catching up with him. The buzz from drinking had worn off, leaving him lethargic and slow to grasp nuances. What clues was he missing to explain the way Ethan was alternating between pushing him away and teasing him closer? "Is this your idea of slapping me down for saying I wanted to have sex with you?"

"No. I already knew that. You're not exactly subtle. If I'd wanted you, I could've had you on the day of your interview."

"Probably, yeah." Andy raised his eyebrows. "You think I'm a slut? I always use a condom. I don't poach and I don't break hearts. I'm not going to apologize for having fun."

"I don't recall asking you to." Ethan gave him a quizzical look. "*Is* it fun, though?"

"Yes, of course—" Under that steady gaze, Andy couldn't finish the lie. "It's okay. It's sex. I get to come. That's what it's all about, right?"

"So it's scratching an itch. But the more you scratch, the worse the itch gets, because it's not a real cure, only a temporary moment of relief."

"Got a better idea?" *Please. And let it involve both of us naked.*

Ethan set his glass down on a low, square table beside his chair. "Plenty, but I'm not a life coach. I'm your employer. And I'm still not interested in you, especially now I've seen you naked."

Secure about his looks, ego uncrushed, Andy retorted, "That's not the usual reaction I get."

Ethan looked him over, a cool appraisal lingering on certain places, such as Andy's chest and feet, but not his cock. "You're attractive enough, and I don't mind you being younger since you're hardly an innocent virgin, but you're scruffy. Huge turn-off for me."

The critique took his breath away. "Excuse me? Scruffy? What? I don't meet your standards outside work either?"

"That's about it." Ethan yawned. "Sorry. Long week."

"I know. I was there."

"In body, but you're still not committed to the job and it shows." Ethan picked up his drink. "How serious are you about acting?"

"What? I *am* an actor. It's not a question of being serious. It's who I am." He patted his chest. "Me, actor. You, neat freak crossed with control freak. Double freak."

"If you think you got across anything useful there, you'd be wrong."

Andy pressed his lips together. "I've been the lead in every school play since kindergarten. I graduated in the top ten percent of my class. I'm having trouble clicking when it comes to making it big. That's all."

"Are you in a union?"

"Not yet. You see—"

"Have an agent?"

"Yeah. Well, I'm on the books of one. She calls when something comes along that's right for me."

"When did she call last?"

"She hasn't—not recently, but she—"

"Film, TV, stage? What paid work have you done?"

Floundering under the relentless assault of questions, he was at a loss for words. Hell, he was close to tears. "What do you want me to say? That I'm getting nowhere? Fine! I'm a failure. Is that good enough or do you want it in writing?"

Ethan shook his head. "I didn't mean to upset you. I want to know what stage you're at in your career."

Naked, he was vulnerable enough without exposing his failures. "I'm spinning my wheels now, because I'm working for you, so I can't go to auditions or get experience acting for free. When I saved up enough, I'll focus on it more. But I've got to eat."

"You do. Though less junk food wouldn't hurt." Ethan stared at Andy's stomach. "You're out of shape."

Andy leaned back against the couch, the cool leather sending a shiver through him, tightening his nipples. "I'm down and you're kicking me. Great. How about some sympathy?"

"Your problems have solutions." Ethan sounded indifferent. "I'll save my sympathy for people with ones that don't."

"Yeah? Enlighten me."

"You expect people to do your work for you."

"Meaning?"

"Like getting Niall to deal with the delivery on Tuesday so you could get a look at that soap star checking in?"

"I didn't—"

"He likes you," Ethan continued. "He's young, romantic, and God help him, he has a crush on you."

"I know, and I'm flattered but he's *so* not my type. I haven't done anything to encourage him." Niall barely registered on his radar and that would be the case with or without his feelings for Ethan, but he didn't share that fact.

"Believe me, that's all that's saved you from my wrath. And I would've gotten pretty damn wrathful. I don't like romantic complications screwing up my team."

Stung by the unfairness—it wasn't his fault Niall had a crush on him—Andy asked, "What? I can't date at work?"

"Not Niall," Ethan said. "You'd break his heart and he'd leave. That's unacceptable. Anyone else, go for it."

"The only one I'm interested in is you, even if it proves I'm a fucking masochist since you treat me like shit."

"I saved you from a night on the street, cold and wet. I gave you a job. I fought for you to keep it when—" Ethan broke off. "I think we've taken this conversation far enough and I'm tired. I'll get you some water."

Indignant and confused by Ethan's disclosure, Andy shook his head. "Not thirsty."

"Yeah, you are. A glass now and one for when you wake in the night with a mouth like sand." Ethan stood. "Want a painkiller too?"

"No."

With Ethan standing over him like the gay Mary Poppins making sure he took his medicine, Andy drank a large glass of water and settled down on the couch, too tired to fight. It would wait until the morning. Then he'd pin Ethan down and get answers to every question buzzing inside his head. Ethan refilled the glass and pulled the small table close to the couch, setting the glass down after sliding a coaster under it.

"Solve one problem for me," Andy said through a yawn. "One. Go on. Bet you can't."

"Already done. I made your hangover go away."

Smug bastard.

Sleep came easily with Andy wrapped in bedding that smelled of Ethan—or smelled of the detergent Ethan used. Andy hadn't reached the point of sniffing out the brand at the supermarket, but if he ever came across it, he was buying it. He had nightmares, not dreams. Monsters chased him, his legs not working as he ran up a hill. He called for help on his phone, tapping out an endless number he kept getting wrong so he had to start over.

He woke, disorientated, parched, body rank with sweat. He'd thrashed around and turned himself into a mummy with the quilt, arms and legs constricted by the thick, soft material.

Panicked, he fought free and lay gasping, the cooler air of the room drying his sweat. His disjointed thoughts lumbered from one recollection to another. Couch. Ethan's couch. Vodka. Too much, but he didn't feel terrible, only thirsty. Water on the table. Yeah.

He stretched out his hand, struck the glass and knocked it flying to shatter on the wooden floor.

Shit, water on the floor would ruin it. Ethan would get mad at him and he didn't want that. Didn't ever want that.

With no other thought in his head, he scrambled off the couch, then headed for the kitchen. He'd get a cloth, mop up the water and take care of the mess before Ethan saw it.

Or, when a shard of glass dug into the sole of his left foot, he'd scream, step back, embed another shard in the heel of his right foot and scream again.

Frozen, trapped by the darkness and fear, he drew a breath to call for help, but even as he sucked in air, he heard Ethan's feet hit the floor, followed by rapid footsteps as Ethan ran along the short hallway and took the stairs at reckless speed.

"Glass on the floor," Andy called out in warning, shivering from reaction. Cold. Dizzy. Couldn't faint. "Turn on the light."

The wash of brightness scalded his eyes. He screwed them shut then opened them a crack, blinking until they'd adjusted.

Ethan took in the situation with a single glance. "Stay there. Do not move."

"Glass in my feet," Andy told him through chattering teeth. God, Ethan looked good. Even dazed and in pain, that registered like a blow. Black muscle T-shirt and boxer briefs clinging to a strong body, pared down, lean and powerful. "Got to sit."

Except the path to the couch required navigating through a dozen chunks and God knows how many tiny splinters of glass and he was too unsteady to manage it.

"Andrew." Ethan's voice was compelling, hypnotic. "Do as I tell you. Stand still."

Do as I tell you. He'd heard that command from teachers, parents and babysitters, always barked out, annoyance coating each syllable. Ethan had said it with a reassuring firmness, bare of anger, certain of Andy's obedience.

From a place deep inside, Andy said, "Yes, sir," and was rewarded by a slackening of the tension in Ethan's shoulders.

He stood, feet throbbing, stomach twisted by pain. Ethan went to the closet and shoved his feet into running shoes, leaving the laces untied. Without looking down, he crunched over the glass and reached Andy, swinging him into his arms with a grunt.

Andy cried out, the pain in his feet flaring hot, and clutched at Ethan's bare shoulder, digging his nails into warm flesh as if inflicting pain would lessen his. "Hurts. Shit. Am I bleeding everywhere?"

"I'll take a look." Ethan deposited him on the couch with another grunt of exertion. "I need to work out more."

"Look fine to me." Andy bit his lip. "God, I'm so sorry. I woke up and I reached for the glass and –"

Ethan tapped his finger against Andy's lips. "Shut up. Lie still and I'll take care of you."

Even through the haze of pain, he registered that light tap, resonating through him until he quivered responsively like a struck bell. He lay on the couch, wincing since every involuntary flex of his foot brought a spike of fresh discomfort. To distract himself, he watched Ethan, who had kicked off his shoes at the edge of the scattered glass to gather supplies.

The practicality of taking off his shoes to avoid carrying splinters into the kitchen struck Andy. That was so Ethan. The guy never panicked, thought things through. He admired that about him. He dunked his feet in a bucket of warm water, blood dripping onto quilt and floor when he swung around.

"It's got Epsom salts in there. Don't press down. Let them float. I'm boiling a kettle to sterilize the tweezers."

"Oh, God."

"Don't be a baby." Ethan grinned at him, a quick flash of humor. "Be a brave little soldier and I'll give you some candy."

"Fuck you," Andy said without heat.

"Candy or nothing."

Andy soaked his feet and Ethan swept the floor then went over it again with a handheld vacuum. The light glinted off missed splinters and Andy pointed them out when he saw them. When the floor was clean and dry, Ethan dropped his shoes into a plastic bag and set it aside. "I'll clean the glass out of them tomorrow. Time for your feet."

Gritting his teeth when Ethan went to work with a pair of tweezers, Andy did his best to earn the candy, wondering what form it would take. A kiss? A ruffle of his hair? Or had it been a joke, nothing more?

Ethan worked in silence. Andy concentrated on not throwing up.

"I think that's all of it." Ethan dried Andy's feet with a soft towel, blotting the water away rather than rubbing at wet, torn skin. "The bleeding has stopped and the cuts don't look deep enough for stiches." He smeared on antiseptic cream, then taped a padded dressing over the two deepest cuts. "Okay, all done. I'll tidy up what's left and get you another quilt. This one's soaked."

With blood and water.

Andy submitted to Ethan's deft, if impersonal, handling, during the swapping of the quilts. He'd never been nude around a man for so long without either of them taking it somewhere, but Ethan seemed unmoved by Andy's body. That wasn't a guess. The briefs Ethan wore would've showcased an erection, but when Andy sneaked a peek, he saw nothing but the soft mound of cock and balls. Pain had kept him from responding to Ethan's handling and proximity. An erection waving in the wind would've been all kinds of awkward.

"Anything else you need?" Ethan asked, punctuating it with a yawn that he smothered.

Andy shook his head. Ethan turned to go, and he leaned forward, snatching Ethan's hand. "Wait. One thing."

Ethan glanced at their linked hands, freed himself with a gentle tug, and faced Andy. "Yeah?"

"You promised me candy. Okay, unless you meant it literally, give me an answer instead. If we didn't work together, if we met at a club or something and I chatted you up, asked you to come home with me for sex — would you turn me down?"

"Yes."

"You said that without thinking about it."

"I know the answer. What is there to think about?"

"Why? Don't give me the whole scruffy excuse. You could tidy me up if you had to. Give me a makeover until I met the Ethan standard of desirability."

Ethan drew in a breath and stepped back, holding up his hands. "You can get lucky any night of the week. Don't obsess over me."

Andy sent his gaze south. "You're getting hard." He watched the soft shape grow firm. "From what?"

"Go to sleep."

"No." Andy sat upright. "I want to know what's wrong with me. I'm not obsessing over — well, yeah, okay, I am — but I swear if we hooked up it would be on the down-low at work. I wouldn't put you in a difficult position or gossip about you. I wouldn't, okay?"

"I believe you," Ethan said. "That's not the reason."

"Then what is?" Andy threw back his head, releasing his frustration with a groan. "Gah! It's sex, Ethan! Throw me a pity fuck and let me get you out of my system. I haven't been with anyone since I met you and celibacy isn't healthy." He met Ethan's gaze. "I'm begging here, in case you haven't noticed. I'd get on my knees if my feet weren't cut to ribbons."

Seemingly indifferent to the erection straining at his briefs, Ethan said, "That's not going to happen. Any of it. And the cuts aren't deep."

"Tell me what the fuck is wrong with me!"

"You? Nothing in most men's eyes. And before you ask, there's nothing wrong with me either, but I don't see why I should suffer through mediocre sex to kill off your crush."

"Why do you think it would be mediocre?"

"What works for you doesn't do a damn thing for me," Ethan snapped. "I'm kinky, okay? I'm hard now. You've pushed some buttons without realizing it, but we wouldn't get far before you'd do or say something to turn me off. I could keep it up, even come, but I wouldn't get anything out of it beyond a few seconds of physical pleasure and that's not enough. I don't settle for second best when it comes to sex or my partner. I never have once I worked out what got me off. Now take your selfish demands, shove them up your ass and accept you're never getting any part of me in there."

With long strides, Ethan crossed the room to the light switch, flipped it then went upstairs, leaving a speechless Andy alone in the dark with a dozen more questions to ask and no one to answer them.

* * * *

Waking up on the couch, Ethan's palm cupping his cheek for an instant, was a huge improvement on Henry hammering on the door. Andy smiled, eyes bleary with sleep, and yawned widely, jaw cracking. "What time is it?"

"Do you have plans?"

If he did, they were lost in the fog blanketing his brain. "No."

"Then it doesn't matter. I'm going to grind coffee. It's noisy so I thought I'd wake you first."

Wow. Considerate or what? Andy yawned again then left the couch and his warm nest of quilt and cushions for the bathroom, treading gingerly. His feet hurt less than he'd expected. Some twinges, yes, but no throbbing. His dry clothes were in a neat pile outside the bathroom door, the contents of his jeans pockets on top. The square condom packages stood out. He'd gone for fruit-flavored and colored to match — grape, strawberry and pineapple. The tiny bottle of lube looked less juvenile at least. He refused to feel embarrassed. At least Ethan knew he had the sense to play safely.

Ethan had set out a toothbrush still in its wrapper and, after taking care of business, Andy brushed his teeth, cleaning the toothpaste from the square bowl with scrupulous care and a handful of toilet paper. He stared at his reflection. Did he look like a man who had badgered his boss into an admission of being into kinky sex and had blown his chances? Depressing. Maybe a guy with a mild hangover who could use excess alcohol as an excuse for his actions?

Mostly, he looked red-eyed and pale. It wasn't an attractive combination.

So what next? Fake amnesia and slide out of the door, abandoning his pursuit?

Hell, no. Ethan was kinky? He could handle kinky. Maybe. It wasn't putting him off, anyway. In fact, if Ethan had wanted to pique his curiosity, that was the way to do it. Forbidden fruit was the sweetest and juiciest.

He got dressed and joined Ethan in the kitchen — a barefoot Ethan in loose sweatpants and a short-sleeved T-shirt. Casual suited him and it had the benefit of making him seem more approachable. Andy gave him a toothpaste-commercial-worthy smile, papering over the cracks their frankness had left, then drew in an appreciative breath. Coffee brewing, orange juice in a jug and was that an omelet being prepped and the smell of cinnamon buns wafting from the oven? Throw in some bacon and hash browns and he'd be in heaven. He'd pictured Ethan living on granola and fresh air with his lean frame. Knowing him, Ethan probably planned to work out later and burn off the calories.

Ethan darted a quick look his way. "Sleep well?"

"Would've slept better in a bed." *Hint, hint.* "The couch is comfortable, though. Thanks for letting me use it and taking care of my feet." See? He had manners.

"No problem." Ethan nodded at the table. "Sit. Breakfast will be ready soon. No allergies or violent dislikes?"

"Nope. If it's edible, I'll eat it. If it's sweet, salty, greasy and deep-fried, I'll love it."

"Hmm." That noncommittal sound meant something, but Andy hadn't figured it out yet. He accepted coffee and a tall glass of juice. A moment later, Ethan placed a steaming cinnamon bun, the frosting melting off the sides, in front of him.

"If I proposed on the basis of breakfast, would you say it was too soon?"

Ethan blinked twice, then matched Andy's mood without missing a step. "Yes. After the omelet? No."

Their conversation flowed easily, never touching work, never delving deeply. Andy ate until his stomach strained against his jeans, devouring a fluffy, thick mushroom and cheese omelet with a side of fried potatoes, golden brown and crunchy on the outside, meltingly soft inside. Ethan refilled his mug and glass, courteous as a waiter, and cleared his plate too, though it had contained less than Andy's by a long way.

"I'm so full you'll need to roll me down the stairs." Andy patted his stomach. "Do you eat like this every day?"

Ethan snorted. "I don't have time to cook. But when I get a Saturday or Sunday off — which doesn't happen often — I make the most of it."

"Carpe diem."

"In my case, I get a Saturday to seize once every two months, if that."

"Which sucks. Since you're in charge of the timesheets, I've got to wonder if you're a masochist."

And that was the peaceful morning ripped in half to expose the night before. Andy didn't kick himself, though. Sooner or later, it was going to come up.

"Interesting theory," Ethan said lightly. "I have a system for loading the dishwasher, so why don't you clear the table and I'll take care of it from there?"

And when it did, it would be on Ethan's timetable. Figured.

When the place looked as if no one had ever cooked in it, even the lingering scent of cinnamon banished by the fan, Ethan nodded at the couch. "Sit."

With Ethan across from him in the armchair once again, the fire flickering, defeating the encroaching damp of an overcast February day, Andy prepared himself for a difficult conversation.

"Last night a lot got said that maybe should have stayed unsaid." Ethan gave him a questioning look. "Do you want to agree to forget it?"

"No." Shit, this might screw things up beyond repair but he had to say it. Had to. "It didn't go far enough. I told you I wanted you. I could've gone into detail. Shared every fantasy I have with you center stage and asked — no, begged — you to make a couple of them come true. But you shut me down before I got that far.

You're kinky? Do you know how often I've beat off in the men's room at work after I called you sir and you smiled at me like it'd given you a happy? How close I came to going to my knees in your office last week when you were bawling me out and offering you my mouth to fuck as a kind of—I don't know—penalty?"

"It wouldn't have been," Ethan said after a brief, charged silence. "You'd have enjoyed it."

Hard to argue with that.

"Anyway, the point is, when it comes to you, I'm not ready to fasten a collar around my neck, but I sure as hell get off on you being"—Andy swallowed—"uh, commanding? Anyone else orders me around and I fight it, but it's different with you. I want... I want to please you and yeah, that's all kinds of weird and you can laugh if you like, but it's true." He exhaled, wiping his hands over his jeans. "Okay. Soul-bared, kinks exposed. Your turn."

"I don't remember agreeing to that."

"Please," Andy pleaded. "Throw me a bone here. Look, if you tell me what cranks your motor and it works for me too, are you telling me you wouldn't want to do me?"

"I should if only to see you burst into tears."

"I would," Andy said. "Crushed. I'd crawl out of here a broken man."

"Yeah, I can see that happening." Ethan stared at the fire, his expression unreadable. "Your ego can stay intact."

Fist pumping would be so immature, but since Ethan wasn't looking, Andy shaped a silent 'yay', elation fizzing through him. Learning he wasn't in this alone did more than boost his ego. It soothed a raw place in his emotions he hadn't known was there.

"So tell me what gets you going," he prompted.

"Any experience in the scene?"

The porn he watched didn't count. "Personally, no. I'm friends with a couple who play at it. Maybe more than that, but I've never liked to ask questions."

"Color me amazed."

"Hey, back off." Andy scowled at him for the mockery. "This is hard enough without you being sarcastic."

"I'm sorry. Your friends…"

"They've got this whole Dom/sub vibe going on. Paul always has something around his neck. Not a collar, but it could be, you know? And the way he looks at Adrian, you can tell he's paying attention to every move he makes. He's…aware of him and it goes both ways." Andy shook his head. "I think I'm reading too much into it."

"I doubt it. If it's something that calls to you, then you're probably picking up on their signals without realizing." Ethan exhaled, the soft sound close to a sigh. "You think I'm like Adrian? Or hope I am?"

"I guess," Andy said cautiously. "Are you? You give off plenty of signals yourself."

"Sorry to disappoint you, but no. I don't have a dungeon tucked away behind a secret door and I've never put a collar around anyone's neck." Ethan looked at him, his gaze compelling. "I've worked out what gets me off by trial and error, but it's not easy getting my particular itch scratched."

"All you'd have to do is walk into one of the fetish bars on Davie and you'd have your pick of subs." And if he was in the club watching, he'd dissolve into a puddle of jealousy and longing.

"Who'd expect a nice spanking, some pain play or bondage, a lot of kneeling and a hard fuck." Ethan rubbed his thumb slowly along his index finger. "I could satisfy them, but they wouldn't come close to pleasing me."

"If you're into something hardcore, I wouldn't either." Andy smoothed his hands over his thighs, nerves getting the better of him. "I've seen kink online that turned me on, yeah, but some of it made me feel more like throwing up than jerking off. Blood and piss don't mix with sex for me. And fists are for fighting not... Well, you get the picture. Not judging, just saying."

Ethan laughed unexpectedly. "If you knew how wide your eyes were. No, nothing like that. You want to know? It's complicated and simple at the same time. I can't enjoy sex unless I'm the conductor. Every note originating from me with my partner performing perfectly." He narrowed his eyes, pure predator in that moment. "And I'd be lying if I didn't say part of me enjoys punishing failure. Maybe there's a healthy dose of the sadist in me after all."

"Some people would say healthy and sadist don't go together." Andy threw the words out there almost at random to cover his mounting excitement. Fight or flight didn't apply to him. If Ethan wanted to pounce, he'd let him. Ethan getting fussy over napkin folding and the number of ice cubes in a glass turned him on, but the thought of Ethan applying that level of precision to sex had him drooling.

Ethan rested his arm along the back of the couch, stroking the leather with a fingertip. "I don't plan to visit a therapist or a priest. The few times I've hooked up with someone on my wavelength, they didn't leave because the physical pain was too much—other way around with one of them—and they didn't leave with scars. I'm at peace with my kinks."

"So why didn't it work out with them?" He hated to think of Ethan with other guys and he didn't enjoy the idea of Ethan being hurt when they left, but he'd be lying if he said he wasn't overjoyed they were out of the picture.

"Submission sounds sexy when you're reading about it—even relaxing. Let someone else make all the decisions." Ethan changed position, hunched over, hands clasped in his lap. "It's hard work. You said your friends pay attention to each other. Yes. Exactly. And how many people can be bothered to do that? We're taught we matter most. That our needs come first. Giving that up to please someone else and making them the center of the world isn't easy." He looked at Andy, a hint of warning in his eyes. "And I'm not an easy man to please. I made mistakes, too. I was inflexible when I should have listened more and I didn't make allowances for real life affecting events. I screw up all the time, Andrew. I'm not perfect either. But it doesn't stop me trying to come close."

Andy leaned back. He was hard without remembering it happen, as if his body had absorbed Ethan's words and used them to feed an arousal too new for him to recognize it. He couldn't wrap his head around this—any of it.

"I want us to fuck."

"You said." Ethan's voice was flat, hiding, what? Disappointment, regret he'd shared so much with Andy for nothing? "It's not going to happen unless it's on my terms, my way."

"I could tell people about you. You'd lose your job. No, let me finish—" Andy sat up, shoving his hands out, palms facing Ethan as if that would keep Ethan in his seat. "You trusted me with all this personal shit. Why? You can count on me to keep my mouth zipped, but you didn't know that. I'm the wannabe actor screw-up who gets into trouble at least once a shift and keeps staring at your ass. Why did you *tell* me all this? Get me turned on, make me want—make me—"

Out of nowhere, he was crying, the unresolved emotions from the night before rising, spilling over. Tears slid down his cheeks. This was throat-scratchy, nose-blocked crying, like a brokenhearted kid. He stood, looking around wildly for an escape route, a hiding place. Too much. All of it. The arousal, Ethan's revelations, his cut feet, this stupid fucking wetness stinging his eyes—

There was only one refuge from his confusion, one source of comfort. He stumbled toward Ethan, went to his knees and buried his face in Ethan's lap, the smooth fabric of Ethan's trousers soaking up his tears.

He'd never done anything as difficult in theory and easy in practice.

Chapter Seven

He knelt. Each inward breath, each gusty exhale marked another moment when Ethan wasn't touching him. There were three. He counted. Then Ethan rested his hand against Andy's head, light but firm, holding him in place. His position, forehead pressed to Ethan's thigh, became Ethan's choice, not his. He stayed like that for a while, his tears over, though his cheeks stayed wet, his spinning thoughts calming, a dozen questions evaporating, leaving his mind empty, waiting for Ethan's words to fill it.

He waited.

Ethan stroked his hair, but when Andy sighed with pleasure, the next stroke ended with Ethan's hand on the back of his neck, squeezing it in a warning not to take gentleness as weakness. The slow rub of Ethan's thumb against the strip of skin under his ear sent a flash of heat over Andy, scorching him, searing away his doubts.

No one had ever touched him like this. Men had kissed, caressed, and fucked him, but never with this lack of haste. If he opened his eyes, he'd see Ethan's erection molding the front of his trousers into interesting shapes—he knew it—but Ethan seemed content to explore what he could reach of Andy's head, shoulders and back with maddeningly light fingers and once or twice his nails, leaving behind a faint sensation and a need for more.

Andy reached the point of daring to lift his head and open his eyes. He twisted to glance up at Ethan and caught a glimpse of turmoil and doubt, as if Ethan wasn't sure of him. That hurt.

He coughed, clearing his throat and gave Ethan a tentative smile. "Thanks." The word scraped his dry throat and he coughed again then swallowed. "Sorry for melting down. After that and last night, you must be wishing you'd left me on the bench."

"Are you sorry I didn't?"

Good question. Excellent, even.

"I like being here. Don't like crying."

"Shame. Seeing your tears turns me on."

"You're joking, right?"

"No."

Andy pushed away, kneeling with his back straight. If they were going to talk, he wasn't doing it slumped over. "If I agree to go along with your kinks, will you fuck me?"

"Not interested in a one-night stand."

"I can't commit to more when I don't know what you want!"

"To tell you what to do. I control the sex."

"There's more to it than that," Andy said shrewdly. "You got a boner last night at the idea of tidying me up."

Ethan didn't flinch. "Yeah. That's kind of first base for me."

"So what would you do?" God, this was weird, yet arousing.

Ticking them off on his fingers, Ethan said, "Haircut, waxing, manicure. Start you off on a diet and exercise regime. Get you in shape."

Speechless, Andy gaped at him. "All that *before* you fuck me?"

"No. Only the haircut and such. The rest would be ongoing."

"Sure gives new meaning to being someone's boy toy." Andy sat back and crossed his legs. The pads on his soles reminded him of how well Ethan had cared for him. That hadn't aroused Ethan, but he'd done it without hesitation, taking responsibility for easing Andy's discomfort.

"How do you feel about it? Interested? Turned off?"

Ethan tried to sound casual, but Andy saw through it to the tension underneath. It was hell sharing something personal and waiting for mocking laughter. He touched Ethan's knee. "Curious. It's kind of hot thinking about you playing with me like that. I wouldn't mind trying it. Don't expect me to turn into some kind of life-size doll with no mind of my own, though."

"Hell, no." Ethan shook his head. "We're talking about a few hours a month on maintenance and the rest you should be doing anyway if you're serious about acting. It's a physically demanding job."

It was impossible to argue with that.

"I'd set goals, targets," Ethan said slowly. He tapped his lips twice with his index finger then rubbed it against them. "Agree on consequences for doing well or failing."

And the glow from imagining those consequences went out. Andy had never been good at living up to expectations.

"There's no point in starting this. I'd fuck it up inside of a day, like I do with my New Year's resolutions every year."

"Okay, start there. Tell me what they are."

Andrew stared at him blankly. His resolutions, not his fantasies? What for? Then he realized he was keeping Ethan waiting and he knew from experience that never went down well. "Generally, to sort out my life. Get on track and stay there. Do the laundry. Keep the place clean. Pay bills before they're due. Stop getting drunk and ending up in bed with strangers. Find an agent who can do more for me than the one I have. Get a good part—"

Ethan held up his hand. "Enough. I get the idea. You're disorganized and drowning."

"More like I'm falling down a mountain. I grab at bushes, rocks or other climbers, and that slows me down, but sometimes what I grab at pulls free so I'm falling faster. And I want to get to the top, you know? See the view. But I always end up at the bottom, covered in bruises."

"Always means you try again, though." Ethan pointed out. "You don't give up."

"No, but I climb knowing I'm going to fall. Guess I'm my own worst enemy." Parents, teachers, and friends had told him that so often over the years he had no choice but to believe it.

"Yes," Ethan agreed. "You're good at convincing yourself failure's not an option but a certainty. I don't accept that."

"So what do you want to do? Train it out of me?"

Ethan drew in a sharp breath. "You—God, yes. I'd love to. I've never taken it that far before. If I'm being honest, it's never been on the table. With the handful of men I did this with, it was mostly about the sex. They weren't—"

"Losers like me?"

"Calling yourself names wouldn't be allowed. But you'd have to want it too. I'm not interested in nagging you or bullying you. Helping you, sure, but not forcing you into anything."

"And we get to have sex?"

"We'd get to do a lot of things," Ethan replied. "But you're not in any shape to agree to this. You're tired, hung over and horny. Think about it."

"I don't know what I'm agreeing *to*," Andy complained, though he appreciated Ethan giving him space. "Tell me a rule. Something basic you'd expect me to do or not do. And tell me how you'd punish me if I were to break it."

His heart beat faster when he mentioned punishments. His parents had never spanked him. If he misbehaved, they'd sent him to his room or docked his allowance and privileges. Would Ethan take a more hands-on approach? God, Andy hoped so. He wanted punishment as needed and to pay for fucking up. Life offered his generation carrots and easy ways out. He craved the stick.

"I don't deal with rewards and punishments, I told you. Just consequences for actions."

Andy clung to his fantasy. "Same thing."

"Not entirely. If you break a glass when you're juggling with it and it cuts you, the cut's a consequence, not a punishment. The glass doesn't have feelings that you hurt."

"You had to pick broken glass as an example?"

"Sorry." From the grin that went with the apology, Ethan wasn't contrite.

"So if I broke something of yours by being careless, you wouldn't do anything to me?" Andy asked.

"For breaking a rule we'd agreed on, yeah. For breaking an object? No. But again, I wouldn't punish you. That implies anger or a need to make your pain equal my disappointment. That's all kinds of fucked-up."

"Oh, yeah? What about making me strip after I threw a T-shirt at you? You called it payback, remember?"

Ethan spread his hands. "Did I look angry? Did you have a choice? No and yes. And you loved it. You wanted me to see you and I liked looking."

"Well..." Andy let that one go. It was true Ethan hadn't retreated into glacial disapproval or lashed out with a bitingly sarcastic comment. "You still haven't told me a rule." He patted his cock though his jeans. "No jerking off?"

"I love how your mind goes straight to sex," Ethan said. "You make it easy to find your pressure points. Sure. Why not? No more jerking off without permission." He raised his eyebrows. "Now tell me how I'm going to know if you disobey me."

Andy gave into the urge to play pussycat and sprawled out on his stomach, head resting on his folded arms. The rug yielded to his weight, cushioning him, and the heat from the fire soaked into him. "Don't know. I always wondered about that when people did it in books. I jerk off in the morning. By night... Hell, an hour later, I'll be horny again. And I'm an actor. I can look you in the eye and lie without blushing."

"So it's a rule that's impossible to enforce." Ethan scratched the side of his jaw, his gaze drifting away to the view outside before returning to Andy's face. "Not interested in those. When you're with me, yeah, you'd keep your hands to yourself unless I said otherwise, but when you aren't, it's your cock. You could do what you wanted with it when it comes to jerking off."

"I thought you'd be more in control of me than that." Andy felt obscurely disappointed by Ethan's lenience.

"If I'm forcing your obedience, I'm not sure it'd be satisfying. I want it given to me. Offered to me, not extorted from you."

"Oh."

"I'd enjoy fucking you and not letting you come," Ethan offered. "Have you over for the weekend if our shifts allowed it and keep you begging for a climax you would not get until it was time for you to leave, maybe not even then. I would love sending you home with a rock-hard cock, tears in your eyes."

"Oh, *shit*." Andy rolled to his back, erection jutting up, constrained by his jeans. "You'd do that to me? God, please."

Ethan laughed, and how much did Andy love making him do that, the harsh, lean lines on his face softening with amusement? "You're taking the fun out of tormenting you."

"Yeah?" With one eye on Ethan, Andy scratched idly at his ribs. "Your rug tickles." He continued to scratch, moving lower, to his stomach, the hollow of his hip, the top of his thigh. He was dressed, but Ethan knew damn well what lay under the clothes.

Ethan raised his eyebrows. "Is this supposed to drive me into asserting my mastery over you here and now? Bringing out the cane and cuffs I'm sure you think I've got hidden away?"

The gentle mockery deflated Andy's belief that Ethan was easy to manipulate. He balled his hand into a fist and hammered it against the rug. "I'm already frustrated and we haven't even started."

"Get used to it. Frustration is a great motivator."

"I want to do this. Submit to you. Let you take charge."

"Of what?"

"Me. My body. My life. My choices." It was reckless but Andy was an all or nothing kind of guy. "Train me. Discipline me. Spank my ass. Torment me. But don't…"

"Don't?"

Andy squeezed his eyes shut so all he saw was sparks and darkness. "Don't ignore me. Don't give up on me."

"You don't like being ignored?"

"Hate it."

"I wouldn't do that. If anything, you'd complain I was paying you too much attention."

"Yeah?" Andy opened his eyes. "I can't see it happening. I kinda get off on being the center of attention. It's the actor in me."

"Come up here," Ethan said unexpectedly and patted his knee. "Sit facing me."

"Okay." Andy straddled Ethan's lap, the armchair deep and wide enough that he was able to kneel on it, saving Ethan from taking all his weight. He wasn't sure what to do with his hands, so he rested them on his thighs then gave Ethan an expectant look.

Ethan stared back, his expression calm, though Andy sensed a reserve he guessed wouldn't disappear until they'd made this official.

"You're pretty, but scruffy, like I said. I'd tidy you up."

"Mmm." Andy swayed forward.

"Cut your hair. Shave you properly. Groom you until you looked presentable."

"Anything," he said on a sigh. He knew this. Why was Ethan repeating it?

"Dress you better. Choose your clothes."

"Sure." His mouth was an inch from Ethan's. Where was his kiss?

"Your diet is appalling and you don't exercise enough. I'd fix that."

Andy bit his lip so hard that when he released it, there was a throb of pain. "I know. You said. I want it. *Please*." What was he begging for? Everything Ethan was outlining and more, that was what. Invisible, intangible fetters settling around him, holding him as Ethan wished, no one knowing but them...

"Fuck you. Use you." The swell of Ethan's erection rubbed against Andy's balls when he shifted forward. "Whenever I wanted. However I wanted it. You'd have no say in that. I'd let you tell me you didn't want to have sex, but once it started, you'd never be in charge. I'd train you. Tie you up so you could only move the way I wanted you to. Gag you so you couldn't argue. Forbid you from coming or make you jerk off until your balls were empty."

"Want you to do it now. All of it." It was hard to force the words out through the constriction in his throat, or to hear them through the roar of blood in his ears. His skin burned for a touch. One word from Ethan and Andy would unzip, take out his cock, and leave the evidence of his obedience on Ethan's clothes, thick white splatters of spunk all over the fucking place. He'd never been this turned on—ever. Offered a climax or a million dollars, he'd have walked away with his balls as empty as his pockets.

"And I want you to—no, you tell me. You said your memory was excellent, so I'm never going to accept you've forgotten an order."

Dazed with lust, Andy pulled back. "Huh?"

"What did I tell you to do?"

Andy dug around in his brain and supplied the answer. "Think it over then decide. I don't want to. I've decided. Want you. Want this." He lunged forward, trusting Ethan's control was close to snapping, and kissed Ethan on the mouth, sliding his tongue between lips parted to speak.

Andy expected some resistance from Ethan. A token moment of stillness, even a reproving slap on his ass. But after that, Ethan would kiss him back, he was sure of it, and after *that*, well, the rug was right there.

His thoughts flashed through his head as he gloried in the taste of Ethan's mouth, intoxicatingly arousing in a way that told him they'd be good in bed. If someone didn't taste or smell right, they made a lousy fuck in his experience.

Ethan was faster.

Andy cried out when Ethan took a handful of his hair and used it to pull his head back. Shit. He'd screwed up. Already. Again. Like always.

"What part of me being in control was unclear?" Ethan asked in the deceptively mild tone he used when he was pissed. "I don't mean the kiss, though in general I'd prefer to initiate them, but the idea behind it. You thought it'd trigger something. Weaken my resolve to the point where I'd give you what you want right here and now."

His scalp burned from Ethan's grip. The only way to lessen the small pain was to yield, lean back, stop trying to get closer, but Andy couldn't do it. Surrender would ease his discomfort and please Ethan, but he wanted another kiss.

"Spoiled," Ethan said with flat disapproval. "Willful. Disobedient."

Yeah. Talk dirty to me.

Panting, struggling, Andy reached out to grab Ethan's sweater, but Ethan showed his ruthless side, pulling strongly on Andy's hair and forcing him to arch his back. Thigh muscles screaming, his spine about to crack, Andy beat the air with his fists.

"Let go! Please, I'm sorry. Okay, I'm sorry. God, you're fucking killing me. *Hurts.* Ethan, for the love of—"

"Consequences." Ethan seemed outwardly unmoved by Andy's babbling. "I did warn you."

He drew Andy's head even lower then ran his fingertip from throat to navel, a slow drag. "If I release you, can you hold this position by yourself?"

"What?" Andy's eyes were watering. That was a consequence of having his hair ripped out at the fucking roots too. "No! I told you. It hurts."

"That doesn't answer my question."

"Shit!" Andy howled. His thigh muscles had been dipped in acid by the feel of them. "I'll try. Okay?"

"Better hope you succeed. Ten seconds."

And the son of a bitch let go of Andy's hair and stared at his watch, not Andy suffering for him, being obedient. He was sitting in Ethan's lap, so Ethan wasn't ignoring him, but it came close. Then he realized part of Ethan's attention was on him. Ethan's gaze flickered between the watch and Andy, over and over.

Ten seconds was a long time. Sweating, trembling, he clawed at his thighs, jaw locked to hold in his moans. From the depths of his need, Andy found the strength to maintain the torturous backward bend until Ethan snapped his fingers.

And it was worth it, every single agonizing moment. Ethan pulled him close, turning him so Andy lay with his back against Ethan's chest, his legs outstretched.

Andy sniffled. He couldn't help pushing for remorse or sympathy he knew he wasn't going to get. "All that for one kiss?"

"All that—which was nothing, trust me—for trying to take my place then being stubborn." Ethan ran his hand over Andy's stomach, petting him absently. "From your reaction to some mild discipline, I know your answer."

"Yeah, so do I." Andy captured Ethan's hand and brought it to the stiff spike of his erection, pressing against his jeans. "Does that feel like a no to you?"

Ethan stroked Andy's cock, then shook his head. "Too much, too fast. My fault. Seeing you on the bench looking damp and forlorn... Let's say I have a soft spot for strays. But our situation at work—"

"I'll quit."

"The hell you will." God, he loved it when Ethan growled. "I've got you to the point where I'm considering letting you go behind the bar. Unless you get the lead in the next Bond movie, you're not going anywhere."

"I wish. Haven't had an audition in weeks." Andy contemplated that sad fact then shoved it aside. "The point remains, I can leave if it gets awkward."

"If it did, we might both find ourselves looking for work."

"No way would they fire you. We're not breaking any laws and—you know what, fuck work. This is between us. You want someone to get your kink on with and I want, well...you, and a firm hand. I'm drifting. My life's a mess. You have everything smoothed out. Teach me how to do it. Punish—no, you don't use that word, do you? Make my screw-ups have consequences so I think twice before making them. Spank me. It's traditional for a reason."

"I still want you to think it over."

"I don't work like that," Andy said. "I know what I want and I want you, kinks and all. I'm sober, sane and consenting to whatever you have in mind. Don't leave scars and don't cross lines and we're good."

"Such as?"

Andy threw his hands up. "God, I don't know." Henry's face came to mind. "Friends. If you meet them and you don't approve, don't even *try* to say I can't hang with them."

The shock on Ethan's face was answer enough. "Jesus, I'm kinky, not abusive. Of course I wouldn't. And that blanket permission you gave me to do anything I wanted, let's consider it never said. We'll play it by ear. If there's an area of your life you want me to stay away from, I'll respect that."

"Start with you in control of the sex and add to it bit by bit?"

"Yes, except there's no sex until you meet my standards when it comes to appearance."

"The hell? What, so I'm not pretty anymore?"

"Think about it," Ethan said and the barriers were down, padlocked and impenetrable. "Conversation is over. I'll drive you home."

Chapter Eight

Andy limped into his place and collapsed on the couch, Ethan's final words on a loop in his ear. "I don't want a yes for a week at least. You need longer, take it. If it's no, you can tell me any time. You have my number."

"What are you hoping I'll say?" Andy had asked and got a lazy roll of Ethan's shoulders by way of reply. It would've hurt him if he hadn't seen the longing in Ethan's eyes.

It helped to know he wasn't the only one with something to lose if this didn't work out.

He checked his messages when he sat. It was testament to Ethan's ability to hold his interest that it hadn't been his first action of the morning. He scrolled through texts from everyone he'd messaged the night before without bothering to reply. They could wait. One from Henry made him grin. Henry scolded him in the first line, apologized in the second and used the third to tell Andy he was spending the weekend with Mahito at his place.

"Go, Henry," he murmured and forgot about him a moment later, mind occupied with Ethan.

He'd thought it would be easy. He'd wait a week, tell Ethan yes and be naked a few minutes later. But as the hours ticked by, what had been a simple answer became fuzzy around the edges.

Ethan wanted a lot and it was difficult to fit those demands into a framework Andy was familiar with. If Ethan had said he was a Dom looking for a sub, Andy would've known what to expect, though it wasn't what he was looking for in a relationship. Fun for roleplay, but he couldn't see himself committing to it in a meaningful way. From a porn perspective, it turned him on, but applied to his life? No.

Ethan didn't want him kneeling or submissive. Ethan wanted him perfect. By whose standards, though? Andy tugged at a lock of hair, brooding over Ethan's assessment of him as scruffy and out of shape. It was true he'd lost a part because he wasn't buff enough and they weren't prepared to give him time to train, but not every role called for abs of steel. Fast food featured too often on the menu, but he was active, walking around the city, running if he was late, and that burned calories.

Some help tidying up his life would be nice. He'd read about Hollywood stars with personal trainers and turned the page with a dismissive comment to disguise his envy. With a stern, uncompromising guy telling him to drop and do fifty push-ups, he'd be in shape in no time. Ethan could be that guy. Tough love. Yeah. Okay.

But the sex would take some getting used to. How would that play out? Would Ethan freak if Andy's hand was an inch too low or high or his moans too loud? Then there was the question of punishments.

Ethan could call them consequences, but Andy knew applied discipline when he saw it. Ethan would exact a penalty when Andy screwed up and the idea held an appeal he didn't want to examine too closely.

Except Ethan had told him to. Ordered him to. Made it a condition of going farther.

His head spun. He went online, entering a string of search terms leading him from eye-watering images to earnest chat rooms.

He kept his hands off his dick, ignoring the boners his research produced and suffering through the ache in his balls. Ethan hadn't demanded it of him, but it was worth trying it to see if he could hold off until Ethan was there to see him come apart.

And there was one reason it appealed — the novelty value. Patting himself on the back for his honesty, Andy made a mental note and moved on.

* * * *

Henry returned at noon on Sunday, eyes hazy, neck marked with a love bite, clothing rumpled.

"The walk of shame," Andy said. Henry would expect some teasing. "Enjoy yourself?"

"I think I rather liked it." Henry broke into a grin. "Mahito's amazing, isn't he?"

"Based on our extensive acquaintance of ten seconds in the same room, sure. He's cute. Cool hair."

"He says I should do something with mine." Henry grabbed a chunk of his hair—brown, thick, straight, boring—and studied it. "I don't think so. It is longer than it's ever been though."

"So get a trim." *And this time get someone who uses scissors not gardening shears and who keeps their eyes open when they snip.*

115

Henry looked at him properly for the first time, myopic eyes focusing. "I could, yeah. Heading into work or just back?"

"Out."

"Oh." A disappointed look crossed Henry's face. "Maybe we can talk later?"

"About how perfect Mahito is? Or do you want blow job tips?"

"No," Henry said with a certain dignity. "You're not interested in him and I managed fine, thanks. You're all washed-out and pasty-looking. Did you get any sleep this weekend? Or was it one long party?"

"Haven't left the house since I got back on Saturday," Andy admitted. "I cut my feet on a broken glass."

"Ouch. Both of them?"

"Alcohol involved," Andy said laconically, knowing disapproval would stop Henry asking questions. "They're okay. No stitches, scabbing over nicely."

Henry gave a sigh as if Andy's attitude was a weight on his shoulders and wandered away to text Mahito. Dude had it bad.

* * * *

Once at work, Andy settled into a routine Ethan and Joel had taught him. It made it easy for his thoughts to wander, but he'd done all the difficult thinking earlier. Now he was picturing his life in a year. Room clean, a steady acting job bringing in serious money he would, of course, invest wisely. Body a temple. He could take up yoga. Give up drinking. And the sex would be out of this world good.

"You're cleaning the cutting board with a floor cloth," Ethan snarled in his ear and rosy dreams of what Andy would say accepting his Oscar or Emmy dissolved into gray reality.

Except Ethan glaring at him spiced it with red. Did penalties, consequences—whatever the fuck they were—apply to work-related mistakes? Wouldn't it be interesting if they did?

"Sorry." He smiled beguilingly, swaying his upper body toward Ethan without moving his feet, half deliberate invitation, half instinctive response to Ethan's scent. The guy turned him primal. "Got a lot on my mind."

They were alone in the prep room, but Ethan didn't seem inclined to take advantage of that. "Disinfect the board and oil it. Don't let me ever catch you doing something so disgustingly unhygienic again."

"Or?" Andy asked, hope filling him the threat would be jerk-off worthy. Except he'd sworn off that. Damn.

"There is no or." Ethan stood close by, voice dangerous, eyes glinting. Jesus, the man intimidated as if it was an art form and he was Picasso. "You're not going to do it again. Are we clear on this?"

His assurance popped out free of insinuation. Saying it didn't turn him on even a little. It was impossible to wet water, and he was drenched, drowning. "Yes, sir."

Ethan studied him then nodded brusquely before turning away.

Andy let him go. Message received and understood. Work wasn't where they played.

Except he was achingly hard with no prospect of relief unless he broke his self-imposed rule a day after making it.

Oh, yeah. He needed an Ethan in his life like, now—right now. And Ethan wanted him to spend a week like this? Still clutching the damp, smelly rag, Andy took a step toward the door then stopped. He could do this. And proving his self-restraint and obedience would please Ethan and that couldn't hurt.

Joel came in and Andy shoved the floor cloth in the trash. "Joel, how do you sterilize the chopping boards?"

"Lemon juice."

"Figures," Andy said with a resigned sigh. "I think I'm developing an allergy to citrus fruit."

"Tell Ethan that." Joel all but rubbed his hands. "But not until I'm there to see what he does to you."

"Pervert," Andy muttered.

* * * *

By the time Friday night rolled around, Andy was alternating between telling Ethan where to stick his offer and whimpering in need. Ethan had ignored the multiple texts he'd sent saying he agreed to everything and could they start the relationship like now, please. At work, he treated Andy like any other employee and refused Andy's attempts to lure him into personal conversations or quiet corners. How was that helping Andy make a decision? And what was wrong with trying it and seeing how it worked? If it did, they moved on. If it didn't, they called it quits. Simple.

Andy did it all the time.

A text came in from Ethan when Andy was putting on his jacket. Heart beating faster, Andy opened it. They hadn't arranged a time and place for Andy to give his answer, but he'd assumed it would be at Ethan's on Friday night. He'd turned down Simon's proposal of a movie followed by a club with a vague reference to other plans and told Henry he'd probably be gone for the night.

Sorry. Got to work tonight.

Without censoring his reaction, he replied.

Wtf?! Get out of it!

Can't.

The answer was yes, if that helps.

Was?

Is. Shit. Is. I want to see you.

Tomorrow.

No. Put me down for a shift tonight or I'll hang around. Meet me on your break. Got to be somewhere we can go to talk.

Wait.

Been waiting a week! Need you. God, is it only me who wants to get this thing started before we're too old to get it up?

No. And if I were with you right now, you'd be finding out how much I don't appreciate your tone.

Not. Helping.

A moment later, he stared in disbelief at a smiley face.

You have to be fucking kidding me.

Behave, Andrew.

Make me. Seriously. Make me. Need you to. Yes, yes, yes. Want this, want you. I'm yours to do whatever the fuck you like with. So do it! Please, sir?

Consider yourself mine. First order, stop nagging. Go home. Now.

Andrew struggled with that, processing his elation and disappointment. He'd signed up for hot sex with a man who only had to look at him to turn him on, not endless waiting, but whining about Ethan needing to work would make him look like a spoiled brat.

And the conversation had plenty for him to mull over later.

With a sigh, he ended the conversation with a dutiful *Yes, sir,* and walked down the hallway leading to the staff entrance. Rounding the corner, he came to an abrupt halt. Ethan was by the door, leaning against the wall as if he had nothing better to do, which was never the case, no emotion showing.

Footsteps quickening, Andy hurried forward, a grin he couldn't force back spreading over his face.

"You did as you were told," Ethan said when they were face to face. His eyes warmed with approval. "Very good, Andrew."

"I live to please," Andrew said then wished he hadn't. Would Ethan get that he was flippant out of nerves?

He must've done since Ethan kissed him, a firm, brief press of lips. "You please me more often than you realize."

Andy swallowed, lightheaded with need, dizzy with pleasure. Fuck, he was a total junkie for praise. "Ethan…"

"Come to my place tomorrow morning at nine. Don't be late."

"Yes, sir."

He'd hoped for another kiss, but Ethan nodded, face expressionless again, and walked away.

Okay. It was on. They were doing this.

Please don't fuck this up.

* * * *

Nine. On the dot. Andy didn't wear a watch but his phone assured him that he'd timed the first rap of his knuckles on Ethan's door to perfection.

Ethan opened it and Andy stepped in, already filled with the sense of expectant peace Ethan's place inspired. He smelled coffee overlaid with clean, as if every molecule in the place had been scrubbed and buffed until it shone.

"Two Saturdays off in a row," Ethan said. "Guess the double shifts were worth it."

Andy toed off his shoes and put them inside the hall closet then hung up his jacket. "Double shifts were invented by the Devil. They're twice as long as normal shifts." His brain caught up to his mouth. "Okay, that came out wrong. I mean a single double shift is twice as long as — oh God, tell me to shut up!"

"I get what you mean." Ethan gestured at the kitchen area. "Coffee?"

"With one of your cinnamon buns?" Andy asked. Ethan studded them with soft, juicy raisins then added a luscious cream cheese frosting.

"Without calorie-laden baked goods of any description."

"You were serious about the diet?"

Ethan raised his eyebrows.

Andy groaned. "Of course you were. Coffee would be great."

He followed Ethan over, then perched on one of the stools at the counter. "So we're doing this? You and me?"

"Unless you've had second thoughts."

"No, but…" He picked at a ragged cuticle. "Suppose I don't like it? Or you get bored of riding my ass?"

"We won't know until we try. The question is, do we want to take that first step or not?" Ethan set a mug of coffee in front of him. "I do. You attract me. You seem to need what I get off on giving. If we've got a future together, I don't know. I'm pretty sure we've got some things in common, but other areas there's not much overlap. We'll see."

"I'm worried about you getting into trouble at work."

"I am too," Ethan admitted. "It's straightforward if I'm harassing you. That's totally forbidden. It's less clear-cut if we're in a relationship."

"I read the handbook." He'd memorized one line. "'The hotel discourages romantic relationships between supervisors and subordinates and prohibits any such conduct if it is unwelcome.' And it isn't. Unwelcome, I mean."

"Yeah, that's the part." Ethan sighed. "Not against the rules, but not a good idea."

"I'll transfer," Andy suggested. "Work for housekeeping instead or in the kitchen. That way you wouldn't be my supervisor."

"Leave me shorthanded?"

"Better than fired or with a mark on your record." Andy put his hand over Ethan's. "It'd kill me to be the reason your career dead ends."

Ethan captured Andy's fingers in his for a moment before releasing them. "I've never kept a relationship secret before, but I don't want to lose you off my team."

"Well, until we're sure this is going to work, it makes sense to keep it between us. If it's looking good after a month, I'll transfer or get another job, and if anyone finds out, we'll say it started after I left the team." Andy blew out a breath. "Listen to me being all responsible and forward thinking. Impressed?"

"Totally. So. One last time. In or out?" Ethan asked.

"In."

It wasn't romantic, but Andy's heart thudded with painful excitement.

Ethan exhaled. "In," he repeated. For a moment, he looked lost. Then he gave the wicked grin Andy both dreaded and anticipated. "Okay."

"So what happens now?" Andy could make demands too, especially after a week of waiting.

"I print off a copy of the plan I drew up for the next time a stunning man became my sex slave. No, two copies, one for each of us. It runs about seven pages with the footnotes."

It took entirely too long for Andy to realize Ethan was joking.

"You don't have a clue, huh?"

"I have a dozen fantasies, but since I never expected them to become reality, I'd say that was a good description, yes." Ethan ran his thumb over his bottom lip. "Why don't we start by sealing the deal?"

"How?"

Ethan came around to Andy's side of the counter. "Like this."

A kiss from someone determined to control every detail was different from the kisses he was used to. He waited for Ethan's mouth to meet his, for Ethan to part his lips with a questing tongue. Let the kiss develop at Ethan's pace, as a slow exploration became a demanding possession. It should've inhibited him or at least made him restive, but it didn't. Ethan's pleasure with him was reflected in the kiss and Andy did his best to respond, echoing every shift in intensity. He wrapped his arms around Ethan, holding onto the man's lean, strong body, soaking in the sensation of being wanted, thirsty for approval.

It was easy. So fucking easy. Why had he worried he couldn't do this? Giddy with success, he wanted to victory dance his way around the room when the kiss ended, but he curbed the impulse and waited for Ethan to do whatever the hell he liked.

"Very nice." Ethan drew his thumb across Andy's lower lip. "Of course, it's early days."

"Hey!" Andy smacked Ethan's ass playfully. "Don't rain on my parade."

Ethan gave him a cool look. "And don't hit me, even in fun."

"Shit, is that me in trouble *already*?" Andy groaned. "Sorry. I'm used to it with my friends. The only way to make Gary see sense is to sit on him and tickle him to death."

"Apology accepted." Ethan kissed him again, a light brush of his lips. "I don't want you walking on eggshells. If you do something I don't like, I'll tell you. If you do it a second time—"

"Consequences, I know."

"Interrupting me is definitely on the don't-do list."

"Oops?" Andy asked. Ethan didn't seem pissed or even ruffled, so Andy forgave himself. After that knee-weakening kiss, he was in a great mood and he wasn't about to spoil it. "And does that work both ways?"

"You telling me if I do something you don't like?" Ethan brushed a strand of Andy's hair into place, the gesture done unthinkingly, without hesitation.

Andy wasn't used to being touched so freely, but something told him he'd better adjust fast to losing his personal space around Ethan.

"Sure. I'm not a mind reader. And this only works if we're both getting something out of it."

"If it's fun."

"Fun?" Ethan grinned. "We can do better than that."

"So, if it's official, can I ask you to do something?" Andy swallowed when Ethan nodded. "Spank me? Please?"

He expected Ethan to ask why or tell him he hadn't done anything wrong so it wasn't appropriate, but Ethan nodded again, no surprise showing. "You're curious, huh?"

"Spanking virgin, more or less." Andy tried to smile but it turned wobbly. "If it's going to be a...uh...a consequence, I want to know what it's like for real, not a few swats from someone playing around."

"It's something I enjoy," Ethan said. "Less a consequence, more part of our sex life."

"So I couldn't stop you doing it?" Part of him loved that idea a little too much.

"Yes and no." Ethan scratched the side of his neck with one finger, his face screwed up in thought. "If I do it now and you get zero out of it, then I'd take it off the menu when it comes to sex. What would be the point? We have to both enjoy it. But I might use it as a discipline method *because* you didn't enjoy it. I'm not sure I like twisting something I enjoy into a punishment for you, though."

"I wouldn't get to say no if you did decide to use it that way?"

Ethan wiggled his hand. "We're back to yes and no. If I spanked you and you asked me to stop when you'd reached your limit—assuming I hadn't seen that for myself—then, yeah, I'd stop. If you said you weren't in the mood for a spanking, I'd tell you to remember actions have consequences and to get over my knee."

Overwhelmed by the implications and his reaction, Andy took a step back. Being forced to behave—he hated that. *Hated.* So why did Ethan telling him he'd be disciplined for fucking up and had to accept it with a good grace turn him on? "I need to pee."

"You know where the bathroom is." Flat, cool voice. Ethan wasn't happy with the interruption, Andy could tell.

"Yeah." Andy took another step back then shook his head. "I do need to go. Already had two coffees before I came here. Over your knee, all that pressure…things could get messy. Hold that thought."

"Which one?" Thank God, Ethan sounded human again, a smile flickering over his lips.

"All of them!" Andy called out, taking the stairs quickly. After peeing, he hurriedly washed his hands. He avoided looking in the mirror. He didn't want to see what he looked like anticipating a spanking.

How many times had he stood in front of a teacher he'd had a crush on, wishing they'd shut up with the lecture and whip out a ruler instead? Plenty. Dragging them into his fantasy had come with a corresponding guilt, but not much. Teenage lust had no conscience.

No need to feel guilty now. Not when Ethan was so matter-of-fact about it being one of his favorite activities. Shit, how hot was that?

Chapter Nine

"When was the last time you did this?" he asked when he was back in front of Ethan, shifting from foot to foot, full of nervous energy.

"Too long," Ethan said with feeling. "Six months, eight?"

"Don't make up for lost time by whaling on me."

"You'll get what you asked for." Ethan took a seat in the middle of the couch. "A trial run. Come here."

"Just like that?"

"Exactly like that." Ethan tilted his head. "Second thoughts?"

"No. Do I need a safe word?"

A muscle in Ethan's cheek twitched, as if he was holding back a smile. "For this? No, but you can tell me what yours is."

"Are you laughing at me?" Andy asked.

"A bit, yes. Well?"

A dozen words darted like minnows through his head, gone before he captured one. "My mind's gone blank."

"Then think of one later. Say stop and I will."

Andy reached for the button on his jeans then paused. Ethan was in control. Better ask first. "Do you want me to undress, sir?"

"Nice," Ethan said approvingly. "Yes. Everything off, please. Fold each item and put it on the floor beside you."

Ethan made him fold his jeans three times. By the third time, Andy was torn between desperation and rebellion, but he listened to Ethan's instructions carefully and got the jeans to lie smooth, seams lined up.

"Better. Stand straight now, feet a little apart. Let me take a look. No, hands behind you." Ethan stood. "Like this." He turned away from Andy and folded his arms behind him so they rested in the small of his back. "Are your feet okay now?"

"Yes, sir."

Ethan circled him as he'd done once before in his office. It had gotten Andy hard back then and it did the same now. Being inspected with Ethan's trademark thoroughness—as if he was a glass about to go behind the bar—made his breath catch in his throat.

Without warning, Ethan kissed the back of his neck, the warm imprint of his lips sending a convulsive shiver through Andy. Nothing could soften his cock, but the rest of him melted at the tenderness of the kiss. Then Ethan slapped his ass, a brisk crack of his palm against one vulnerable cheek.

Andy gasped from shock not pain, digging his fingernails into his forearms and fighting to hold position.

"If I did that for every time you've made me want to spank you, your ass would glow like neon by the time I was done."

Andy swallowed. "I piss you off that much?"

"You have no idea." Ethan caressed the ass cheek he'd struck. "Starting with walking into my office for your interview and lying to me."

"I didn't—ow!"

Same place, but harder. His skin smarted, but the sensation faded. He found he didn't want it to. It was like an arrow pointing at somewhere he needed to be and when it disappeared, he was lost.

"Try again," Ethan advised him.

"I lied. I'm sorry."

"And that's another lie." The third slap rocked him forward, destroying his balance, but Ethan's hand on his hip steadied him. "You're not sorry at all."

"It got me a job. It got me here with you, so no, I'm not sorry. But I won't lie to you again. I promise."

"Hmm." Ethan patted instead of slapping and yet the burn intensified, as if all Andy needed to go up in flames was Ethan's touch. "Over my knee, Andrew."

He'd expected a last chance to get out of it, but not being offered one was a relief. Take away his choice and make this Ethan's choice, Ethan's responsibility.

Except…he was the one who had asked for it.

Ethan sat on the couch again, at the edge so there'd be room for Andy. He didn't crook his finger, just waited.

Andy got into position. It was similar to jumping into icy water. Think about it too long and he'd stay on the edge, shivering. Launch himself into the air and he'd endure the initial shock then realize it wasn't that cold after all. So he bent and wriggled until he found his balance, hands on the floor, feet braced, ready for Ethan's hand.

Ethan sighed with pleasure and Andy pictured him smiling. It gave him the courage to raise his ass an inch, mutely begging for more of those sweet, sharp slaps. With infinite gentleness, Ethan pushed him flat again, his message clear. Andrew groaned, frustrated, needy as hell.

"Impatient?"

"I guess."

"That's a shame. I wasn't planning on rushing this."

"It's been months," Andy pointed out. "You can rush if you like." Weird how sometimes it seemed right to add a 'sir' and sometimes not.

"And if I needed your permission, I'd thank you, but I don't." Ethan traced the mark he'd left on Andy's ass, making Andy conscious of the heat trapped in the skin. "It'll all be this color soon—then darker red. It'll fade, but tomorrow you'll be bruised, tiny purple bruises under the skin. I'll want to see them."

"Yes, sir." Definitely the right answer then. "I'll show you."

Ethan smoothed his hand over Andy's ass, raised it then brought it down. The jolt of pain brought a cry from Andy, but it was one of relief. Finally. *Yes.*

There was never any doubt he'd enjoy it after those first slaps. He'd planned to pretend he did anyway rather than rob Ethan of something he enjoyed, the same way he'd sworn he loved sushi, subtitled movies and jazz in the past, but he didn't need to fake it.

The slaps, crisp as a green apple or a soft curl of palm against quivering, burning flesh, went on and on. He tried to count them, treasure them, but they rained down, too fast to register at times, striking his skin in a flurry of blows so the sting on one flowed into the burn of another. Then Ethan slowed, placing each slap precisely, mercilessly, targeting the site of his first slap, building up a venomous sting.

It hurt. Andy sucked in air, legs flailing. Ethan held him pinned in place with a strong hand, but Andy could still kick his legs and grab Ethan's sweat pants in a death grip. He sobbed out words that even in the depth of his torment he made sure didn't include 'stop'.

His flesh cringed in anticipation of the next spank, the rest of his ass cool in comparison. That one marked place burned, as if Ethan had branded him. He heard the repeated crack of hand on skin, loud, lost sometimes in his open-mouthed gasps for breath and smelled the musk of sweat from both of them.

He was aroused, but there didn't seem room for it. It was irrelevant. The pain mattered — and Ethan's relentless blows — but the stiff, swollen cock trapped against Ethan's lap was nothing to worry about. He couldn't come, so what difference did it make?

Ethan stopped and Andy cried out for the first time, a wail of loss, lifting his ass again in a forbidden, shameless plea. His ass was like an overripe fruit, close to bursting, heavy with heat and swollen with agony, but he needed one more, just one more —

Ethan placed his hot hand on the back of Andy's thighs, and pushed him down. "That's enough for now." His voice shook, but his hand was steady. "Lie there. Catch your breath. There's no rush."

"Need to move. Need you to hold me." He could ask for that, couldn't he?

He could. Ethan shifted back on the couch and rolled Andy over, spreading his thighs so Andy's ass touched air not fabric. Still hurt, but seeing Ethan's face was worth it.

Ethan looked dazed, but only momentarily. He focused his gray eyes on Andy, the expression in them warm with approval. Blessedly, Ethan didn't ask questions, but pushed a cushion behind Andy's back and offered his arm for support. Andy drifted for a while, processing what had happened from the throb and burn of his ass to the dreamy lassitude softening the edges of the pain.

"Too much?"

"Not enough."

"It was plenty for your first time." Ethan studied his scarlet palm. "Maybe too much for me."

Without thinking, Andy captured Ethan's hand in his and brought it to his lips, not for a kiss but a lick, wetting the hot skin then blowing on it. "I wish it didn't hurt you too."

Ethan curled his hand into a loose fist, as if capturing Andy's attempt at comfort. "So do you want me to use a paddle next time?"

The arousal he'd pushed aside flared to life at that. Realistically, his ass was toasted, buttered and burned. He was done. It didn't seem to stop him from craving another hit, literally.

"Oh, well now." Ethan ran his finger over Andy's cock from root to tip, drawing a choked groan Andy couldn't hold back. "Look at this."

"I'm looking." His cock was flushed dark, the tip shiny, beads of fluid welling up to glaze it.

"Is that from the spanking or are you suffering from lack of attention?"

"It's you." Andy was certain of that much. "Everything you're doing to me. Everything I want from you."

"You can want, but who decides what you get?"

Andy closed his eyes before looking at Ethan's expectant face made him shoot. "You do."

"Open your eyes. Stop hiding from me."

"Yes, sir." That got easier to say every time, but no less of a thrill. "Are you going to decide I can come? Please? Begging's allowed, right? I can do that."

"Begging, possibly. Nagging, no. There's a fine line." Ethan tapped Andy's balls. "I said no sex until you were presentable, but—"

"Then let me jerk off for you."

Too late, he remembered the rule about not interrupting and winced. Ethan clearly hadn't forgotten it. He inhaled sharply, nostrils flaring, lips tight. "You have permission to come from this, if it's enough."

The stinging flick of a fingernail at the precise, exact spot under the head of his cock where it was most sensitive hurt, but the intense flash of pain was a lit match thrown onto dry paper. On the heels of the spanking, it overloaded his system, desire and discomfort melding into a single driving need for release.

When he came—cock jerking, balls squeezed by an invisible hand—it was for Ethan's pleasure too. He didn't hold back a single moan or whimper, letting his face contort as unselfconsciously as if he was alone. He wanted Ethan to see how turned on he was, how grateful for this small mercy.

He lay back, stomach wet with spunk, heart beating fast. "God." As an afterthought, he added, "Thank you."

"No need. I was satisfying my curiosity, not being kind." Ethan pinched Andy's stomach, seemingly indifferent to the wet streaks decorating it. "Flabby."

"Hey! I work out."

"When? Where? Details."

Unable to provide any, Andy settled for folding his lips before they formed a sulky pout.

"I thought so. There's a fitness room for the staff at the hotel, you know."

"Like I want to sweat more after a shift," Andy muttered.

"You don't have a choice now." Ethan stared at him, a question in his eyes, doubt shadowing them. "Is that sinking in and you're regretting asking me to take it farther than the sex?"

More answers he didn't want to share with the class. Andy rested his forehead on Ethan's chest. Boneless after the spanking and the orgasm, he wasn't thinking clearly, but he was damned if he was bailing this soon. "It's sinking in. It's sunk. Ignore me."

"No. That's one of the things I agreed not to do, remember?" Ethan kissed him. "I'll run you a bath. Soak for a while, then I'll put some gel on your ass. It'll ease the sting."

"A bath? I already showered. And I like the sting."

"It won't make it disappear. Don't worry."

It didn't. The warm water, redolent of balsam bath salts, stung his ass when he eased into it, but that passed. Ethan sat on the edge of the bath, running his hand through the water and sometimes over Andy's body, gentle touches that made him feel cared for.

"Did you get off on it? Spanking me, I mean?" Andy gave Ethan's groin a covert glance that could've been sneakier because Ethan caught him.

"I loved it. And yeah, it got me hard, but I'm a patient man. I'll think about it the next time I jerk off."

"Wow." Andy blushed, flustered. "I guess someone out there must've fantasized about me when they beat off before, but I never knew about it. That's pretty cool."

"You seem to have a fairly high pain threshold, but your skin soon shows the effects of a spanking. You were bright red within minutes. Beautiful."

"Can I see?" Andy jerked upright, only to have Ethan push him back.

"Another few minutes of soaking. And yes, of course you can. I want to look too. I put those marks on you and I'm..."

It wasn't interrupting when Ethan paused for that long. "Proud of them?"

"Proud of you," Ethan said.

Sweetest moment *ever*.

After the bath, they admired his butt in the mirror. It was mottled red and pink, a faint hint of bruising here and there, but nothing that wouldn't fade. Ethan bent him over the counter and spread aloe and arnica gel over his ass, the cooling sensation instant, the gentle smoothing of the gel deliciously erotic. Ethan slid a finger between Andy's cheeks and yeah, he had hair there. He was a guy. Telling him it had to go, along with whatever he had on his chest, and adding he could spend the afternoon at a salon getting his nails trimmed and cuticles neatened, killed the mood.

"I'm not spreading my cheeks for a complete stranger."

"Unlike most Saturday nights when you get lucky?" Ethan sucked in a sharp breath. "Okay, sorry. That was bitchy as hell. I didn't mean it."

"Yes, you did." Andy pushed past him, hurt souring his mood. So Ethan thought he was a slut? Good to know. Wonderful, in fact. "I'm going to get dressed. I should go. Let you enjoy your day off."

Ethan turned on the basin tap and let the water run over his hands, sticky with gel. "That's an easy way out, not a solution to the bump in the road."

"Bump? More like a fucking roadblock."

"You swear too much." Ethan dried his hands then tweaked the towel straight. "Whatever it is, we can deal with it, but only if we're in the same room. Go downstairs and get dressed while I clean up in here. If you want to leave after that, you know where the door is. If you're still there when I finish, we'll discuss this—no raised voices, no traded insults."

"I'm going home," Andy repeated but he heard the uncertainty in his voice. Why didn't Ethan beg? No, this was Ethan. Why didn't Ethan order him to sit his ass down and listen?

"You want me to forbid it?" Ethan met his gaze squarely. "Not going to happen, Andrew. You're a free agent. If I wanted a slave or a sub, I'd have one. I'm looking for a partner. One who agrees to let me take charge of certain areas of our relationship. I told you part of it was over your body and you asked for it to extend to your bad habits. I never said I wanted to control your emotions or your thoughts. You don't like something? Tell me. Then tell me why. I'll listen. Throw a tantrum and I'll open the damned door for you and call you a cab. Now do as you're told and put some clothes on. You're shivering."

Andy backed away and headed for the stairs and his clothes. *Asshole. Controlling, demanding* —

He got that far in his cursing and stopped. True, all of it, but Ethan had never pretended to be anything else and he'd promised it didn't matter. Sworn it was what he wanted. And Ethan had been so damn hungry, he'd accepted Andy at his word instead of seeing through him to the waste of space underneath.

Hating himself, Andy dressed. The door was right there. He could walk through it and out of Ethan's life. Hand in his notice to spare them the embarrassment of working together and pretend the last few hours had never happened.

Except his butt was raw, his dick was in love with the sensation and if Ethan knew what he looked like in the throes of orgasm, it didn't seem fair the reverse wasn't true.

To sum it up, staying was what he wanted and leaving was what his big mouth had talked him into doing.

Ethan saved him. He was beginning to see Ethan always would, given half a chance.

"Still here? Good. Sit."

Faced with a brisk, unemotional Ethan, it was easy to turn away from the door and make his way to the couch. The view from it was familiar now. When it included Ethan, sitting not in the armchair, but beside Andy, it became fascinating.

"I rushed you." Ethan's words were clipped, brusque. "Gave in to you with that spanking. Too soon. It scared you."

"I liked it," Andy protested.

"Maybe that's what scared you the most. I can't wipe the red off your ass, but you can tell me why a trivial thing like personal grooming has you up in arms."

Ethan leaned back against the couch, relaxed, waiting. Andy focused on Ethan's hand, half-hidden, clenched, bone pressing against thin skin, whitening it across the knuckles. This mattered to Ethan. No, *he* mattered to Ethan.

Andy shifted on the couch, grimacing when his clothing chafed his ass. He wished he was naked.

"You don't look comfortable. Lie on the couch and I'll take the chair."

Ethan rose, but Andy grabbed at his arm. "Don't go way over there. Please." Ethan sat again, his expression dubious, and Andy scooted closer, until his head was on Ethan's shoulder, his weight on one hip. After a moment, Ethan grunted with exasperation and put a cushion in his lap. "Head on that, face me, stretch out."

"Yes, sir."

"Don't call me that unless you mean it."

Andy settled into position, sighing with relief when the burn in his ass subsided. "I've never once said it as a joke. Major turn-on, yeah. How did I miss what a kinky freak I was until I met you? That's the question we should be asking."

"Did you miss it? Or do a good job of hiding it?"

"Hiding," Andy confessed. "And while I'm being honest, got to tell you...no one I've slept with ever came close to rocking my world the way you did walking around me, adjusting my suit."

He would've bet a week's wages on Ethan giving a noncommittal 'hmm' and that was exactly what he got.

"I want you in charge but I'll fight it because, well, because..." He wound down. "Because I'm stupid," he said finally. "Give me lemons and I mangle them. Ask Joel."

"You cut them perfectly for me and I've heard no complaints after I showed you the way to do it," Ethan pointed out.

He rubbed his face against the cushion, wishing it were Ethan's leg. "I don't appreciate charity. If you want me to get a mani-pedi, I'll pay for it myself. The waxing, though...why do you want me to get that done?"

"So I can rim you without getting a mouthful of hair."

Heedless of his ass, Andy sat upright, eyes as wide as his mouth. "No one's ever done that to me. Came close but never all the way." A blow job from Ethan would be incredible, he was sure of it, but a rimming? He'd end up a puddle of goo. "Why didn't you tell me that before?"

"And we're back to you not getting how this works."

"I get it. I do. When it's one of those things, I say, sir, yes, sir, no backchat. But waxing hurts. A lot. I heard my sister and her friends shrieking like banshees when they waxed each other's legs. At least I hope it was their legs."

"It hurts, but so did the spanking."

"Yeah, but that was you doing it to me, not a random stranger."

"And who do you think would be waxing your crack?" Ethan tapped his chest. "Me."

"You?"

"When it comes to your hair and nails, you can see a professional. When it comes to your ass and making you scream? Well, that's my job."

Overwhelmed by the dark intent in Ethan's eyes, adding weight to the joking words, Andy licked his dry lips and nodded. "Yeah. Okay."

Ethan captured his chin between finger and thumb. "Try again."

"Yes, sir," Andy whispered, cock hardening so fast it left him dizzy. "Ethan..."

"Yeah?"

"I'm freaking out here. Do something."

Ethan shrugged, pulled him in and kissed him. Andy opened up, giving everything Ethan asked for without holding back, feeling the difference it made. He had questions and they needed to negotiate boundaries and limits to avoid more arguments, but with Ethan's tongue against his, as Ethan caressed his bruised ass, reawakening the sting, they went to the end of his to-do list.

Chapter Ten

It was odd being outside with Ethan, now dressed in black jeans and a thin green sweater under a black leather jacket. Jeans showcased Ethan's ass to the point where Andy kept dropping back to sneak a peek, and the scent of leather mixed in with the way Ethan smelled made him want to bury his nose in Ethan's neck and snuffle.

Even odder being on his way to get polished up for sex. The sense of insult had faded, lost in wave after wave of lust. Haircuts had always been routine. He'd never considered them foreplay — not until Ethan had run his hands through the mop on Andy's head, studying split ends and experimenting with where his parting should be. To an onlooker, it might've seemed an impersonal examination with Andy playing the part of a living doll, but every pass of Ethan's fingers, every tug at an unruly strand, had been a caress. It had left Andy shaken, skin flushed with heat, fighting back a helpless moan.

They'd compromised on who was paying. Ethan was. Okay, so it was less of a compromise and more complete capitulation on Andy's part, but there was something about being a boy toy that appealed. Andy wasn't one to ignore what his dick thought about a situation.

"When you're sitting in that chair, I want every snip of the scissors down to me," Ethan had said. "Same at the salon. I'm shaping you into my ideal. Yeah, it's a fantasy, but indulge me. If you don't enjoy it or it makes you feel uncomfortable, this will be the last time we do it. If you like it, I'll plan regular maintenance days. There's more I want to do to you than wax. Maybe tie you down and go over you, head to toe."

Yeah, that little speech had done the job.

"Would it surprise you to know there are places in the city a Dom can take a sub and have that relationship respected by the owner? No raised eyebrows at a collar or a sub kneeling, permission asked before the sub's spoken to or touched?"

Andy shook his head. "No, but if they exist, I don't know where they are."

"I don't either," Ethan admitted with a grin. "But it's a nice idea."

"You said I wasn't your sub," Andy pointed out. He detoured around a puddle, splashed when a passing car sent up a spray of dirty water. He swore and shook his wet leg. Ethan took Andy's place closer to the road.

"You're not. It doesn't mean I don't feel possessive about you and protective. Deal with it. In your case, it's a double whammy since you're part of my team—at least for now."

Andy had seen Ethan go up against an irate customer demanding one of his bartenders be sacked for spilling a drink over his wife's designer purse.

He'd apologized on behalf of the bartender, assured the woman the hotel would cover damages, but flatly refused to promise retribution. When the bag had been wiped dry, no damage visible, the couple had calmed down, the woman already mollified by Ethan's genuine concern. And when they'd left, after their bill had been comp'd, Ethan had hauled the bartender off and given him a terse lecture on clumsiness and tact. Andy had eavesdropped for the vicarious pleasure of hearing Ethan growl.

"I can deal with it." Andy ducked around Ethan and back to his original position. "But I'm already wet. You stay dry."

Ethan shot him an exasperated look with a flicker of amusement lightening it. "Suit yourself."

Lowering his voice — not that anyone passing by was paying them any attention — Andy asked, "So I can't jerk off —"

"That was your idea, not mine. We'll discuss it later."

"What about getting hugs from friends? Some of them don't have much concept of personal space."

"Now you're fishing. A question like that insults me, so you've earned a little something when we get home."

"A little something what?" Andy demanded. Ethan veered sideways, heading for the door to an upscale barbers. "Ethan!"

Ethan opened the door and inclined his head with grave courtesy a little overdone to be sincere. "After you."

"You're telling me later," Andy said under his breath. The air in the barbers' was warm and scented with a mix of shampoo and product. Screens hid the customers from the street, but once past them, he saw ten chairs, most of them occupied, with a lounge area at the back, leather couches in front of a plasma TV showing a soccer game. The place was uncompromisingly male, from customers to barbers. Andy relaxed. No way of knowing if anyone here was straight, but his instincts told him most weren't. He got that from the glances Ethan and he received. Straight men didn't let their gazes linger.

"Showing, yes. Telling, no." Ethan walked forward, hand outstretched to the man approaching. "Good to see you again, Tony."

"Always a pleasure."

Tony was short, bald and dapper, in his late fifties with an English accent. He looked like everyone's favorite uncle, but the appraisal Andy got was frankly sensual. "And who's this charming young man?"

"He works for me," Ethan said. "He needs—"

"I can guess exactly what he needs. What a pity I'm spoken for." Tony winked at Andy, who couldn't decide if he was flattered or creeped out. "Why don't we start with a—?"

"Full package," Ethan said flatly. "On my account."

Tony sucked in a breath. "With no appointment? We're rushed off our feet, love."

Ethan arched an eyebrow and that was all it took to have Tony shaking his head with a rueful smile. "Seeing as it's you and he's cute. Wait at the back and I'll fit you in where I can."

Sinking into the leather couch with a cappuccino to sip, Andy let himself enjoy the moment. Ethan had accepted a bottle of sparkling water from the teenager assigned to wait on them and looked completely at home.

"What's the full package?"

"You'll see."

"Why not tell me?" Andy licked foam off his upper lip. "Scared I'll make a run for it?"

"Not at all."

"So tell me."

"I suggest you remember the difference between begging and nagging." Ethan picked up a magazine and turned deaf to Andy's hissed questions.

They didn't wait long. A client rang up to cancel due to a sudden business trip, and a guy named Justin whisked Andy off to the back room for a shave.

It took forty-five freaking minutes and Ethan never looked away.

Being pampered was a revelation. Shaving, for Andy, was a case of hoping his disposable razor didn't chew up his skin too much, and a five-minute job at most. A shave at Tony's involved a straight razor with a blade so sharp Andy's stubble retreated into the pores it came from. He was shaved twice, with and against the grain, then treated to a facial massage hat left his skin tingling. Ice-cold towels were wrapped around his jaw over his protests.

"It closes the pores." Ethan's voice was so tightly controlled it gave away everything he was trying to hide.

"That's right, sir," Justin agreed. Andy repressed the urge to tell him to back off. Justin was being polite, nothing more. "Then some toner and moisturizer, special formula, exclusive to us, followed by a clay mask. You'll like that. Very relaxing. Some gentlemen nod off."

Sleeping with Ethan staring at him in a wolf and rabbit kind of way wasn't likely, but since the razor had disappeared, Andy risked a noncommittal grunt.

Justin left them alone after applying the mask, cautioning Andy not to speak, a warning Ethan converted to an order once they were alone.

He hitched his chair close to Andy's and said quietly, "I'm so hard right now. I'd like nothing better than to straddle you and feed you my cock. Make you take it deep, fuck your face so fast you couldn't do anything but swallow when I come."

Mindful of the thick clay, Andy replied with an anguished whimper. Ethan was hard? Yeah, well he wasn't the only one.

"Sitting here, watching you take all this after I told you I wanted it? Do you have any idea what a turn-on that is? When we get home, I'm going to show you."

Andy couldn't speak, but he was an actor with expressive eyes. He used them, meeting Ethan's heated gaze and getting across how completely down he was with that idea.

Ethan ran his palm over Andy's erection, straining against his jeans, and Andy parted his legs an inch, raising his ass, the movement instinctive, offering himself. Ethan caught the change in position, a slow smile building, satisfied without being smug. "Hold that thought."

If Justin noticed Andy's boner when he returned, he was professional enough not to betray it by even a flicker of his eyes.

Manicure, pedicure, eyebrow waxing, shampoo, scalp massage, cut and styling... Andy was sometimes bored but the glow of Ethan's approval and pleasure carried him through. When they emerged onto the street many hours later, he turned to catch another look at his reflection in the window.

"I look fucking amazing."

"You do," Ethan agreed, not commenting on the swearing. No reason why he should. Ethan cursed up a storm at work when needed. The man had a filthy mouth on him. Telling Andy he swore too much was a case of 'do as I say, not as I do', and Andy didn't intend to obey that particular rule.

"So where now?"

"Are you hungry?"

Andy shook his head. "Still full from breakfast. I usually skip lunch."

"Need anything while we're out?"

"There's a sex shop around the corner. Feel like stocking up on anything?"

"Not a chance."

"Come on," Andy pleaded. "I'll pay for it. There's something in there you'd like to use on me — got to be."

"Yes. A gag."

Andy pouted, but rallied. "That's the start of a shopping list right there. What about something to spank me with? Or put up my ass?"

"I have two hands and a cock. I think we're covered. If you want something *in* your ass, my cock will work just fine."

"Jesus, Ethan, I own like three butt plugs and a pair of handcuffs, though they're broken so they don't count. You're seriously telling me you don't have any sex toys at all?"

"No, but I am saying I don't want to browse some tacky —"

"It's not. Gay-orientated, friendly staff. Nice place, I swear. It's on the way back to the car. Down here, on the right. Please? Not nagging, just using my puppy dog eyes."

"I'm more of a cat person." Ethan heaved a resigned sigh. "Okay, we can check it out. I know the one you mean and yeah, as sex shops go, it's better than most. But anything you want I'm paying for and that's not up for debate."

The gray sky had cleared to pale blue, wispy clouds shredding like cotton candy in the wind and a watery sun raising the temperature a few degrees. Or maybe Andy's face was warm because he was about to browse a sex shop with Ethan. He'd gone in alone or in a large group, unembarrassed and willing to goof around many times, but this was different. Ethan wouldn't buy gag gifts.

The outside of the store was discreet without pretending to be something it wasn't. Black fabric draped the window, and coiled chains and whips glittered under spotlights. A pair of metal cuffs attached to a stark, steel pole completed the display. Minimalist S and M décor.

Inside, discreet gave way to uncompromisingly kinky. Andy nudged Ethan. "How many dead cows are we looking at?"

Ethan snorted. "A herd or two. Wander around by yourself. Pick three things that interest you and find me when you've chosen them."

"Yes, sir." The place was so over the top, he couldn't say that without his lips twitching, but Ethan only grinned and swatted his ass lightly before walking away with purposeful steps, a man on a mission, leaving Andy wondering how much of his reluctance to come here was genuine.

Andy went in the opposite direction. The store was busy, but music blasted out. The lighting was intimate rather than bright and it was easy to feel invisible.

He'd seen a dozen items he wanted before he'd wandered up and down two aisles, but he went for the three that sent a jolt through his balls at the thought of Ethan using them on him—a wicked looking paddle in wood a match to the floors in Ethan's place, a posture collar in black leather, padded on the inside, decorated with a single ring at the front and a pinwheel, gleaming steel points promising all kinds of sensations.

Too much? Too mainstream BDSM and not what Ethan liked? He wasn't sure. But they intrigued and aroused him without pushing his boundaries too far out of sight. Ethan didn't have to buy them, after all.

Ethan's expression when Andy caught up with him in the restraints' section told him he'd hit the jackpot with one of his items at least. Ethan looked ready to drag him to a dark corner and Andy wouldn't have struggled. "Interesting selection. Okay, add them to the basket." He nodded at the assistant beside him, a curvy young woman wearing a collar and a tight leather corset over tiny leather shorts, all in screaming scarlet. He'd seen her here before and she gave Andy a conspiratorial wink before arranging his purchases in the basket she carried.

Andy tried to peek at what else was in there and got a light smack on the ass. Ethan had to stop doing that in public. It didn't piss him off, but it made him want to drop to his knees, arms behind him as he'd been taught and open his mouth.

Ethan tossed a handful of lube bottles into the basket. Andy spotted one that warmed up on contact. He'd tried those, unimpressed by the mild tingle, but that particular brand was new to him. The erupting volcano on the label hinted at incendiary heat levels.

"We're done." Ethan smiled at the assistant. "Thanks for your help, Sally."

"It was my pleasure, sir."

She made it sound genuine, eyes downcast, voice demure. Andy wasn't sure he could achieve anything similar in the subservient line, but he'd do his best.

They left the store with the two bags Andy got to carry — lucky him — and walked the short distance to Ethan's car. Bags stowed, Ethan asked again if Andy was hungry.

"Not for food. I know that sounds cheesy, but it's true. Can we go back to your place?"

Ethan nodded. "We can do that."

They seemed destined to drive in silence. Ethan's car wasn't fancy, a Saab, four years old, but the interior was immaculate and it had heated seats. Ethan flipped a switch and the leather under Andy's ass turned warm, then hot, making his bruises wake up and throb. "That's not helping." He wriggled, wincing. "Turn it off."

"No. Sit still. Show me you can be obedient."

Ethan's tests were diabolical. Andy drew in a deep breath and settled into his seat, hands clasped in his lap. "Yes, sir."

Ethan smiled. Andy saw him out of the corner of his eye, but he didn't reply, his attention seemingly on the road. When they stopped at a red light, though, he reached across and cupped Andy's jaw. "You're being good. Thank you."

Andy huffed. "It's torture. If my ass was red before, it'll be visible from space after this."

"In addition to not moving, you could be quiet," Ethan suggested with a slight edge to his voice.

He didn't get a 'yes, sir' after that. Lip jutting in a pout, Andy stared out of the window until they arrived, suffering in stoical silence. His jeans stuck to his ass and the back of his thighs and his spanked skin burned. In the last few minutes of the drive, his discomfort had become real, but he hadn't voice it. Ethan left him there and retrieved the bags. Andy could've taken the opportunity to peel his ass off the seat, but he didn't. He wasn't obeying Ethan. This was pigheaded stubbornness at work. He knew the difference and so, by the grim expression on his face, did Ethan.

"Out," Ethan ordered, opening the door.

Once in Ethan's loft, some of Andy's resentment at being told to zip it seeped away. It was peaceful there, the glittering expanse of water offering horizons to explore, the muted, warm colors around him soothing his emotions.

"Brat," Ethan said when Andy relaxed and gave him a sheepish smile. "Don't make a habit of sulking, okay? It pisses me off."

"Being told to shut up does that to me too."

"Duly noted." Ethan stared at the bags he'd dumped on the kitchen counter. "I think I overdid it."

"Kid-with-a-new-toy syndrome. And I'm not talking about what's in the bags."

"I'm not saying that's how I think of you, but if I did, would it bother you?"

Andy shook his head, walking up to Ethan. "Only if you put me in a box and never play with me." He wound his arms around Ethan's neck. "I don't mind you calling the shots in bed, but I want to kiss you without asking. Touch you like this. It's too cold otherwise. Too one-sided."

Ethan pursed his lips then hunched a shoulder. "Fair enough."

"Thank God." He wanted to show Ethan he was grateful, not for the staggering amount of money Ethan had spent, but for the time Ethan had lavished on him. He rubbed his smooth cheek against Ethan's. "Feel that? Want to feel it against your cock? Let me suck you? Please. Want to be on my knees for you. Wanted it all fucking day and I couldn't do it."

"You don't need to kneel to me. You're not my sub and I'm not your Dom."

"You do a good impression of one. You like spanking me. Will you enjoy tying me up?"

"Yes," Ethan said, his reluctance to admit it showing, "but I want you to stay where you're put without rope or cuffs."

"You'll love it and I will too. And we both know who's in charge of the remote. So why doesn't me kneeling work for you?"

Andy slid to his knees, a slow, graceful descent. Ethan didn't stop him.

He tilted his head back. "I like the view from here." He breathed in the scent of Ethan's arousal, the sharp musk of a man in rut. "How about you?"

Ethan folded his arms across his chest, his body language screaming closed-off. "I think I want you naked when you're here, assuming we're alone. No one can see in and I keep the place warm. Undress then leave your clothes folded neatly on the chair by the door. I'll put away what we bought."

"No blow job?" Andy groaned, biting back a retort that would've made the situation turn stormy. "Am I ever going to see your dick?"

"No." Ethan walked over to the stairs with the bags. "Yours is twice the size of mine. I'm intimidated."

"I've seen enough of it to know that's not true," Andy called after him, but the only reply was a mocking chuckle.

So that was what happened when he suggested something. Shot down in fucking flames. And seriously, who said no to a BJ?

Ethan wasn't there to see it, but Andy pursed his lips in a pout anyway.

Chapter Eleven

Ethan placed the three items Andy had chosen onto the coffee table then sat beside Andy on the couch. "Talk me through what you picked."

"Why don't you use them on me?" Andy countered.

"Nope. Are they things you're scared of and you're daring me to use them? Things you're curious about, aroused by? Or are they nothing special and you were trying to keep your secrets to yourself? I'll understand that. Sharing a fantasy, especially a kinky one, can be scary."

"No! I liked them all. They turned me on for different reasons." Andy reached for the wheel. "I tried this on my arm. It doesn't hurt unless you push down on it, but if I—if you tied me, blindfolded me, I wouldn't know until it touched me where you were going to use it or how much pressure you'd apply."

"And it wouldn't matter because you'd have no choice about taking it." Ethan gave him a quizzical look. "You like having your choice taken away. Are a lot of your fantasies centered around that? Guilt-free submission after you've been put in a situation where you've lost the ability to refuse?"

"Maybe." He couldn't meet Ethan's gaze, even though there was zero condemnation in Ethan's eyes or tone. "The collar's a special one. They had labels on the shelves. It's a posture collar —"

"I know what it is." Ethan picked it up. "It'll hold you in place. Keep you from lowering your head." He tapped underneath Andy's chin. "Nowhere to hide. Is that something you think you'll be tempted to do and you want that choice taken away too?"

"Wow, look, you found a theme. Want a gold star?" Andy bit his lip after speaking, the sarcastic words hanging between them. "Look, I'm going to mouth off if you hit a nerve. Don't take it personally."

"Too late." Ethan set the collar on the table and pulled Andy facedown across his lap in an awkward tangle of limbs. "And we're back to those consequences we discussed."

A spanking over a spanking hurt in a different way — or perhaps Ethan hadn't been punishing him before. He got half a dozen slaps — no more — none of them particularly hard, but by the fourth, his face was hot and it was hard to breathe. Shame suffocated him, closing up his throat. It took the last slap to loosen the constriction and let him call out an apology in a shaken voice he didn't recognize.

"Stay here." Ethan moved Andy so he lay more comfortably. "I'm not puzzled by why you wanted the paddle. I think it's time you got a taste of it. Pass it to me, please."

The act was simple. Extend his right hand, and curl his fingers around the handle of the paddle. He couldn't give Ethan the means to inflict more pain on his ass, though. It asked too much of him. Take the paddling, yeah. Initiate it? Not so much.

"Don't make me."

"Andrew, if this is going anywhere, I need trust between us, not a word that rhymes with it."

Lust. Ethan lusted after him? Well, for sure, but since when? That was an important question. Vital even. He needed the answer. Ethan would understand why everything had to wait until they'd thrashed out — discussed — the matter.

He opened his mouth then closed it again, squeezing his eyes shut. He knew where the paddle was. He didn't need to look.

Ethan took it from him. "Thank you."

"Welcome," he whispered into the darkness. This would break him, splinter his shell and reveal him to Ethan's gaze. Much though he dreaded it, his toes curled with anticipation. He'd chosen the smooth, heavy paddle, and he'd known exactly what he was doing.

Ethan placed the paddle against Andy's ass, the cool weight of it a shock. He cried out, startled, but the paddle didn't move. It rested against his skin, leaching some of the burn. Ethan rocked it, spreading the balm, then raised it.

Okay. Here it came. Time to suck it up or give Ethan, the sadist, a nice pitiful wail.

The paddle descended and came to rest against another part of Andy's ass, the only weight behind it that of the paddle itself.

"What're you doing?"

"You sound indignant that I'm not paddling you when a moment ago you were terrified I would. You're a hard man to figure out."

"You tricked me!"

Ethan placed the paddle across the top of Andy's thighs. "No. You thought you knew what I'd do and you were wrong. But in the end, you trusted me. I said thank you, remember? You can't think it was for handing it to me."

"Are you seeing how much of my ass you can cover with it?"

"More indignation? Yeah, of course I am. But I won't use it on you until your ass recovers from this morning and until I have an idea of how heavy it is."

"How will you do that?"

"Spank a pillow. Try it out on myself."

"Now *that* I'd pay to see," Andy muttered. "Need a hand?"

Ethan sighed. "You don't learn, do you?" The paddle landed on the table with a clatter and Andy yelped when his backside received three spanks, these hard enough to match the worst of the ones he'd received during his morning spanking.

Once delivered, Ethan tipped Andy off his knee and to the floor. "You wanted to kneel? Kneel. Head down, ass up. Spread your knees. Wider."

The humiliation of the position forced a sob of protest from him, but he'd never been harder. Ethan shoved the table away, making room. He nudged the inside of Andy's knee with his foot, pushing it out leaving Andy splayed, ass, hole, balls, all on display. His face burned, his head oddly light. Ethan handled him with such care at times, then so unceremoniously. It was difficult to predict and it threw Andy off-balance emotionally. His former partners wanted a climax, no more than that. Ethan took the long way around.

"You do like to push me, don't you? It can move us along at times, but I wouldn't advise making a habit of it."

"Gag me," he said it in all seriousness, craving the enforced silence. "Please. You bought one. If not, hell, shove a sock in my mouth. Use a dishcloth. I don't care. Don't let me spoil this."

"I won't." Ethan crouched behind him, his palm soft against Andy's bruised skin. "And yeah, I bought a couple of gags, but they're not for today. I want to hear you, Andrew. I'm getting to know you and that's tricky if you can't answer my questions." Ethan fondled Andy's balls with casual intimacy. "Speaking of which, any questions?"

Difficult to think in this position, keenly aware of the view Ethan had, but Andy tried. "When am I leaving?"

"Up to you. You've got a shift tomorrow, but if you want to stay the night, you can."

"Sleeping on the couch?"

"No."

"On the floor?"

"Jesus, no. In my bed. With me."

"Are you going to fuck me? Let me come again?"

"If I say no, will you leave? Maybe I will, maybe I won't." Ethan patted his ass. "Get up."

Andy straightened, turning to Ethan. "Why don't you want to fuck me? Are you worried about it being safe? I always use condoms and I get checked every couple of months."

"Good to know you're careful. And no, that's not it."

Andy smiled wryly. "Let me guess. Along with the butt waxing, you're into clean inside and out?"

"Yeah," Ethan admitted. "Though that's something you can deal with in private. There's an unused douche in the bathroom, second drawer down. Is it a problem?"

"No. I don't use one every day, but before I go out, if I think I'm going to get lucky, sure." Andy cleared his throat. "I don't want you thinking I'm a slut, but I'm not a blushing virgin either. I've been fucked a lot."

"You like it?"

Andy scrunched up his face. "Kinda, but I'd like it better if I was with someone who knew what they were doing." He ran his hand down Ethan's arm. "Am I?"

"I've never had any complaints."

"If I don't enjoy it, I'll tell you," Andy warned him. "I promised I wouldn't lie. If I stick to that, you can forget about me being tactful and not hurting your feelings. I'm so done with smiling and telling guys it was great when it wasn't anything much."

"Listen, if my dick's inside your mouth or your ass and you don't love it, I want to know." Ethan leaned against the couch, legs stretched out. "From the way it's gone so far, I don't see that being a problem for you."

Andy mirrored Ethan's position, ignoring the throb from his ass. "I don't mind being naked, but am I ever going to see you?"

"Hard to avoid."

"And yet you have."

Ethan peeled off his top and socks then pushed down his trousers and briefs without getting up, going from clothed to naked in less than thirty seconds under Andy's fascinated gaze. "Happy?"

Lean, flat stomach, a subtle strength in arms and legs... Ethan naked reflected his personality. Everything under wraps but nothing missing. Including a cock that even half-hard had Andy envious. Ethan wasn't porn star huge, thank God. A man with a nine-inch cock had fucked him once and it'd been wince-inducing. Ethan's was closer to eight, a thick, straight column flushed with color, surrounded by neatly trimmed dark hair.

"Finished looking?"

Andy nodded, entranced by the slow thickening of Ethan's erection. "You're hot."

Ethan twisted to show his back. "Still think so?"

Scars, pale and ropy, marred the smooth expanse of his back. A starburst under his shoulder blade and a long, curving line leading from it, ended an inch from his spine.

"*Shit*," Andy said. "Who the fuck did that to you? Bastards. Tell me they got what was coming to them." He trembled with the force of his reaction, clenching his hands. It had to have happened years before, but he wanted to comfort Ethan even so. Tell him it didn't change a thing. "And yeah, I still think you're hot. The scars don't change that."

Ethan turned to him. "It was years ago in a fight and it's done with. I forget they're there most days. It's only when someone sees them for the first time —"

Andy surged forward, arms around Ethan, hands flat against the once-torn skin, and kissed him hard. "So I've seen them. It's done. Go back to forgetting them."

Ethan patted his shoulder as if Andy was the one who needed comforting. "I'm thinking about returning the gags."

It was an oblique compliment, but Andy tucked it away to gloat over later anyway.

* * * *

If Ethan had turned the waxing into a ritual with candles and music, Andy would've bailed, but he didn't. It took place in Ethan's bedroom after they'd eaten, the bed covered with an old sheet still twenty times nicer than anything on Andy's bed, and with the lights on and sunlight streaming in.

He was nervous when Ethan set up the wax melter with a box of wooden spatulas beside it, but he remembered how being shaved with Ethan watching had aroused him and his nerves steadied into an anticipatory buzz.

Ethan glanced at Andy's erection and slapped it lightly with a gloved hand. "Lucky for you, I'm not waxing around this."

"Why not?"

Grasping some of the wiry hair low down on Andy's stomach, Ethan tugged it gently. "So I can do *this*. And I'm not a fan of the shaved look when it comes to balls. A smooth crack, though — definitely. But I'll start with your chest. Those few lone hairs here and there look messy."

"So tidy me up."

"Plan on it."

It hurt, but in a different way from the spanking. It wasn't sexual. Ethan might be getting a charge from it, but Andy wasn't. What aroused him was being the focus of Ethan's attention, so even as Ethan daubed hot wax on one side of his crack, allowed it to cool, then peeled it off, he didn't complain.

Knowing what it was like made the second side hurt worse, though.

"All done," Ethan reported, cleaning off the wax with a damp cotton pad. "Shouldn't itch, but you'll want to apply moisturizer. I'll check it next time I see you."

"Do I tip you now?" Andy rolled to his back, wincing. Ethan had deemed his ass cheeks smooth enough, thank God. Hot wax on spanked skin would not have been fun. "Or is that against the rules of the spa?"

"What did you have in mind?" Ethan asked, taking the equipment into the bathroom. He returned, gloves stripped off, smiling. "Well?"

"Mmm." Andy raised his ass for the removal of the sheet, then sprawled out on the bed. "You're in charge, yeah? So whatever you like, whenever you like, but please make it now."

Ethan was already undressing. "I think it could be now. No toys, just me."

"You're plenty," Andy said, voice husky even to his ears.

Lube and condoms landed on the bed. Plain lube, standard condoms. Andy's balls tightened, his cock stiff. Weeks of wanting, of wondering, and now all he had to do was follow Ethan's lead. He couldn't go wrong. Okay, he was still fretting he'd manage it somehow, but Ethan's whispered, "Hey, relax," when he joined Andy quieted the voices in his head.

They kissed for long enough that Andy grew restive, needing more, but Ethan countered every move he made with a word or a touch. The kisses disturbed him with their intimacy, the taste of Ethan's mouth and the soft curl of his tongue a subtle invasion. He could've accepted the thrust of Ethan's cock into mouth or ass without feeling possessed, but the kisses dissolved barriers he hadn't known were there.

Eventually, Ethan propped himself up on an elbow. "You don't like being kissed?"

"I don't do it much," Andy admitted. He ran his tongue over his lips, reclaiming them. "When I was a teenager, sure, but mostly when I'm with someone, we fuck."

"Get used to it," Ethan told him. "If I'm in the mood for a fast, hard fuck, you'll get friction burns, but I'm in no rush now."

He moved over Andy, straddling him. "Link your hands behind your neck."

"You're not planning to wax my pits too, are you?"

"I'm waiting."

Pouting, his untouched cock stubbornly hard, Andy did as he was told. "Don't tickle me," he begged. "Hate that."

The exasperated look he got was reassuring in a way. "Pity. I'd planned that after the pillow fight and hair braiding."

"There's no need to be—"

Ethan's mouth on his ended his attempts to finish his sentence. Andy closed his eyes and tried to submit to the kiss without responding, in the hope Ethan would get bored and move on, but Ethan's patience seemed infinite. The kisses weren't a matter of mashed together lips and a probing tongue. More a slow, dreamy slip and slide, Ethan teasing at Andy's tongue with his, his teeth catching at a lip his kisses had sensitized.

Impossible to stay still, unmoving. With a sound that remained caught in his throat, Andy surrendered, lost in the moment, as he'd never been before. He wanted to run his hands down Ethan's back, cup his ass, bring their bodies together, but he didn't even try to move. Offering his mouth then his throat for Ethan to brand with a kiss, he moaned his appreciation when his mouth was free, then he eagerly returned Ethan's kisses when it wasn't.

His reward came with Ethan tugging at his hands to release them. "Touch me."

"God, yeah." The scars on Ethan's back interrupted the glide of his palms but he skimmed over marred skin, cursing whoever was responsible but forcing his thoughts away.

Ethan explored Andy's body with fingers and mouth, nodding from time to time as if committing every result to memory, from the texture of the hair around Andy's balls to the shiver Andy gave when Ethan scratched lightly at the hollow beside his hipbone.

At a word from Ethan, Andy rolled to his stomach for the cataloguing to continue. This wasn't sex the way he knew it but there was no denying it was a turn-on. Even face down, he sensed Ethan's gaze on him, a shadow of a caress.

Then abruptly, Ethan placed his hands on Andy's ass and split his cheeks open. Andy tensed when Ethan squeezed the tender skin but when Ethan drew his tongue over the freshly waxed skin, he spread his legs wider, inviting more. Ethan used his tongue like a finger, stroking, flicking, prodding at smooth flesh and the whorl of Andy's hole. Andy melted like licked ice cream.

He realized he was rubbing his cock against the quilt, close to coming, and forced himself to stop but it wasn't easy. He squirmed, panting, garbled entreaties for Ethan to do more, go deeper, don't stop, pouring from his lips.

He heard Ethan chuckle, but it was a small sound lost in the roar in his ears.

Aware of how close his climax was, he drew in a deep breath and choked out, "Gonna come."

"No, you're not." Ethan pulled back, drawing his thumbnail across Andy's hole. The small, sharp pain grounded him, jerking him back from the edge. "Breathe. Calm down."

"Yes, sir."

That was a mistake. Saying it ramped his arousal higher again.

"I'm going to—" A ringtone played, shattering the moment. Andy's phone was downstairs with his clothing, so it had to be Ethan's.

"Ignore it," Andy begged.

"Can't." Ethan got off the bed. "If it's that ringtone, it's work."

Andy focused on the tune and rolled his eyes. The 'dig, dig, dig' song of the dwarves from *Snow White*. Cute.

He rolled to his side and took in the view. Nice. Naked Ethan, dick up, thick and red, hair tousled, a flush fading from his face. He waited for Ethan to end the call and get back to him, body humming with arousal. Would Ethan appreciate him lubing up to save time? He could catch Ethan's eye, and groan when he pushed his fingers inside him make a show of it.

He reached for the bottle of lube then held it up, raising his eyebrows in a question. The scowl Ethan gave him had him dropping it even before Ethan's mouthed 'No!'

With a sniff, he settled back against the pillows and listened in on the conversation. After an initial exclamation, a grim-faced Ethan was mostly murmuring yes and no which wasn't informative. "I'll be there in twenty minutes, traffic permitting. On my way." He ended the call and jerked his thumb at Andy. "Up. I've got to go."

"What the fuck? No! Call them back and tell them it's your day off!"

"I can't." Ethan picked up his briefs. "Sorry. This is—"

"This is bullshit," Andy snapped. "Why're you getting dressed? We were in the middle of something, in case it slipped your mind."

"This is urgent." Ethan pulled up his briefs, then dipped his hand inside to angle his softening cock to the side. A cock Andy hadn't even touched yet.

"And I'm not?" Andy saw Ethan's attention slip away, as impossible to capture as a soap bubble caught by a breeze. "You're not a fucking paramedic. It's not life or death if one of the bars has run out of ice or if someone asked for a single malt we don't have. Jesus. Get your priorities straight."

"Enough," Ethan said, the word dragged out as if speaking was an effort. "This isn't the way I wanted the day to go, and I understand you're disappointed, but it can't be helped. There's been—"

Forgetting the rule about interruptions, Andy said, "At least get me off before you go."

"No." And there was the familiar snap of an annoyed Ethan, facial muscles tense, rocking forward onto the balls of his feet, ready to fight. It was intimidating, but Andy was in a reckless mood and that bestowed a spurious courage.

"Excuse me?" Andy slapped his cock hard enough to leave a sting. "Look at me! It would take, like, three seconds. Hand or mouth, I don't care, but do something with it before my balls explode."

"It won't kill you to wait."

"No. It won't. Because I'm not going to." His hand was where it needed to be. With the stink of smoke from burning bridges thick in the air, he gave his cock the few strokes needed. He knew his body and what it enjoyed. Even with Ethan watching, eyes wide, expression forbidding, he could get himself off in a matter of moments when he was this close to climaxing.

As orgasms went, it was mediocre. He pretended to enjoy it, but with Ethan impersonating a thundercloud, arms folded across his chest, lips pressed into a thin, pale line, it became no more satisfying than a sneeze. From heaven to blah. Knowing he was behaving badly, he used the quilt to wipe the spunk off his stomach and hand then stood, legs wobbly.

"Think I'll disappear then." He aimed for nonchalant and hit insolent by accident.

Ethan turned away and continued dressing, acting as if he were alone in the room. Infuriating.

Andy wet his lips. "So do we want to do this again?"

"Stop talking," Ethan said tersely. "Unless it's an apology— No, you know what? I don't even want to hear that. Get dressed and leave."

"You're kicking me out for jerking off?" His voice could express every emotion but he forgot that training in his guilt and anger. "Unbelievable. I've kept my hands off my cock for days and I was going to wait for you to say I could shoot, but under the circumstances—"

"And what circumstances would they be?" Ethan, dressed now, faced him, eyes cold. "You don't know, do you? Didn't bother to ask what was important enough for me to be called in like this."

"Some work emergency anyone with half a brain could handle by themselves. Big fucking deal."

"Try a drunk pulling a gun and shooting a guest and a member of the staff in the lobby."

"What?" The words made no sense. This was Vancouver. People had guns — *some* people — but gun-related incidents were rare. Aghast, Andy blurted out, "Oh, my God. Are they — are they *dead*? Who was it?"

"Victor, the lobby security guard. The guest was a woman. The drunk's ex-wife, they think. The paramedics took them to the hospital. I don't know more than that. The shooter is in custody." Ethan walked away, moving quickly but with an urgency untainted by panic. Ethan never freaked out. Andy trailed after him, unsure of what to do.

"Should I go with you?"

"I can't see what good you'd be," Ethan said with flat finality. "Get dressed. Hurry, please."

Throat tight with misery, Andy did as he was told, dragging on his clothes at speed.

"I'm sorry I was an asshole about it, but if you'd told me —"

Ethan ushered him out of the door, locking it behind them. "Any apology with a 'but' in there doesn't count for much. I don't have time for you now, but we'll deal with this, trust me. Now go home. And don't gossip about this with your friends."

"I wouldn't do that," Andy said, but he was talking to Ethan's back.

Chapter Twelve

He made his way home, nerves jangling from the shock of the day's events. He wished the walk were longer. After spending more time at Ethan's place, orderly yet warm, he couldn't think of a bad enough word to describe his home. It smelled funky. Nothing was new, nothing matched. It didn't not-match in a designer way and it wasn't shabby chic. It was a dump, a patchwork of castoffs, and the sole saving grace was the vodka in the freezer.

Except using it to smooth the jagged edges was a method he shied away from. He got drunk to have fun, not blur his emotions. He made coffee instead and sat slumped on the couch, TV tuned to the news channel, watching coverage of the shooting play out, the meager details stretched endlessly. No fatalities, but Victor's arm had been broken and a bullet had grazed the woman's skull. Seeing the familiar surroundings of the hotel lobby swathed in police tape made him shudder. No Ethan, though the hotel manager was interviewed — Charlotte Dawes being dignified and eloquent without gushing, saying all the right things.

It had been a good day up until the call. Dinner had been nice. Chicken stir-fry, nothing fancy but tasty, with Ethan making a sauce of soy, black beans and garlic that had tasted better than any takeout. They'd talked, and yeah, doing it naked when Ethan was dressed had been on the freaky side but he'd become used to it surprisingly fast. He'd only noticed when Ethan dropped a napkin in his lap with a grin.

He should be there now, lying on Ethan's bed, dreamy with lust, obeying every order, begging for permission to do so much to that strong body, that mouth-wateringly thick cock. Ethan had bought two freaking bags of sex toys and they were still in their packaging, waiting, like him, for a touch.

If he'd behaved himself and had acted more maturely, Ethan might've let him stay there or better yet taken him into work—not that arriving together would've been wise.

He pictured the scene when the man burst in, heading for the ex-wife he'd texted and told to meet him in the lobby. Was that premeditation? Hell, it had to be. Who walked around with a loaded gun in their pocket? The police statement didn't give the man's name, but said he had been furious over losing his boat in the divorce settlement. A boat. A fucking *boat*. And now two people were hurt, traumatized, along with everyone else in the lobby, and the man himself was looking at years in prison.

"Stupid fucker," he said aloud. It didn't help.

Restless after answering a worried text from Henry wanting to know if he was okay, he wandered around doing some desultory tidying but he couldn't settle to a task

He should be at the hotel. He was new, but even in less than two months, the hotel had crept under his skin. It was a beautiful space and it did something useful. He'd seen people check in, frazzled, exhausted, then an hour later come downstairs faces bright, refreshed, rejuvenated, ready to walk out of the huge doors, opened for them by a doorman, his uniform impeccable, and into the beautiful city.

His city. And the hotel was his too. If outrage filled him after this violation, the people within its walls endangered and hurt, what were Ethan's emotions?

The guy loved the hotel. Loved his job. And when it came to his team, well, they were family.

Ethan was firm, yeah, totally fucking anal about his rules and methods. Cross him and the result was freeze-dried employee, reeling from Ethan's icily worded lecture. The man was a hard-ass, no argument there — and his team loved him. They knew Ethan had their backs. They respected his competence and work ethic. The week a stomach bug had reduced the bar staff by a third, Ethan had moved into a staff room for four days and had taken over so many shifts Andy could've sworn Ethan had a twin. Everywhere he looked, there was Ethan — serving drinks, clearing tables, organizing a delivery and spraying down every flat surface to kill any lurking germs.

With him, though, Ethan had been different. He'd taken time to train Andy, releasing Joel from the job after the first few days and seeing to it himself. He'd called Andy to his office at random times for an inspection, requiring Andy to stand still while Ethan examined his clothing for wrinkles or stains. Once he'd held out his hands for Ethan, who'd grasped them, turned them over and sniffed disapprovingly at the dirt under Andy's nails. Pointing out he'd been in the middle of clearing out a stockroom when he'd been summoned hadn't saved him from being sent to wash them. The second inspection, his hands red from hot water and scrubbing, had sent him to the men's room to jerk off in a stall. Not his finest moment, but it was either that or combust.

Expecting Ethan to spare him a thought after hearing about a gunman in the hotel was unreasonable. Andy saw that now. But telling Andy to stay away was worse.

So did he obey Ethan or go to the hotel?

It might've been his second bad choice of the day, but he grabbed his jacket and left.

* * * *

A police officer guarding the staff entrance did his best to persuade Andy to leave but Joel spotted him and came to the rescue. Andy slipped inside before the cop changed his mind.

"What a day," Joel said. "Can you believe he did that in our hotel?"

He sounded indignant over the location more than the act but Andy picked up on the strain in his friend's voice and cut him some slack. It wasn't as if he never chose his words poorly.

"It sucks," Andy replied. "The man's nuts. Have we heard how Victor is?"

"Not officially, but word is he's home already. He wasn't shot like people thought at first. He dodged — dodged a bullet! Can you imagine how many times he'll hear that?—and slipped. That's how he broke his arm."

"Wow."

"Yeah." Joel cast a puzzled look his way, taking in Andy's casual clothes. "Thought you were off today."

"I was, then I heard about it and I... Well, I wanted to be here, you know?"

Joel leaned against the wall, a sprinkle of freckles over his nose standing out sharply against the pallor of his face. "Yeah, I hear you. I was in the lobby bar when it happened." His voice dropped to a whisper, as if confessing a sin, "There were kids around, Andy. Hell, there was a baby in a stroller. And he walked in and started yelling, then the shots..."

Helpless to comfort him with words, Andy embraced him impulsively. Straight guys weren't usually on his hug list no matter how cool they said they were with him being gay. He was surprised and pleased when Joel returned the hug without thumping him on the back or getting flustered.

Having Ethan appear was another surprise. Andy had assumed he'd be in meetings and hoped to avoid bumping into him. It wasn't the time to continue their argument and giving them time to cool off would've been a good idea.

Which made coming to the hotel doubly stupid, but he didn't regret it.

"Boss." Joel disentangled himself from Andy with a final, grateful pat on Andy's arm. "How's it going?"

"Fine," Ethan said, his gaze locked on Andy. "Did you need something, Andrew?"

"He wanted to be here," Joel answered for him when Andy stood mutely.

What he needed wasn't anything he could discuss with Joel around.

"Jenna and Niall came in too. I guess everyone wants to help, if they can."

"There's nothing that needs doing the staff on shift can't handle." Addressing Andy directly, Ethan added, "And you won't get paid for being here, so it's best if you leave."

He strode away, leaving Andy's feelings bruised to the point where he wanted to curl up in a corner somewhere, protecting himself from any more unkind words. His skin felt thin to the point of splitting open. When it came to Ethan, he had no defenses.

Joel whistled. "Okay, even for him, that was cold. Ignore it. He's upset. We all are."

"Yeah," Andy said. "I'm getting that."

"It'll be fine," Joel said. "The security cameras in the lobby caught it all and the guy confessed—not that he had any choice. Part of the lobby's cordoned off— blood on the floor—and housekeeping put up screens while they clean it, but it's business as usual. I mean, it's a crime scene, but there's no reason to shut us down. By tomorrow, you won't know anything had happened."

Andy nodded. "Yeah. One of those things."

Joel plucked at his lip, a nervous habit of his. "I hope it's a once-in-a-lifetime one of those things."

He left and Andy stood in the hallway, undecided. Home? A bar? Or should he track Ethan down and deal with the awkwardness before it solidified into a wall he'd never be able to break through?

His phone beeped and he dragged it out. Ethan.

Go home. Now. If I see you on the hotel property before your shift tomorrow, the consequences won't be pleasant.

In a weird way, it cheered him up. Ethan was pissed, clearly, but he hadn't given up on Andy. Not if he mentioned consequences. On the other hand, Ethan had said several times he didn't consider Andy his sub. He wasn't obliged to obey him outside the limits they'd agreed on, and telling him where he could be...no. That wasn't acceptable.

Not trying to annoy you but I'm not leaving yet. Going to hit the gym. Start that fitness routine of yours.

The idea appealed. Get sweaty. Burn off his nervous energy and switch off his thoughts. He wasn't dressed for it, but his running shoes and T-shirt were fine. He needed to swap his jeans for a pair of shorts and the lost and found would provide those. Andy wasn't squeamish. He'd worn costumes reeking of sweat or cologne and had sucked it up. Besides, as a courtesy to the guests who claimed their belongings and a matter of hygiene, housekeeping washed anything wearable before it went into temporary storage.

Ethan didn't reply. Ominous silence or tacit permission? With a shrug, Andy tucked his phone back in his jeans. Workout time.

The floor with the employee fitness room was so high he expected to see clouds floating by the window. It wasn't busy and there was only one topic of conversation though exertion made for choppy, breathless comments about the shooting rather than eloquence. Andy warmed up on a treadmill, staring out at the glimmering water and mountains, and let his thoughts drift anywhere but in the direction of Ethan, which meant they took abrupt zigzags a lot. Everything led to him.

The shorts chafed his spanked ass, but he got a kick out of that. It was as if Ethan was still spanking him in a way and Andy wasn't ashamed to admit he was a fan. It hurt—oh God, did it ever—but the high from it wasn't dissimilar to the one he was trying to achieve through running. Same high, different route, and he liked the view over Ethan's knee much better.

Ethan had mentioned the—small!—roll of flab around Andy's waist. He resolved to save money and eat better by following Henry's example, cooking instead of ordering in. Kicking around his bedroom somewhere was a cookery book aimed at students that his sister had given him. He'd browsed through it, mildly interested in some of the recipes, but unwilling to make the effort to cook them. That would change. After he'd finished exercising, he'd hit the supermarket and buy actual veggies, fruit and meat and see what he could do with them.

And he'd clean his room, sort through his clothes and wash some of them. Yeah. Buoyed by his plans, his speed increased.

The room emptied out during his run, leaving him alone. Next time he'd bring his headphones and listen to something more to his taste than the piped-in music.

"Having fun?" Ethan asked.

"God!" Andy jumped, stumbled and would've fallen if Ethan hadn't steadied him. Panting, he said, "Thanks for nothing. Do you *have* to creep up on me?" He turned the machine off and stepped down, glaring at Ethan.

"So you weren't lying about exercising."

"Hate to break it to you, but lying isn't something I do often. And I promised I wouldn't lie to you again, remember?"

"I remember."

"But I didn't promise to ask how high when you said jump. Not about everything."

"Understandable."

Andy eyed him suspiciously. "Are you still mad at me? It's hard to tell with the stone face and the chipped-off words."

"Let's just say if you asked for a spanking, I'd turn you down."

It took him a few seconds to figure out why. No spankings in anger. Right. And if a dark, secret part of him wondered what it would be like to get one with Ethan furious, he didn't have to provide an answer.

"I need to keep going." He pushed past Ethan, walking over to the weights' machine.

"I'll spot you," Ethan offered.

"I'm not going to use anything heavy. Bulking up isn't a good idea."

"Then I'll watch."

"No," Andy said, facing him. "You won't. I get that shaping me physically is a turn-on, but this was my idea and it's on my time. I'm not happy with you, either, and I'm not going to provide you with jerk-off material until things are right between us. Yeah, I was a dick, but I didn't know what had happened. When I did, I behaved. And sure, you had to drop everything and come in—I *get* that. Finishing what we started wouldn't have been the right thing to do. But trying to send me away, shut me out? That was…that was mean, Ethan."

"You're an actor. This is a job. This place doesn't matter to you."

"Yeah, well, I'm an actor who's resting more than performing, and this job and the people here are more important to me than you think." Andy gripped the bar linking the weights. "Now are you going to let me work out in peace or keep harassing me?"

Poor choice of words. Ethan flinched and stepped back. "I didn't—you can't think I was—oh, fuck it."

He slashed the air, drawing a metaphorical line between them. "We're done."

Andy watched him leave. Calling after him would be a waste of time. "And that's how to cap a shitty day, folks," he muttered to himself.

The hell with shopping healthy. He was buying ice cream.

Chapter Thirteen

He was a mess. And Ethan would take one look at him and know he'd inflicted damage. That was unbearable. He'd surrendered his pride over Ethan's knee, offering up his ass for a spanking, giving Ethan his tears, his honesty, but he was taking it all back. Ethan would see him smiling, unruffled, a guy who had moved on. He could say he was doing it so Ethan didn't feel guilty, but it would be a lie. He was doing it for himself, looking out for his best interests since no one else was.

He signed in and pasted a smile on his face when he saw he was down to serve drinks in the lobby bar, accepting Joel's slap on the back with a nod and Niall's less welcome but fulsome encouragement with a weak grin. Niall was a pain in the ass, always hovering, dropping hints about clubs he went to and asking if Andy went there. Leaving subtle behind, Andy avoided him, vaguely guilty, but unable to warm to the man.

"First time serving solo. Way to go. It's never too busy," Joel told him between sips of coffee in the break room. "It's more for people who want a quick drink while they're waiting for someone. You'll be fine. Text me if customers start to pile up and I'll swing by to help out."

Joel had recovered his equilibrium since yesterday and was back to normal. Everyone was, on the surface at least. Less pretending it didn't happen and more choosing to ignore it. The guests deserved normality, not staff speaking in hushed tones or endlessly discussing the shooting. Word from on high was to deflect questions and guide a curious guest away from the subject. No one had died but the hotel's reputation was at stake.

Though a few people had canceled their reservations, there wasn't an empty room in the place since even more people were clamoring to stay somewhere they'd seen on TV. Go figure.

"Thanks."

Joel raised his mug to his mouth then paused, studying Andy over the rim. "Are you feeling okay? Not coming down with something? You look as if you're about to throw up."

"He looks fine," Niall chimed in before Andy replied, stepping sideways to block Joel's view of Andy.

Andy took a few steps of his own, placing himself closer to Joel and with his back to Niall. He so didn't need rescuing. At least not by Niall. "It's the lighting in here."

"Can't be." Joel wandered over to the mirror by the bulletin board. "I look handsome as ever."

Not touching that one. "I've got to go. My shift starts in five."

"Yeah," Joel said absently, peering at his reflection. "Hey, I didn't notice yesterday, but did you get a haircut?"

"No," Andy said before Niall answered for him again. "Nothing's changed."

Biggest lie *ever*.

He took over from Tanya, listening to her explanation of what went where with half his attention on her, the rest on the people in the lobby. Some avoided the patch of cleaned carpet as if they knew why it had been steamed three times. Others walked across it without noticing. Andy, with an actor's superstition, took a detour.

Ethan had shown him every bar in the hotel so he knew his way around this one. What he didn't know was who would be his first customer.

After Tanya left, he stood alone for five minutes, straightening bottles, wiping down the bar—busy work to occupy his hands and calm his nerves. It helped to pretend there was a camera on him and this was the start of a scene in a movie. A man would come in, order a drink, then leave, slipping a flash drive into Andy's hand along with a tip. Andy would chase after him only to see the guy get shot, then it would be one long chase after another. He'd fight off bad guys and rescue the girl, all without mussing his hair or picking up more than an artistic cut or two.

A little girl, no more than six, walked around the screening wall and stomped up to him. She had a round face, hair in two braids and held a battered doll upside down. Kids still played with dolls? She wore a wool coat, green plaid, buttoned to her neck. It had ketchup smeared across it. Messy eater. Andy glanced past her, expecting to see a harried parent, but she was alone.

"I want a root beer."

"Uh..."

"These chairs are too high," she announced after a fruitless attempt to climb into one without letting go of her doll. "Lift me up."

Lawsuit waiting to happen. He'd pick her up and she'd scream about bad touching or fall off the stool and break a bone.

"I don't have root beer, miss, and this area of the lobby is for adults only. Would you like me to page your mom and tell her where you are?"

"No. She was mean to me. And you do so have root beer. Everywhere has root beer."

Andy picked up the soda gun and showed it to her. "Nope. See? I have buttons for club soda, cola, tonic and lemonade, but no root beer. Look, you shouldn't be wandering around on your own. What's your name?"

"I'm not supposed to talk to strangers." She shot him a darkly suspicious look. "My mommy said if anyone tries to take me somewhere I should scream and kick them—hard."

He held up his hands. "No screaming or kicking needed. My name's Andy and I work here at the hotel." He showed her his employee pass. "See?"

"I can't read." She pursed her lips. "Well, some words. Easy words."

"Never mind." Andy looked around helplessly. He couldn't leave the bar unattended and shepherd her to reception. She'd scream the place down if he tried, anyway. Better to keep her there where he knew she was safe and shoot off a quick text to Joel when she wasn't looking. "Suppose you tell me the name of your doll instead?"

"Isabella." Isabella landed on the bar with a thud, staring up at Andy with one glassy blue eye. The other was missing. Creepy as hell. Her owner tried a second assault on the bar stool, this one successful, then lowered her head like a bull preparing to charge, gazing at him, eyes screwed almost closed. "She's mine."

"I don't want it—her." Isabella wore a diaper and nothing else. Ketchup matted her short, curly hair. Gross.

"No root beer?"

He shook his head. What the hell? She was his first customer. "How about a cola? Same color."

"They don't taste the same, at all," she said, curling her lip. The gesture needed work. She hadn't quite mastered the art of raising one side of her lip in a subtle sneer.

Andy had spent hours in front of a mirror practicing until he could produce anything from a barely noticeable twitch to a full-blown Elvis impression.

"Gin and vodka are the same color too and neither do they," she informed him when he didn't reply.

How did she know? "True."

He picked up a glass, filled it with ice—using a scoop, not the glass itself as Ethan had trained him to do—and held the gun poised over it. "Lemonade then?"

She punished him for daring to assume he knew what she wanted by demanding club soda after he'd half-filled the glass with lemonade, then asking for a cherry in it, not a lemon slice.

While she sucked it through a straw, he took out his phone and texted Joel with a cry for help and a description of the girl he tried to keep factual. 'Demon spawn' wouldn't be helpful.

"What're you doing?"

"Nothing." He slid his phone into his jacket pocket. "How's the drink?"

"Boring. It doesn't taste of anything. You were texting someone. Was it your girlfriend?"

"No."

"Do you *have* a girlfriend?"

He dredged up a memory of Ethan telling him a bartender listened without offering personal information—an ear, not a mouth.

"No. So what do you think of the hotel, miss? First time staying here?"

"Are you gay?" She peered at him, straw stuck to her bottom lip. "A girl in my class has two daddies. Melanie. I don't like her. I used to but she said Isabella was a dumb name for a doll."

"I think it's a, uh, pretty name."

"You didn't say no," she observed. "You probably are. You're in denial."

Stung, he opened his mouth, prepared to fly the rainbow flag, but a shriek had him jerking his head around. "Katy!" A woman, teetering on insanely high heels and swathed in designer everything, flew across to scoop the little girl into her arms. The exhibition of maternal love ended abruptly when she noticed the ketchup. Katy's feet hit the floor fast after that. "Oh God, did it get on me? Did it?"

"Some of it did," Katy replied with sublime indifference, retrieving Isabella from the bar. "They don't have root beer here. Can we go now?"

The woman turned on Andy, gaze dropping to Katy's drink. "Is that *alcohol*?"

"Club soda. Look, I'm sorry if you were worried, but I—"

"Worried? *Worried*?"

Jeez, what a drama queen. Andy would've been sympathetic if her distress was genuine but it came over as fake as her hair color.

"She's been missing for hours! I've searched *everywhere*."

Katy checked a Hello Kitty watch. "Twenty minutes," she said to no one in particular before darting a smug look at Andy. "I can tell the time."

Katy's mother took a deep breath, shedding the artifice and getting a boatload scarier in the process. Eyes narrowed, she snapped, "You had to know she shouldn't have been here alone. Why didn't you tell someone?"

Okay, that was reasonable and thank God he had the text to back up his story. He took out his phone. "I couldn't leave my station, but I sent a text to Joel—"

"Joel's his boyfriend," Katy said. "Andy's gay."

"He works here," Andy said. "And he's not my boyfriend."

"I see you've found Katy, Ms. Harrison." Ethan walked forward, smiling, relaxed. "That must be a relief."

Andy forgot Katy, her mother and his predicament, lost in a haze of longing and renewed resentment because Ethan looked great. No shadows under his eyes, no bloodstains from a broken heart showing.

"This man served her drinks and didn't have the common sense to tell someone she was here." Her nostrils flared. "Too busy discussing his sex life with her."

"Hey, wait a minute—" Andy got that far before Ethan glared him into silence.

"I'll discuss his choice of action later, but the important thing is you found your daughter."

The woman bent over. "Katy, tell mommy what happened."

Katy swung Isabella by the foot. "You yelled at me for getting ketchup on my new coat."

"Of course I did! It's Marc Jacobs!"

"So I did what you did when you're in a bad mood and went to a bar for a drink." The satisfied gleam in Katy's eyes had Andy hoping to God his sister's kids were nothing like this little horror when they got past the toddler stage. "But they don't have root beer, so he got me a club soda instead."

"And I texted Joel to tell him to alert security," Andy blurted out, waving his phone at them. "Look, you can read the text yourself. And I didn't say anything about—"

"Thank you, Mr. Naylor." Ethan silenced him with a look, freezing the words he'd be about to say. "That's enough." He turned to Katy's mother, acquiring a professional but sincere smile on the way, back straight, head inclined, blending authority with flattering deference. "I'll have room service send a bottle of root beer to your suite with your permission. And we can clean Katy's coat, free of charge, of course. We want all our guests to be happy during their stay."

"I suppose she can have it," Ms. Harrison said ungraciously. "Well, Katy, what do you say after causing all this trouble?"

"I'm sorry." Katy didn't show a shred of guilt. "Can we go now?"

"Yes, but if you think I'm taking you shopping after this, young lady, you're very much mistaken."

"Don't care," Katy said when her mother led her away. "Isabella's tired anyway."

Andy gave Ethan a helpless look. "Tell me that was a setup because it's my first shift? Traditional hazing or something?"

Ethan didn't crack a smile. "We don't do that here."

"Then where the hell's Joel? I texted him ten minutes ago!"

"I know. He was with me when you did and I decided to rescue you myself. Just as well. You were in over your head." Ethan turned to go then paused. "Come to my office when you take your break. I'll need to write this up and I want to know exactly what happened."

"You already do. Jesus, why is everyone making such a big deal out of it?"

"My office," Ethan repeated. "And try to stay out of trouble for the remainder of your shift, or it'll be your last."

Andy watched him walk away. He'd wondered if their first meeting after breaking up would be awkward. Guess he had his answer. Ethan didn't give a fuck.

* * * *

Standing in front of Ethan's desk reciting everything he remembered saying to Katy was an exercise in humiliation. Ethan glanced up at him sometimes, but mostly he made notes, his writing too small for Andy to read upside down.

Talking to someone whose attention was elsewhere, forbidden from taking a seat though after standing behind the bar for hours, his feet were throbbing, Andy seethed inwardly and kept his voice toneless. He took a small revenge by folding his arms behind his back as he stood, the way Ethan had taught him.

He'd left his suit jacket in the break room, so the position made his shirt strain across his chest. The memory of the last time he'd stood like this had his cock hardening but he didn't care if Ethan noticed. He wasn't going to pretend nothing had happened between them, even if Ethan was suffering from convenient amnesia.

"That should be enough—" Ethan looked up, then froze when he took in Andy's stance. "What the hell are you doing?"

"You said I couldn't sit."

"I said it wasn't worth it, since this wouldn't take long."

Andy let his arms fall to his sides, point made. "Yeah, well, it has. My break's almost over and this is a complete waste of time."

"Getting an accurate account of what could've been an awkward situation while it's fresh in your mind is a waste of time? The woman's an idiot, but she stays here seven or eight times a year in a suite. She's a valued guest."

"Money talks. I get it."

"We're in the service industry. Yeah, money talks, but we don't want anyone walking out of here and bad-mouthing the hotel, especially not after yesterday, which was a PR nightmare, as well as traumatic, in case you hadn't guessed. I've calmed her down, luckily for you."

"Huh? She's the one who yelled at her kid then lost her!"

Ethan set his pen on the desk. "You can go now."

"That's it?"

"That's it," Ethan confirmed. "We're done here."

Those words again. "I got that message loud and clear yesterday."

Ethan narrowed his eyes, sending a clear warning. "Please don't bring your personal life to work."

"*My* personal life? Only mine?"

"Out," Ethan said tersely and picked up a file from his in box. "I'm busy."

The flat dismissal on top of the stress of the day combined to shred Andy's self-control close to breaking point, but he held it together. "Fine by me." At the door, he couldn't resist a final gibe, turning his head to say, "Remember you wanted to see my bruises? I don't have any. Guess you didn't leave much of an impression after all."

He turned back to the door, heart thudding fast, a sick sense of satisfaction filling him, though he'd lied through his teeth. Tiny purple bruises peppered his ass. He'd stared at them in the mirror, then caressed them with an ache of longing.

He heard Ethan's chair scrape over the floor and snatched at the handle, then fumbled to open the door. Before he could, Ethan slammed his hand against the wood, forcing the door to stay closed, trapping Andy with his body.

Andy sucked in a breath, dizzy with panic and exultation. Ethan shifted to the side without moving his hand, fingers spread. Beautiful fingers, straight and strong. God, he wanted that hand on him again, punishing him, awakening him.

"I told you not to push me," Ethan said into his ear. His free hand swept across Andy's ass, too light to count. "No marks? I doubt that, but it's an easy fix, isn't it?"

"Yeah," Andy said, gasping the word. "Except you're busy pretending you don't want to do it. Don't worry. I know where to go to get marks that last. There's this club—"

Ethan moved his hand from Andy's ass and slapped it across Andy's mouth to silence him. Andy bit at it, catching flesh between his teeth, willing for any retribution if it got Ethan looking at him, not through him.

Ethan spun him around and this close, there was only one way it could end. The kiss was a messy clash of teeth and tongues, a heated battle for dominance Andy had no wish to win but was damned if he'd throw the match. Ethan had abdicated. If he wanted his crown back, he'd need to do more than ask politely. Andy wanted to be conquered, his body the spoils of the war between them. He moaned into the kiss, trying to find skin. Ethan grabbed the hair on the back of his head with one hand and Andy's ass in the other, holding him in place for a kiss.

"You pushy little fuck," Ethan muttered, fastening his mouth to Andy's throat.

"Chicken-shit asshole," Any hissed back, rubbing the heel of his hand over Ethan's erection, solid and unyielding. "You going to use this or is it only for show?"

For a moment, when Ethan tightened his grip to the point of pain, Andy thought he'd gone too far, but the risk factor amped up his arousal. All or nothing. He had to get Ethan to a point where denying their attraction was impossible.

"I told you to get out." Ethan wasn't talking about what he'd said a few minutes before, Andy knew.

"Any regrets?" He shaped his hand to Ethan's cock. "Yeah, I found one."

Ethan rocked his hips into the touch, lips parted on a groan, but it was a momentary surrender, no more than that. He released Andy, stepping back and wiping his mouth. "We're not doing this here."

"So find us a room," Andy said. "You did it before to yell at me."

The look he got was incredulous. "Are you fucking kidding me? You expect me to leave my desk and screw you in one of our rooms? No way."

Another rejection. Great. Heart racing, Andy smoothed down his hair then tucked in his shirt. His hands shook a little, but it wasn't noticeable. "My break's over, boss. Okay if I go back to the bar?"

He got a wince out of Ethan with the 'boss' at least. "Andrew—"

No. Not his name spoken with that pleading, yearning intonation. No more. He couldn't be here with Ethan and not lose it so spectacularly they'd have people hammering on the door wanting to know what the shouting was all about. He opened the door wide, letting the outside world back in again. Seeing Joel walking toward the office, he said, projecting his voice, "We're running low on gin, by the way. I'll grab a bottle from the storeroom, if that's okay?"

His actor training paid off. He didn't sound like someone about to explode into a million pieces with frustration at all.

* * * *

Shift over, Andy had left the luxury and warmth of the hotel, walking through the cool night, apathy dragging at him like a physical weight. His throat ached and he couldn't stop shivering. Was he coming down with something? God, he hoped not. Being sick when you were alone in the world sucked. His friends weren't the kind to come over with chicken noodle soup. They'd keep their distance in case they caught whatever he had. Henry would be sympathetic and brew him noxious herbal teas, but he'd lecture Andy on poor diet and too much alcohol. Apparently, Andy's lifestyle made him a germ-magnet.

He'd planned to browse the Vancouver Actor's Guide webpage to see if there was a decent role, but it didn't appeal now. He was non-union, so he was a free agent, but that limited him in some ways too. Doing a student gig for pizza and experience was getting old. He needed new headshots. The agency he was with hadn't sent him anything in weeks.

As an actor, he was a great bartender.

When he got home, he made himself a hot toddy. His dad swore by them and though Andy rarely drank whiskey, mixed with honey, lemon and hot water, it didn't taste bad at all. He sipped, inhaling the fragrant steam, a throw wrapped around his shoulders, and dissolved into a self-pitying mess.

Henry found him sitting in the dark an hour later and snapped on the light, prompting an anguished yelp from Andy.

"Bright light fright, man! Turn it off!"

Sighing, Henry did as he was told, but turned on a lamp instead. "Sick?"

Andy sniffed experimentally. His nose wasn't snot-clogged and two toddies had numbed the rawness in the back of his throat. "Mostly miserable."

Henry pushed Andy's feet to the floor and sat beside him on the couch. "I'm happy. If you avoid bringing me down, I'll listen."

"Hooked up with someone. Found out I'm a kinky son of a bitch Saturday morning. Got kicked out of his life Saturday afternoon."

"Hmm," Henry said, triggering immediate Ethan flashbacks. "I thought you were brooding over that Ethan guy?"

To betray or not to betray? Andy settled for a noncommittal hum.

"How kinky is kinky? On a scale of one to ten, are we talking eleven?"

"Calibrate it for me," Andy countered. "Wax play."

Henry threw back his head and stared at the ceiling. "Dripping hot wax onto people? Umm, eight?"

Eight? The hell? "Spanking."

"For fun? Like a birthday spanking?"

"Over the knee, hard, bruises."

"Nine," Henry said firmly which guaranteed Andy wouldn't be sharing anything else with him. A spanking rated a nine? Did Henry look at online porn *ever*?

"I'm a four," he lied without hesitation. "This guy wanted to tie me to the bed, then blow me and I kinda got off on it."

And there went Henry's glasses, pushed up hard. "I think I stopped being comfortable with this conversation a few numbers back. Do you still like this guy? Why did he kick you out anyway?"

"Don't know to both of them." Andy gave up. The only person he could talk to about this was Ethan and that wasn't going to happen. "Forget about it. I have. When are you seeing Mahito again?"

"Tomorrow in class, then we've planned to hang out after and play some games. You should see his place. Huge plasma, thousands of DVDs and games. He's into all these anime shows but mostly they're the original Japanese, not the English dubs. No subtitles, so it's hard to follow."

"Sounds great." Andy shrugged off the throw, yawning widely. "I'm going to bed. See you."

"Good talk." Henry patted Andy's knee. "Glad I helped to cheer you up." The sad thing was, he probably thought he had.

As usual, feeling sleepy switched off when he was in bed, teeth brushed and lights out. He tried to lull his body to sleep by reciting his classic audition speech in his head. He polished the intonations of the Lord's speech from the prologue of *The Taming of the Shrew*, until he reached the line, 'And if he chance to speak, be ready straight, And with a low submissive reverence Say 'What is it your honor will command?''

Even Shakespeare was making it impossible to forget what he'd been for a few shining hours.

His phone was on the nightstand. He had Ethan's number. A text was easy to send, simple to ignore if that was what suited Ethan best. Honesty, not pride, shaped his words.

Can't sleep. Can't forget you. We both screwed up. Fix it.

He was used to his friends replying within seconds but after holding his phone for five long minutes, he put it back, fumbling in the dark. Maybe Ethan was asleep. No, it wasn't late enough. Even Henry was still up, pottering around in the kitchen washing dishes and wiping surfaces. Ethan's phone might be dead, but that was a remote possibility. The guy was too organized for that.

He wasn't sending another. Except somehow, his phone was back in his hand, the glow from the screen bright, and he was typing.

Sir, sir, sir. Been calling you that in my head for wks. Feel like a car you filled with gas, started engine, then walked away. Never got to touch your cock, suck it, ride it. Don't know what you taste like. Want to.

Shit. He swallowed hard, pretending that he tasted Ethan's spunk, thick and hot against his tongue, the roof of his mouth, his throat. The flat, empty taste of saliva mocked his efforts.

He'd walked around naked for the best part of his time in Ethan's loft, spent hours being pampered and groomed under Ethan's watchful gaze. His ass had been spanked hot and sore and he'd loved it.

He shuddered, moving restlessly, the brush of the bedding against his cock maddeningly arousing. God, he'd worked himself up to the point where the muted sound of an incoming text would bring him to climax. He threw back the covers and rolled to his side, clutching his phone as though it were the crocheted blanket he'd slept with during his childhood. It had been repaired until barely anything remained of the original yarn, then lost on a vacation. He'd been inconsolable for weeks.

Thinking about his blanket — with mild regret now, not the gut-wrenching sense of loss he'd suffered at the time — was oddly soothing. He drifted into a doze, hearing Henry's bedroom door close with a considerately quiet click. True sleep would've followed, but his phone vibrated, startling him fully awake. He raised himself up on his elbow and checked his message, praying it wasn't spam, willing it to be from Ethan.

Go to sleep.

He studied the three words, analyzing them. Ethan hadn't told him to go away, though he'd implied the texts had to stop. And for Ethan to think he had the right to tell Andy what to do...

Is that an order, sir?

Silence. Too hard a push? Too demanding? He knew Ethan wanted to call the shots, but passivity wasn't Andy's specialty and he needed Ethan with a desperation that made calm acceptance impossible. If he belonged to Ethan, held securely by his rules, it would be easier, but he was floating, drifting, drowning and ready to grab onto anything passing by to save himself.

Three words were a light twig, not a life raft.

He muttered, "Come on, come on. Say yes, damn it. How hard is that? Three taps and hit send."

As if Ethan had heard him—though if he had, he wouldn't have been pleased—Andy got what he'd asked for.

Yes.

He couldn't resist sending a final text.

Thank you, sir.

Ethan didn't reply, but Andy didn't mind. Drawing the covers up again, a quiet happiness displacing his misery, he fell asleep.

Chapter Fourteen

Andy stood on the Stanley Park seawall and stared across at Siwash Rock, a tall, narrow rock stack crowned by a tree. It was millions of years old, majestic, immovable, and with the cloud shadows painting it with patches of darkness, he almost believed the Squamish legend that it was a man turned to stone, not as a punishment, but a reward for unselfishness.

What would Ethan think of that particular consequence?

As if mentioning him was all it took to conjure him up, Ethan arrived, the sound of his boots on the path pulling Andy from his reverie. From the direction he'd come, Ethan must've parked at the lot by the Teahouse Restaurant, a short walk away. Andy had gotten a ride to the park from Gary who had asked a dozen questions Andy had no intention of answering. Since when were his friends interested in his love life anyway? Being poked for details of who had tamed him was funny for about ten seconds. After that, unable to defend Ethan or mention him by name,

Andy had become irritated, snapping out answers or terse deflections. It wasn't *that* big a deal if he'd found someone who was more than a one-night stand.

Waking, his phone digging into his hip, then finding a message from Ethan proposing a meeting on the seawall at noon had been more effective than coffee. The site of the meeting put them in a neutral setting with no privacy. They'd be able to talk, but no more than that. Well, this was Vancouver and no one would care if they held hands or kissed, but Andy's sights were set on something less romantic and more intense.

"You must've been early," Ethan said by way of greeting, checking his watch. It had a brown leather strap, brown face and a gold rim. After seeing Ethan's place, his choice of watch made sense. Outside work, Ethan went for earth tones. "It's barely past noon."

"Got a ride here with a friend. He had a dentist appointment so he dropped me off half an hour ago."

Ethan nodded, shoving his hands into the pockets of his leather jacket. He'd stopped a yard away from Andy, out of reach. "Nice day, but we can walk back to the restaurant if you're chilly from waiting. I took the afternoon off, by the way."

"This is fine." Andy took a step forward, needing to bridge the physical gap. Distance between them left room for doubts and questions. Touching brought with it a clarity he appreciated. Naked and touching reduced all their problems to insignificance. Pity they couldn't be in bed for every important conversation. "Are we going to talk? I mean, *really* talk? I meant everything I said in those texts."

"Did you?"

"Yeah. And I wasn't drunk either. Lonely, I guess — and confused. It was going great then you kicked me out on my ass after one row. I didn't see you as someone who gave up on people easily, so why give up on me?"

A cyclist went by in a flash of color, legs pumping and head down. Ethan watched him go out of sight before turning to Andy. "Newton's Law. Every action has an opposite and equal reaction. You pushed me and I pushed you back. Pushed you away."

"Yeah. And I let you."

Ethan exhaled, puffing out his cheeks. "Not for long. You harassed me, goaded me and pushed me again. But this time I was ready for it."

"Can we start over? We can take it slower and keep it vanilla apart from the bit where you're in charge in bed. I don't need all the kinky stuff if it's too much for you."

That got him a huff of laughter. "I have a feeling some of what you'd enjoy may be but if you think I didn't enjoy having you over my knee, you weren't paying attention."

Andy grinned. "I noticed." He threw back his head, staring up into the endless blue of the sky. "There's this exercise in drama class where you scream and yell, let it all out. Supposed to release all the negative energy and free the inhibitions. I'd do it now, but someone would think I was being attacked and come running to the rescue."

"And you don't need rescuing." Ethan moved closer. "You need to be tied down, spanked, fucked, used."

Andy walked into Ethan's hug with a deep sense of relief. "All of that. More." He rubbed his nose against Ethan's neck, breathing in the citrus scent of Ethan's cologne. "When you spanked me, it was as if all these spinning pieces stopped moving and fell, slotting into place. It all came together. Fucking loved that feeling."

"How are the bruises?" Ethan asked, murmuring the words so they belonged to Andy, no one else.

"Fading. I want—" He corrected himself. "Will you put some more on me, sir? Please?"

Ethan tightened his arms. "Yeah. I want to use that paddle you chose. Tie you to the bed, ass up, then fuck you with the tears still wet on your face."

Andy moaned, kissing Ethan's neck over and over, frantic presses of his mouth to skin. The image Ethan's words conjured was like a mirage, tempting but unobtainable, because they were in the park, not Ethan's bedroom. Whose stupid idea had it been to meet here anyway?

"Shh." Ethan stroked his hair then dropped his hand to Andy's ass, slapping it lightly. "Behave."

"God." Andy bit the shoulder of Ethan's leather jacket, worrying it with his teeth, needing to express his frustration. A reproving click of Ethan's tongue stopped him. "You want to see me crying? Tell me we're not heading to your place right now. That'll do it."

Ethan broke free. "That's exactly where we're going." Emotion heightened his color, his eyes bright and fierce, hiding nothing. Ethan often slammed a wall between himself and the world, but he didn't seem to care if Andy saw his arousal now. "And you're going to walk to my car in silence, Andrew. Not a word, not even one of those 'yes, sir's you're so fond of. And if you want to ask why, I'll tell you." He cupped Andy's face, his palm startlingly warm against Andy's wind-chilled skin. "Knowing why you're not talking will drive me crazy and I *want* to feel that way. I want to hurt from it, ache with it and know when I get you home, I can make it stop for both of us."

You sadistic, beautiful fucker. He was too lost in lust to nod. He fell into step beside Ethan, willing him to walk faster—hell, run—but Ethan seemed content to stroll, a half-smile on his lips.

Only the flush of color and the jump of a muscle in his cheek now and then betrayed him.

The parking lot was quiet, a few cars around but no one close to Ethan's. They got in, doors closed, seat belts fastened, and exchanged glances.

"You can talk again, or stay quiet and I'll make the ride back interesting. Your choice."

Andy rolled his eyes. Like that was a choice. He mimed zipping his lips and Ethan acknowledged his choice with a sharp nod. "Okay. No sound at all. Let's see if you make it."

What counted as a sound? Too late to ask now.

Ethan started the engine, but kept the car in park. "Cock out. No touching. Hands behind you. Yeah, it's not comfortable. I don't care."

Jesus. It was broad daylight and once they were on the road, anyone driving an SUV or truck could look in and see him. His rigid cock, liberated from his jeans, stuck up like an exclamation point.

"Nice," Ethan said casually, turning the heater to full-on temperature and power. Air blasted from the vents, directed at Andy's face, but he had a feeling that wouldn't be the case for long and he was right. Ethan adjusted the vents so the hot air played over Andy's exposed cock, the subtlest of caresses, but in his current state of arousal, more than enough to have his teeth gritting to avoid moaning.

Thank God the drive was a short one—a matter of minutes, no more. By the time they left the park, he was sweating and digging his fingers into his thighs. Ethan glanced at him from time to time, but it seemed enough for him to know Andy was suffering. Staring ahead at the road helped distract him, but Ethan took that away from him too, with a terse command to look at his cock.

Staring at the dark red crown and flushed shaft, brought a tortured whimper from him, impossible to hold back.

"Yeah, that counts." Ethan turned on the air conditioning. There was a moment when the temperature mellowed to pleasant warmth, but the air conditioning was efficient and within a breath or two, the stream of air turned chilly. Against his will, Andy grunted a protest, biting his lip too late to prevent the sound being audible.

Ethan sighed, reached across and grasped Andy's cock firmly, jacking it a couple of times before flicking his thumb over the head.

Andy closed his eyes, and arched his back, unable to see the rough fondling as a punishment until Ethan took his hand away.

"Zip up. We're nearly there."

Gingerly, Andy tucked his cock inside his jeans, praying his labored breathing didn't count as a sound. He was uncoordinated, fingers clumsy, a buzz in his ears distancing him from the world. The short walk from the car to Ethan's front door was a case of one step at a time and hope to God the friction of clothing against cock didn't prove too much for his self-control. The dazzle of sunlight on the nearby water gave him an excuse to walk with his head down, blocking out anything that might shatter the mood. The salt-laden air he breathed and the cry of the gulls wheeling overhead were irritants, overloading his senses. He was reaching the point where holding back his climax would be a physical impossibility, but silenced, he couldn't tell Ethan about his plight and ask for permission to come.

Once inside, he gave Ethan a beseeching look that Ethan met with raised eyebrows and a tapping foot.

Oh. Right. Strip at the door. He struggled out of his clothes, watched by Ethan who had done no more than remove his jacket and shoes. Each shed item left him lighter, as if naked he'd lost his concerns and doubts. Clothes folded on the chair, he went to his knees, wrapping his arms around Ethan's waist and resting his cheek against the metal and leather of Ethan's belt.

It wasn't submission. It was where he wanted to be.

"You can talk now." Ethan framed Andy's face with his hands, tipping Andy's head back so he had nowhere to look but up at Ethan. "Andrew."

Hearing his name said like an endearment, Ethan's longing vividly coloring the word, made Andy's throat tighten. Silence was a refuge. He couldn't spoil the mood if he didn't speak.

Ethan stroked Andy's throat with the fingers of one hand, taking a handful of Andy's hair with his other. The position didn't hurt unless he resisted and it was an effective means of focusing his attention, something he guessed Ethan had figured out early on.

"You didn't stay quiet in the car," Ethan said and there was regret there, the same faint disappointment he showed when Andy failed to complete a task at work. "Up. Let's deal with that now. Arms behind you."

Andy tasted anticipation, a bright fizz of it, when he rose and folded his arms behind him, hands resting on forearms. He got off on Ethan's methods of balancing the books. Better to get things right and be rewarded with Ethan's approval plus a deliciously perverse consequence, but this worked too. He'd tried to stay quiet and it bugged the hell out of him to fail at so simple a task. He deserved whatever Ethan decided to hand out.

Maintaining his grip on Andy's hair, Ethan leaned in and licked Andy's left nipple, then blew on it until it hardened obediently. Teeth came next, the sharp pressure of the bite sending a bolt of pain through Andy's chest. Ethan drew his head back, stretching skin taut, the wet flicker of his tongue against the captured morsel of flesh doing nothing to ease the agony.

Andy whimpered, shocked out of silence, his hands tightening to the point where he was probably bruising his arms. Shit, it hurt so fucking much. Ethan couldn't do this and expect him to take it. It wasn't fair. He'd tried to behave in the car, tried so fucking hard.

"God! Ethan — sir, *please* —"

Ethan moved his head side to side, sending a fresh wave of pain through Andy's body, a silent rejection of the plea for mercy.

Stepping forward would've lessened the tension and eased the pain, and for the space of time between one breath and the next, he contemplated it, but he didn't want to fail this test. With that realization, he stopped fighting it and relaxed, sighing out a moan holding pleasure, not protest. As if rewarding him, the sensations radiating from the tiny scrap of flesh transmuted into a steady thrum, shaping his thoughts, rough edges sanded away.

Ethan opened his mouth and straightened. Andy glanced down at his nipple. No blood, not that he'd expected any. Red. Swollen. Wet from Ethan's mouth.

He looked at his right nipple, hard from an echo of pain, but untouched. It ached. Hurt more than the other. With a soft, imploring sound, he twisted his torso, then arched his back, offering himself up for more.

Ethan brushed his thumb over the punished nipple instead. "My choice. Not yours."

That was harder to accept than the tearing pain of the bite but after an inward struggle, Andy nodded, getting a smile from Ethan that held gratitude and approval.

"Upstairs," Ethan said. "Face down on the bed. Keep your arms like that."

Thank God. *Finally*. Ethan walked upstairs behind him, not touching him with anything but his gaze. The wooden floor was cool against Andy's bare feet and he counted each step. With no hands to steady him, walking became a conscious effort, the need to please Ethan filling his head, pushing everything else aside.

The four-poster bed with an intricate metal headboard and footboard offered a multitude of possibilities when it came to bondage. Andy crawled onto it, a thick, soft comforter patterned in deep green and copper welcoming him. Ethan had changed the bedding. No surprise there. Andy closed his eyes, some of the urgency of his arousal leaving him, now that he'd reached journey's end.

He heard Ethan undress then open one of the built-in cupboards along one wall.

"I'm tying you up," Ethan said. "Tell me your safe word."

Andy shook his head, clinging to his silence.

"Andrew."

It was a warning now, and yet he couldn't break through the quietness surrounding him.

"Then I'll do it for you. Yellow if you want a break, red stops everything. Okay?"

Andy nodded, breathing in Ethan's scent, permeating the bedding, indefinable, unmistakable.

Ethan put a pillow under Andy's thighs and attached his wrists and ankles to the bed with easy-release straps. "Struggle. Try to get free."

He obeyed, pleased with himself so far, but his composure shattered when he tugged at his bonds and realized they held him securely. He'd been tied for sex a few times but only his wrists and never for long. It'd been fun, nothing more.

He couldn't break the straps. Couldn't free his hands to touch Ethan. If there was a moment of panic, it was gone too quickly to register. He cried out, a sharp, exultant joy suffusing him. Safe. Impossible to screw this up now. He was how Ethan wanted him, and he'd stay like this until Ethan released him.

He tugged again, craving that wash of pleasure as he processed his limited ability to move. Words poured from him. "Feels so good. God, it feels so fucking good."

Ethan placed the paddle Andy had chosen beside his head, along with a couple of condoms and a small bottle of lube. He waited, giving Andy a chance to protest—like that was going to happen. The bed creaked and Ethan knelt between his spread legs, hands on Andy's ass. He slid his hands higher, along Andy's sides, before lowering himself, fitting his body to Andy's. Supporting some of his weight, he rubbed his cock along the cleft of Andy's ass, his breathing harsh, his need palpable.

Yes. Use me. Rub off on me.

He smelled Ethan's spunk before it struck his skin, the acrid tang of it familiar, known. Spunk striped his back and ass, warm splatters marking him.

Ethan sighed and kissed the back of Andy's neck. "I'll get a towel," he murmured.

Wary of saying anything Ethan could interpret as a challenge to his authority, Andy said, "You coming on me is hot as hell. If you left it on me, I'd love it."

Ethan kissed him again, lips lingering. "You like being marked. Is that it?"

"Like being yours."

"Yeah, I like it too. And I'm going to put marks on you that don't wash off."

Andy waited for a slap or the dull blows of the paddle, but he got Ethan's mouth and teeth instead. Ethan pushed the globes of Andy's ass together, filling his hands with muscled flesh to bite.

Tiny nips, sucking bites that brought the blood to the surface. Ethan raked his teeth across Andy's flesh, leaving a tingling trail of heat. He rolled his head, gasping, squirming, desperate for more, loving the way Ethan covered every inch of his ass. Ethan was thorough, no doubt about it.

"Much better now that it's waxed," Ethan remarked, voice calm, as if he'd spent the last five minutes reading a book or throwing bread for the ducks. "I promised this ass a paddling and it's nicely warmed up now." He dealt out a slap to each cheek, playful blows that had Andy smiling back over his shoulder. He missed the drowsy immersion in the scene, but in some ways, it had distanced him from Ethan. Sharing a smile was a good reminder they were doing this for fun. No artificial accusations he'd been a bad boy, simply an acknowledged need on both their parts.

"The paddle will hurt more than my hand," Ethan told him.

It did. Andy had nothing other than Ethan's hand to compare it to, but after a dozen swats, he decided he didn't like it as much. The effects were bearable, at least for now, but the way it jolted his body broke the mood, making it impossible to sink into the tear-streaked euphoria he craved. He missed the intimacy of Ethan striking his skin with his palm, the heat and pain shared between them. This didn't hurt Ethan at all.

He gave it a fair trial, but when he realized his paramount emotion was boredom, the next word out of his mouth was, "Yellow."

The paddle landed beside him and Ethan had a wrist freed before Andy could stop him.

"No! Yellow, okay? Not red. Yellow."

Ethan collapsed onto the bed, erection at half-mast, expression concerned. "Talk to me then."

"Don't want the paddle," Andy said succinctly. "Prefer your hand."

"Too painful?" Ethan caressed Andy's butt. "It's red, but it doesn't look too bad."

"I can take it, but I don't *like* it. You're…you're too far away. Miss being over your knee."

That got him a slow nod and a faint smile, with more than a hint of tenderness showing. "I get what you're saying. It wasn't doing much for me. Too impersonal. Though you do look incredible tied up."

"If I ask you to tie me up again and spank me, would you do it or say I was pushing you?" Andy craned his neck and nuzzled Ethan's hand. "Not pushing, sir. I swear."

"I know." Ethan tugged Andy's hair gently. "I'd be pretty stupid to say no when it's what I want too." He hesitated. "I'd like to try a different position, though. And fuck you afterward. Okay?"

"Don't ask." Andy scrunched up his face in an effort to express his frustration with Ethan's hesitancy. "Do it. You're in charge, remember? God, I wish I hadn't said anything now!"

And cue the oops moment. Ethan dealt out a stinging slap to reddened skin and gave Andy that personal touch in spades. "If you ever hold back from using a safe word for any reason, let alone a bullshit one like that, you won't enjoy what happens next. Not one little fucking bit. Clear?"

Chastened if wildly curious, Andy whispered a meek, "Yes, sir."

Ethan studied him, narrow-eyed, still steaming, then gave an abrupt nod. He left the cuffs around Andy's wrists and ankles, but unfastened the three straps still attached to the bed.

"Over on your back," he ordered, taking away the pillow under Andy's hips.

Wondering how he was going to get spanked with his ass on the bed but not suicidal enough to ask, Andy rolled over. Ethan fastened the wrist straps to the bed again, then, with a wicked gleam in his eyes, he picked up Andy's right foot. "How flexible are you?"

Oh, shit. Like that? And it wasn't even a punishment. Ethan had planned it before he mouthed off. Face flaming, Andy submitted to having the ankle straps tied above the wrist straps, leaving him spread obscenely wide, doubled up. The straps were long enough to allow him some freedom to bend his legs, raised high in the air, but not much. Not a position he could be comfortable in for long, but holding it wasn't an issue. He had no fucking choice.

"Personal enough for you now?" Ethan kneeled in the middle of the bed with easy access to Andy's ass, but he ignored it for a while, tracing the taut muscles on Andy's inner thighs and the arch of his foot until Andy begged him to stop.

"Ticklish?"

Breathing unevenly, Andy nodded, assaulted by memories of a bully holding him down and tickling him until he peed his goddamn pants. That hadn't been fun at all. The delicate scratch of a fingernail across his sole had come closer to breaking him than anything Ethan had done to that point. He hadn't used a safe word but he was relieved Ethan had seen his mounting distress and stopped.

"I won't do that to you again," Ethan promised. "At least not on purpose."

Mercy from a sadist. He must've sounded freaked. "Thanks."

Ethan gathered Andy's balls, weighing them, jiggling them before running his finger along the seam of Andy's ass to his hole.

"I cleaned my ass out properly this morning," Andy said. "When I got your text."

"Good." Ethan continued an examination clinical enough to make Andy squirm with renewed arousal. Why being objectified turned him on, he didn't know, but it was beyond hot to lay there, traces of Ethan's spunk on his back, his genitals exposed to Ethan's gaze and probing, assessing fingers.

It wasn't romantic, but it wasn't about that, was it? Just the two of them getting off. Did he like Ethan? Hard to say. He didn't know him well enough. Respected him, yes, but strip away the sex and spankings and what did they have between them?

"You're thinking, but not about the right things," Ethan observed and slapped the top of Andy's thigh hard. "Focus, Andrew."

And yeah, that worked. Ethan, the man, was an enigma, but this side of Ethan he knew and enjoyed. That slap hadn't been playful or tentative at all. A skin-scorcher, in fact. He wanted more.

Being displayed like a dead frog in a Biology class shouldn't arouse him this much. His cock, responding to Ethan's fondling, was rigid, bobbing with every gasped breath he took, every slap Ethan delivered.

Ethan paused to study his handiwork and Andy dared to ask, "Can I come, sir?"

"Not a chance in hell until I'm inside you," Ethan said, taking care of that question.

The spanking lacked the intimacy of the over-the-knee one, but it was kinkier and Andy loved it. He saw Ethan's face, the absorbed concentration while Ethan deliberated over his next target, the flash of a smile when Andy's strangled moans grew particularly plaintive. And Ethan saw him. Their gazes locked again and again, usually when Ethan struck Andy's flesh. He held back nothing. Ethan didn't want him brave and stoic. Ethan wanted to break him open and watch the tears trickle down.

Ethan could have that, but only if he took it. Andy didn't want to give in easily. He understood how submitting as a personal choice would work for some people, but right now with this new to him, he needed to be made to shed those tears. Even got off on it.

Look at me. Jesus. Tied up, legs split wide, ass bright red, body aching, back itching from his dried spunk, cock about to blow. Is this me? Do I know this guy?

Yeah. He did. And so did Ethan now. The pain of the spanking and the discomfort of being doubled up had him wailing, sobbing Ethan's name punctuated with a shitload of incoherent begging, repetitive pleas for it to stop, for Ethan to fuck him, let him come.

Stop. Never stop. Which would he chose? The crisp, remorseless slaps kept coming, a steady rain of them on the taut flesh of his ass and thighs. Then Ethan transferred his attentions, slapping Andy's cock—not hard—but he didn't need to. The indignity of it, the way his erection swayed and jerked, struck by Ethan's right hand, batted at by his left, made it a fucked-up game of tennis with his cock the ball.

Ethan stopped and curved his hand around Andy's shaft, squeezing tightly—a warning, not a caress. "Do *not* come. I mean it. You'll tighten up if you do and I won't enjoy fucking you as much."

Andy writhed, held by wrists, ankles and cock. A snappy, snarky reply was there in his head, but it couldn't push past the overwhelming urge to please Ethan.

"Yes, sir. I won't. I *won't*. I want it to be good for you. Fuck, Ethan, please. Please. Need you in me. God, it's too much, too fucking much. Oh, God—"

Saying the words took no effort at all. They gushed from him and when he heard them, they turned him on and he didn't want to stop talking. He was riding the high of his degrading position, relishing his abasement and Ethan's power over him.

Ethan lunged forward and planted his hands on either side of Andy's head, filling his vision. Without a word, he took Andy's mouth in a kiss, swallowing unspoken words like candy, teeth hard, tongue thrust deep.

Andy couldn't breathe. Didn't care. He strained to get closer, pulling hard at his bonds. The cuffs were padded, but still chafed his skin. His fault for struggling. Add it to the list of shit he didn't care about.

The kiss ended and Ethan wiped his mouth, then he used his thumb to spread the spit on Andy's lips and across his face. Andy caught at the thumb when it passed over his mouth, licking it, then sucking at the tip. He whined when Ethan pulled his thumb away.

"If you're good, you can clean my cock when it comes out of your ass." Ethan patted Andy's cheek with a condescending smile.

"Fuck you," Andy snarled, startling himself more than Ethan, who after blinking twice, grinned at him, leaning back on his heels.

"For that, you'd need to be so well behaved you'd have wings and a halo. Not seeing it. How about we stick with the plan of me fucking you? Or doesn't the idea appeal anymore?"

Andy closed his eyes. So close. All that work, all that effort and he'd blown it.

"Hey." Ethan gripped his chin. "No. Open your eyes, Andrew. Look at me. Yeah, that's it. Tell me how I screwed up."

Andy scowled at him. "Don't mind you stringing me up like this. I look fucking ridiculous but whatever. I do mind you being a condescending dickhead."

"Jesus. You go from one extreme to the other faster than anyone I know. Sorry. Apology accepted, or do I ignore the fact you're still hard and untie you?"

Andy pouted, enjoying his moment of power, though Ethan seemed amused more than outraged and the apology was on the sketchy side. "I guess you can fuck me."

"Wrong answer," Ethan said. "Look, I'm ready to come from spanking you. And for the record, you look fucking incredible. Do you see me laughing? I put you like this. I sure as hell didn't do it to amuse myself."

"Really?" Andy tugged at his restraints. "I like it. I do. Gonna ache tomorrow, but it's worth it."

"Good to know, but I'm not finished." Ethan stroked his erection, palming it roughly, then groaning. "I'm so close to coming. Don't need to get inside your hole to do it. I can jerk off over your ass, watch the steam rise and call it a day by the time you've wiped that sulky look off your face. Mouthing off doesn't bother me. You were somewhere good, and I spoiled it. Took it a step too far. I'm sorry. But you *guess* I can fuck you? Seriously?"

"I'm sorry!" He saw the righteous hammering he'd been longing for disappearing like beer from a cooler on a hot summer's day. "Ethan—sir—I'm sorry, okay?"

"Not seeing it," Ethan said flatly. "Annoyed with yourself after you forgot your lines maybe."

"I'm not pretending. Not for any of this. It's real. If I was playing along, I'd have given you an adoring fucking smile when you said I could clean your dick, not said you were being an asshole."

"True. I still think you're more worried about not getting to come than pissing me off. And that's disappointing."

"Oh, give me a break." Andy turned his head to the side, unable to meet Ethan's gaze. "You don't even like me," he muttered. "I'm an ass to spank, two holes to fuck—not that you've even done that."

"Are you insane?" Ethan asked incredulously. "No. We're not having this conversation like this." He got off the bed and reached for the straps, freeing Andy's left ankle and wrist. Being able to move his limbs was a mixed blessing. His shoulder muscles had tightened and bringing his leg to lie flat on the bed meant his ass touched more than air too.

Face grim, Ethan walked around to the other side and took care of the last two straps. Andy lay still, staring up at the ceiling, star-fished out and refusing to move.

Ethan drew in an exasperated breath and unfastened the cuffs, tossing them and the attached straps onto the floor.

"Come here, you annoying brat."

Being rolled to his side and gathered into a hug was unexpected. Andy struggled but Ethan seemed to have reached his limit.

He growled out a terse, "Stop it" and threw his leg over Andy's, pinning him down.

It was a situation Andy could've freed himself from without too much effort, but Ethan's order and the tight grip of his arms were enough for Andy to tell himself he had no choice.

His arms were trapped against Ethan's chest, but Ethan met an attempt to move them and return the hug with a bite to his shoulder.

"Stay still," Ethan said into his ear. "I don't want a fucking hug. I want you calm enough to talk."

"I am. Blue balls, red ass, yeah, but perfectly calm."

"You sound it."

Andy kicked out, his bare foot connecting with Ethan's shin.

"Do that again and you're over my knee saying hi to the paddle."

Andy ground his forehead against Ethan's chest, lost, struggling for the right words to fix this. "If that's what you want, do it. I won't stop you. I mean, I could say red or yellow but what's the point? I want the pain. I can handle that better than the rest of it."

"What can't you handle? Being fucked?"

"I've been fucked more times than I can count."

"When it didn't matter. When it was a quick release with a stranger. Not when you're this vulnerable."

Andy snorted, denying the truth of it as if that would stop it being the case. "It's a dick in my ass. It's not a big deal."

"It was to me." Ethan relaxed his grip then smoothed Andy's hair back off his damp face. "I want to put you over my knee. You spoiled my chance to show you how much it mattered. But if I spanked you every time you pissed me off, my hand would never recover."

Flattered, upset, Andy demanded, "What about my ass?"

Ethan chuckled. "It can take a lot more than I've given it and we both know it."

Andy moved his hand up, tentatively touching Ethan's face. "Yeah, but not today. Listen, what I said about you not liking me—I wasn't acting out. I know this is sex, and I'm not getting clingy on you, but is there a rule that says we can't talk? I don't know anything about you!"

"Not much to tell."

"I don't mean deep, dark secrets or childhood trauma," Andy said impatiently. "Where are you from? Mom and dad still around? Brothers or sisters? Star sign? Do you like fishing, books, hiking, what? What hockey team do you support? Ever been out of the country? Which Avenger would you like to fuck? What—?"

"Enough. God. I get it. Small-talk time." Ethan let go of him and propped himself up on one elbow. "Get into bed. I'm going to get us a drink."

Chapter Fifteen

There was something decadent about being in Ethan's bed in the middle of the afternoon, the downy comforter molding to his body, the glass-smooth undersheet soothing his ass. The lube and condoms had slid to the floor, but he retrieved them before snuggling under the covers, setting them on the nightstand. It wasn't a hint, more a nod to the tidiness of the room. He didn't touch the restraints, though. Those were Ethan's.

The drink was a tall glass of orange and pineapple juice, topped with sparkling water. Andy sipped it politely, propped up on pillows beside Ethan, then realized he was parched and drained the glass. It settled the shakiness he'd been experiencing and he was able to turn to Ethan and meet his gaze without wanting to look away, abashed.

"Are you wishing you'd never seen me on that bench?" He'd asked the question before but was the answer still the same?

Ethan shook his head slowly. "Are you wishing you'd turned down my offer of a bed for the night? And think about it before you answer."

"I don't need to think. I know the answer. No." Andy sat up, ignoring his throbbing ass. "So, do we talk? Or do I walk?"

"Poetic threats. Nice." Ethan didn't seem annoyed, though, a faint smile curved his lips, hands relaxed on the comforter. "Okay. Ask."

"No. Tell me. That way you don't need to spill anything you don't want."

"I wouldn't, but I appreciate the thought." Ethan rubbed his chin. "I'm from Ontario. Kingston to be exact. My father was never in the picture and my mom remarried when I was seventeen, a widower from across the street. We didn't get on."

"Because you were gay?"

"Darin wasn't a bigot. If someone around him made a joke about gays, he didn't leap on a soapbox but he didn't laugh either. No, he thought once he'd married Mom he was the man of the house and that had been me all my life. I didn't appreciate being treated like a kid. But I left to go to college and things got easier when I was away from home most of the year. In the summers, I went home and got a job."

"What did you study?"

"Cooking," Ethan said. "I enjoyed it and it was the kind of career I could do anywhere. I wasn't good enough to own a restaurant, but my knife skills weren't bad and I didn't mind hard work. Then I decided I wanted a change and I came out here."

The gap in the story was wide enough to float a ferry through, but Andy stayed quiet. The scars on Ethan's back weren't visible, but they filled his head.

"Why here?"

Ethan laced his fingers together in his lap. "That was pure chance. There was this elderly couple Mom knew planning to drive across country to Vancouver and visit their son. They weren't sure they could handle that much time behind the wheel, though. They were the kind of drivers you get behind and curse, toddling along going under the speed limit, changing lanes without indicating—you know the type. She had a phobia of flying so that way was out. People told them to take the train, but they wanted to travel on their schedule, plan a route. So they asked if I'd take them there."

"Hell of a long way."

"You have no idea. But it was fun. Took us a month. I traced it out on a map and the route was like this." Ethan drew a series of squiggles and loops in the air. "They'd get to somewhere interesting and stop. If they were tired, it would be for a day or two and someone would tell them about a must-see place they'd never heard of, so off we'd go."

"But you got here eventually."

"Yeah." Ethan blew out a gusty breath. "Fell in love."

"Who with?" Andy asked, careful not to sound the least bit jealous. What was the point? Whoever the guy had been, he wasn't around now.

"The city, not a person." Ethan shot him a glance. "You're from here. You're used to it."

"I guess, but it doesn't mean I don't appreciate it."

"Anyway, I got a place, got a job, made some friends—and when they find out about you, they won't give me any peace until they meet you—and that's about it. So you're all caught up."

"Oh yeah. I know you inside and out now." Andy shook his head. "Bare bones, man. I knew more than that about Henry five minutes after he walked through the door. Never mind. It's a start."

"It's all you're getting. Not down to any — what was it? Deep dark secrets? — but it's boring. I know what happened and I doubt you care. You're curious about your kink, not me."

"I can't be both?"

"Tell me how it usually goes with you when you meet someone. Ever had anyone serious in your life or a relationship that lasted a while?"

"Uh, how long is a while?"

Ethan raised his eyebrows. "A year?"

"I dated when I was a teenager." Andy did some math in his head. "I was with one guy for, oh…six, seven months. But it fizzled and once I was a student, it was an all-you-can-fuck buffet. I'd go out. I'd pick someone up or let them seduce me, and if it was good, we swapped deets. If it sucked, we didn't. I hooked up with this one guy five times in a row, but he didn't… Well, it wasn't…"

"Now I'm interested," Ethan said. "Why him? What did he do that first night the others didn't?"

Andy stared at the pattern on the comforter until Ethan pushed his chin up. "He spanked me," Andy whispered as if he was confessing something shameful, which made no fucking sense given what Ethan had done to his butt. "I was on my knees in his room blowing him and he went too deep and I gagged. Caught him with my teeth. He pulled out, threw me face down on the bed and walloped my ass a few times then fucked me. He wasn't angry and it was only five slaps. I counted."

"And you liked it."

"Yeah. But it wasn't enough, so I went back to him and it was vanilla. Total snooze. But I couldn't forget being pinned down on his bed waiting for the next slap. How much I enjoyed it. Fifth date, I was an asshole, hoping he'd get the message, but he didn't. Never laid a hand on me. So I asked him to spank me. I mean, why not? He — shit, he looked at me as if I was a freak and that was it. I was out of there."

"Good decision," Ethan said.

"Yeah, but at the time it was like a door slammed in my face. Then I met you and the door wasn't open, but I started knocking, I guess."

"And I answered."

"Yeah."

They were talking at random now, swapping words absently. Andy's attention was on Ethan's mouth and the renewed tingle in his balls. The air turned syrup-thick and heavy around them. He waited, his anticipation a slow, powerful thrum, resonating through him. He was warm, muscles loose, ready for sex.

Ready for Ethan to make the first move.

Ethan kissed him, pushing Andy to his back and following him down, never losing that point of contact between them. He used his hands to cuff Andy's wrists, where the skin was tender, and slid his thumbs over the pulse points, quickening the beat.

What would it be like with Ethan? God, if it was more of the same, no different from any encounter he'd had —

"Don't come." Ethan pinned Andy's wrists to the bed, level with his hips. "If you're getting close, tell me. If it happens after that, I'll take responsibility for not stopping you. Come without warning me and you'll regret every drop you spill."

Okay. It wasn't going to be exactly the same.

"Yes, sir."

That got him a twitch of the lips, first cousin to a smile. "You love saying that, don't you?"

"As much as you enjoy hearing it?"

Ethan shrugged, the movement putting more pressure on Andy's wrists. "I don't mind you using my name, but yeah, it's kind of hot." He licked Andy's nipple, still swollen after being chewed like gum. "Love to see these clamped. Nothing too tight at first. Something you could wear for a while. Then I'd take them off and use something nasty. Vicious enough your eyes would be watering from looking at them."

"Yeah? Did you buy some? Never did get to find out everything you had in the basket." How eager did he sound?

"Pain slut," Ethan said. There was nothing in his voice to say if it was an insult, a compliment or a question.

"For you, yeah. If you wanted me like that."

Ethan let go of Andy's right wrist, tapping it in a wordless command to keep it in place. "I love seeing you cry," he admitted, stroking Andy's cheek with a fingertip, mapping the line a tear would take. "Don't know about hearing you scream, but the way you beg is addictive."

"Cool." Andy wanted to lift his ass, rub his erection against Ethan's, but he stayed still. The restraints Ethan had placed upon him with his demand to be in charge turned him on like actual cuffs did.

"But I don't need to get the clamps when I've got fingers and teeth." Ethan pinched the abused nipple with his fingernails, digging in and twisting it from side to side.

The pain was sharp and savage, slicing through Andy like a knife. He didn't scream, but he cried out, clutching Ethan's shoulder with his free hand—not to push him away, but to have someone to hold onto when he fought to surrender.

A shadow passed over Ethan's face and Andy was left sipping air, nipple throbbing wildly.

"What's wrong?" Something was, that was for sure.

"I never knew I could enjoy hurting someone this much," Ethan said. "You scare me. *I* scare me."

Andy stared up at him. "Well, you don't scare me. Want you. Want this. Go as far as you want. I'll let you know if it's too much."

"How about if it isn't enough?"

Packing the words with reassurance, Andy said, "We're nowhere near there. You're pushing me. It's not the other way around. But safe words go both ways. I ask for something that makes you want to throw up, use it. Or, you know, tell me to think of something else."

Ethan chewed the inside of his cheek, trapped in the indecision Andy hated seeing.

"We can worry you're not sadist enough for this pain slut *after* you've fucked me." He drew up his knee and nudged Ethan in the ribs. "Now would be a good time. And don't glare at me. You want to drive the bus? Get behind the goddamn wheel."

"Tell me when you reach the point of regretting you said that. I mean it. Tell me. And trust me, you *will* regret it."

Ethan flipped Andy to his stomach. Five hard slaps rekindled the blaze in his ass. Anticipation sizzling along every nerve, Andy grinned into the pillow. That was more like it.

"Wriggle your ass for me," Ethan ordered. "Give me a moving target."

"Yes, sir."

It seemed like fun at first. He pretended he was in a club, shimmying his ass to the beat. Slaps rained down, never hard enough to do more than leave a fleeting sting, and he tried to dodge them. That didn't work. Ethan always connected and the back of Andy's thighs tingled from a dozen spanks aimed at his butt.

Soon, his muscles protested. It was hard work. Sweat dampened his back and he slowed down until he was barely twitching.

"Lazy. I have a cure for that." Ethan pinched Andy's ass where it met his thigh. "Another day, though. Wriggle."

"I'm exhausted."

Ethan snorted. "Out of shape, you mean. Maybe this will help."

A drizzle of lube, cold enough to form icicles, landed in the crack of Andy's ass. The wriggle he gave was lively enough even for Ethan.

Lube meant fucking. Andy spread his legs and raised his backside, mutely pleading.

"Fingers first. I want to see how clean you are." Ethan worked a finger inside Andy's hole, driving it deep. The initial burn subsided soon and Andy closed his eyes, hoping Ethan would add another finger. Instead, Ethan withdrew, leaving Andy to clench around emptiness.

"Engines are given a white-glove inspection. Let's see if your hole would pass."

Ethan took a tissue from the box on the bedside table, the soft rustle ominous. Andy held his breath while Ethan wiped his finger. A crumpled tissue floated down, landing on the pillow. He squinted at it. Translucent in places from the lube but clean. Thank God. He exhaled, relieved.

"Good boy."

The genuine approval made him shudder with pleasure. Praise from Ethan or punishment—both worked.

"Thank you, sir."

"But you said you were tired, so please don't feel you have to move when I fuck you. In fact, I insist you don't."

Huh? Stay still with that thick cock splitting him wide? Was that even possible?

Ethan put on a condom, then he rubbed the head of his cock over Andy's hole. No prep work beyond that exploratory finger, then. There was plenty of lube running down his crack, but how much was inside him?

Ethan pushed a pillow under Andy's hips. "That's a better angle for me. Remember. Hold still, or I stop."

"I'll try."

"No. You'll succeed. Relaxed, open for me, but be completely still. I want you to take what you're given and show me that you can obey an order."

Inch by torturous inch, Ethan sank his cock into Andy's ass. Immobility became an ordeal. He wanted to drive back, taking in more of the thick shaft, or meet each shove with an answering push. Wouldn't that feel better for Ethan anyway? Who was this punishing?

His fingers ached from clutching at the sheet, but he needed some outlet for his frustration. Slowly the tension in his hands moved to his forearms then his shoulders.

"No. Let go of the sheet. Hands flat."

He tried, but within a minute, his fingers curled into fists. He growled, annoyed with himself.

"You're fighting me," Ethan told him.

"I'm not! I'm trying."

"To do what? Tell me your orders."

"Ass relaxed for your monster cock—"

Ethan chuckled. "I wish."

"The rest of me a statue."

"And instead, you're caught up on making this play out the way you want it to."

Andy twisted his head to get a glimpse of Ethan. "It's more fun if I move."

"I disagree." Ethan turned Andy's head to face the pillow again. "You can do this, Andrew. Submit. Give me what I've asked for. Commit to the gift. Don't hand it over grudgingly."

"Me lying here like a dead body isn't a gift. It's an insult to your cock."

"It's what I want," Ethan said patiently. "I told you to move and you gave up. Think of this as both a consequence of that failure and a second chance. No more talking."

Ethan withdrew most of the way then plunged forward, a slow, deliberate possession of claimed territory. Rebellious not compliant, determined to make Ethan see this was a mistake, Andy went limp. Memories of acting class danced in his head. *Be a bird. Be a tiger. Be a boneless, boring lump with a flagging erection.*

Ethan groaned, pure pleasure coating the sound. It sent a shock of arousal through Andy. He'd caused that groan by giving Ethan a fake surrender. What would happen if he made it real?

He needed to know more than he needed to move.

Willing his body to be receptive to the next deep thrust was easy. Ethan's cock stretched him to the point where more would've been too much, but what he had was just right. He rode the wave of sensation, allowing it to take him to uncharted territory, all resistance gone. Ethan knew their destination.

"God, yes." Ethan stroked Andy's hair. "Perfect. Thank you."

And that made every stroke that followed a victory for them both. Andy counted eight before Ethan abruptly pulled out all the way.

"Huh? What did I do?"

"Nothing." Ethan hung over him, breathing heavily. "Another second in you and I would've come."

Well now. "But I'm still not allowed to?"

"What do you think?"

That wasn't worth answering. But Andy knew his question was equally pointless.

"Up off the bed."

The order came with a caress Ethan delivered to his ass. It ended with Ethan shoving two fingers into Andy's fucked-loose hole. He kept them there while Andy struggled to rise. So this was what a glove puppet felt like. Moving awkwardly, Andy staggered across to the balcony rail. Ethan finger-fucked him at every step, pinching Andy's nipple with his other hand. Andy's cock bobbed eagerly, slapping his stomach, the tip streaked with pre-cum. He didn't feel self-conscious. Not with Ethan in total control.

"Hands on the rail, legs spread as wide as you can get them."

Spreading his legs stretched the skin around his hole taut as a drum. The next thrust from Ethan's fingers hurt. Too dry. He hunched his shoulders, an involuntary protest Ethan picked up on instantly, withdrawing his fingers with infinite care.

"What's wrong?"

"Need more lube."

Ethan rested his hand on Andy's back. "Were you going to tell me if I hadn't asked?"

He could be honest. "Yeah. Dry fucks can be hot at the time but not afterward. I learned that the hard way."

"No argument there. Let's see if you're okay."

"I'm fine. More lube then get back to what you were doing."

Without replying, Ethan knelt behind him and placed his hands on Andy's ass. The wet swipe of his tongue across Andy's hole soothed and aroused at the same time. Fingers had hurt, but he could take Ethan's tongue for hours.

Of course, he'd melt into a puddle after the first ten minutes or so.

After a warm, limber tongue, the application of generous amounts of lube shocked a gasp from him. "Cold! God, do you store it in the freezer?"

"Don't put ideas into my head."

Ethan coated Andy's balls with lube then rolled them in his palm. "Ever been fucked with these clamped?"

"Before I met you, clamps were for bags of frozen peas or clipboards."

"That's no, then. Clamps, light ones, but with weights attached. You'd beg to stay still."

Horrified, unbearably aroused, he blurted out, "You wouldn't."

Ethan leaned over and kissed his ear, whispering, "Why does that sound so much like 'please'?"

Andy closed his eyes, balls tightening in response to the phantom pain Ethan's words had conjured. "Because I want it, but I can't—asking for it is so…"

"Easier to let me tell you it's going to happen, end of story?" Ethan bit Andy's earlobe, hard. "No hiding. Tell me you want it."

Struggling with desire and shame, Andy opened his eyes. Sweat dampened his palms, making the rail slippery. The shame added to the thrill and made his capitulation more intense. He savored his words, as he knew he'd savor the pain. "I want it. Everything you dream up. It's like you're tapping into my fantasies."

"It's good, but give me more," Ethan murmured.

With the rush that came from knowing he had the correct answer, Andy said, "I trust you. With my body. With me," his voice cracked with longing. "God, Ethan, I don't care if you let me come, but hurt me. Make me fucking scream for you. We both want to hear it."

Ethan grabbed Andy by the shoulders, hauled him upright then spun him around. Startled but too deep in submission to struggle, Andy went with the change of position, clutching Ethan's arms to steady himself.

Without a word, Ethan kissed him, drawing Andy against him, his thigh between Andy's legs. Held firmly, supported, Andy gave himself over to Ethan. Kissed until his lips stung and his head swam, he stopped wondering what came next. What was happening right then mattered more.

At some point, Ethan had ditched the condom. His cock, hard and warm, pressed against Andy's stomach. He wanted to slide to his knees and taste it, but he pushed aside any idea of asking for permission. If Ethan wanted his cock sucked, he'd tell Andy to do it.

Ethan broke contact with Andy's lips and stared at him, eyes narrowed, a flush of color in his cheeks. He stepped back, putting a small space between them, his arm still around Andy's shoulders. "Before I get the clamps, give me a preview."

He slid his hand down and cupped Andy's balls again, crushing them with a slow, deliberate pressure, never taking his gaze off Andy's face. The dull pain mounted quickly, accompanied by an increasing sense of how few options he had. One, realistically. He could use his safe word and end it. Andy's initial groan became a howl, emerging from deep in his chest. He writhed, held in place by that punishing hand.

"God! Hurts!"

He went up on tiptoes, instinctively looking for an escape, but the pain followed him. Remorseless, powerful, Ethan tightened his grip until Andy closed his eyes and took a deep breath. Acceptance. Could he? The pain radiating from his crushed balls focused him. Small, pitiful whimpers forced their way past his gritted teeth, but he lowered his heels and opened his eyes to meet Ethan's stare.

Everything fell away. Arousal and agony were forgotten as he saw what Ethan made no attempt to hide—a blaze of pride, a dark satisfaction Andy shared—one giving, one taking, but both joined.

He shaped a word with his lips, a silent 'sir', and reached down, covering Ethan's hand for a moment in acknowledgment of what Ethan had given him.

When Ethan slackened his grip and the intense ache faded to a throb, a stab of regret went through Andy He didn't mind losing the pain. There was plenty more on the way. That shining moment of connection, though...

It turned out he was right about the pain. Ethan brought out a small box of tiny clothespins, a piece of string and small fishing weight attached to each one.

Certain he could handle the bite of something so small, Andy gestured at them. "How long did it take to do this?"

Ethan sat on the bed and motioned Andy to stand in front of him. "About thirty minutes. I prepped them a few nights ago. Why?"

"Just picturing it. Did it turn you on?"

"Yes." Ethan picked up the first pin and held it so the weight swung freely. "Very much so."

"They're cute."

A faint smile passed over Ethan's face. "I tried one on myself and that wasn't the first word that came to mind."

"You did? Why?" And where were the pictures?

"Part curiosity, but mostly to gauge their effect." He squeezed, opening the clip, then let it snap shut. "Surprisingly strong."

"Uh, yeah."

Ethan grasped Andy's erection, bringing it to full hardness with a few strokes. "I've got plenty in here. They won't all fit on your balls, but it's a shame to waste my hard work."

Before Andy framed a question, Ethan attached the first clothespin to the base of Andy's cock, capturing a piece of loose skin.

"Jesus!" Andy flailed at the air to stop himself from taking it off. The sharp, piercing bite was savage and the drag of the weight added to it. "H-How many are there in there?"

"Thirty." Ethan exhaled, smiling. "I'd love to spin this out, but they can't stay on for too long. Pity."

It still took a torturous span of time. If Ethan was dissatisfied with the placement of a pin, he removed it and reattached it. Andy lost count of how many vicious nips he endured. Clamps lined the underside of his cock, two went behind his balls, then Ethan crowded the remainder on the delicate, ultra-sensitive flesh he'd tormented earlier.

Andy held as still as he could. Moving brought a crescendo of agony. His skin was hot, as if he'd stepped out of a scalding bath, sweat prickling it. If he concentrated, he could focus on an individual starburst of pain, but it was easier to accept it as a whole. Coherent thought or speech was beyond him. He babbled, pleading with Ethan to hurry, to take them off, to fuck him. Begged for mercy, clutching then releasing air, spasmodic movements that gave a small measure of relief. His cock remained rigid, deeply red, the smooth head glossy with clear liquid.

"Beautiful," Ethan said finally. He ran a fingertip across the taut strings and the weights swayed.

Andy sucked in a breath and released it in a moan. He tasted salt. He was crying. Unnoticed, tears had gathered and fallen, wetting his face. "I can't take it. If you fuck me, I'll die."

"No," Ethan corrected him. "You'll scream." He tugged gently on one piece of string, sending a flare of fresh agony through Andy's balls. "Regrets?"

Unable to answer, Andy shook his head, blind to anything but the sheer impossibility of movement.

"Back over to the railing."

He couldn't. Impossible. But Ethan had a new condom in his hand, ready to roll onto an erection that hadn't flagged and an expectant look in his eyes.

Step by step, he covered the short distance, but bending over caused the weights to clash together, ripping a hoarse cry from him.

"Easy." Ethan ran his hand over Andy's back. "You can do this. Open up for me."

Panting, Andy edged his feet wider. Oddly, that helped for a moment or two, allowing the fog to clear from his brain. He felt the blunt head of Ethan's cock nudge at his hole, fresh lube trickling down his crack. That helped too, cooling his burning skin.

Ethan sheathed himself fully in two strokes, each sending a warm rush of sensation through Andy. Sparks lit the darkness behind his screwed-shut eyes.

"Move for me." Ethan slapped Andy's thigh, urging him to respond. "No, come for me. You wanted pain? You've got it. Use it. Fuck my cock. Show me you want it."

With a strangled cry, Andy shoved his ass backward, grinding down on the thick shaft. The goal wasn't a climax. That would end this hellish, heavenly ordeal and he never wanted it to finish. Heedless of the wildly swinging weights amplifying his suffering, he drove forward then back, the guttural sounds he made bringing an answering growl from Ethan.

Another moment with Ethan's cock embedded deep. Another. He collected them, greedy for more, knowing they were limited. They couldn't sustain this level of ecstasy for long and he knew Ethan was close to coming from the subtle hardening of his cock.

Ethan pumped his hips strongly, taking control back then froze. He clamped his hands on Andy's hips, his body rigid in the instant before a climax shook it. Their bodies were so close, the front of Ethan's thighs against the back of Andy's legs, that Andy felt every tremor.

He came, cock swelling with the force of his release, cum escaping the confined prison of his balls to jet out, each surge jolting the clamps, twisting his pleasure into new shapes.

The removal of the clothespins was excruciating. Even flying from his orgasm, suffused with delight in his success, Andy suffered. Ethan didn't prolong his torment, but he didn't rush, either. After removing a clamp, Ethan wound the string around it before replacing it in the box. Knowing Ethan, he'd throw the used clothespins out and salvage the weights, so there was zero point to his finickiness, but Andy didn't point that out.

Andy lay on his back on the bed for the removal, a small mercy granted after he staggered and came close to falling. The fuck had left him exhausted but peaceful, the clamor of questions and doubts silenced.

Clothespins put away, Ethan brought out a tube of arnica. He applied it to the bruised, swollen skin with gentle touches, pausing sometimes to exchange a glance with Andy. They didn't speak. What was there to say?

Andy sipped the fresh juice Ethan gave him then curled into the haven of Ethan's body to sleep.

Yeah, it was different with Ethan.

It was better.

Chapter Sixteen

'*When you're at work, forget you know what my cock looks like and we'll be fine.*'

Ethan's last words before dropping Andy off outside his house stayed with him until the next day when he started his shift. He'd wanted to spend the night with Ethan, but it wasn't practical. He didn't have his work clothes with him and Ethan had an early managers' meeting.

He'd stayed late, content in the aftermath of sex, pleasantly full from the meal Ethan had cooked while Andy lazed in the bath, spending hours teasing more information about Ethan's past without going near potentially fraught topics.

Without malice or betraying confidences, Ethan had shared some stories about the hotel and the staff and guests that had left Andy helpless with laughter or wide-eyed. The Totally Five Star was high-end, a plush retreat for the wealthy, but that didn't mean the guests were well-behaved.

Ethan had refused to attach names to some of the stories if the people involved were famous or powerful, but Andy was more interested in the stories themselves and what they revealed about people.

"They don't think it counts if it happens in a hotel bedroom."

"The housekeeping staff cleaning up after them might have a different view, but yeah." Ethan had pulled Andy's feet into his lap, massaging the soles with strong fingers, never coming close to tickling him. "I get it. The few times I've stayed in a room with someone, we've barely got through the door before we were stripping off and heading for the bed."

"Hey! No stories about exes." He'd freed his foot and nudged Ethan in the ribs, scowling. "Not cool."

"No exes. And no new ones either. I don't share."

"Does that mean you want to do this again?" Andy had asked, scared of the answer but needing to know. "Keep seeing me?"

"Yes." Ethan had rested his arm along the back of the couch. "Of course I do. It's a terrible idea in some ways, but I'm ignoring that—"

"Because I'm irresistible and you adore me."

"That's it exactly," Ethan had agreed gravely, earning his ribs another, harder poke. Andy didn't let anyone laugh at the idea of him being irresistible.

And now Andy was a twitchy, jumpy mess, listening for Ethan's voice, glancing up every time someone walked past. They had to get the first meeting over and done with. Okay, in some ways it was the second time around for the first meeting after sex, but this one mattered more. They knew where they were with each other and they'd committed to making it more than a one-off. Not exactly a relationship but close.

Oh my God. Ethan's my boyfriend.

Ethan might not take kindly to that description, but Andy didn't intend to share his revelation.

"What is *wrong* with you today?" Joel asked, grabbing a box out of Andy's hands. "These are new glasses. Dusty. Need washing. Why are you taking them into the bar?"

"Huh? Oh! Sorry." Andy gestured vaguely down the corridor in the direction he should've been going. "Didn't sleep well. I'm dead on my feet. I'll grab a coffee at break and wake myself up."

"No, you'll wake up now," Ethan said from behind him.

If he'd still been holding the box, his next job would've been sweeping up glass.

He turned to meet Ethan's cool stare. How would he normally react to it? His brains were melting around the edges from a blast of lust. Ethan wasn't naked, or in the muted earth tones he favored off duty. He was an intimidating slice of elegance in a dark gray suit, a pale blue shirt and a sleek strip of silver and blue silk for a tie.

Hot. So fucking hot. Power and authority and sternness in one package and he didn't need to fantasize about Ethan now that he'd experienced the reality.

Punish me. Show me the consequences. All of them. Right here. Ignore Joel. Send me to my knees. Make me serve you. Make me beg.

"Yes, sir." It shot out of him, automatic, unthinking. And yeah, that was exactly what he would've said a week ago, so they were safe, but he couldn't look away, which wasn't.

Ethan did what Andy couldn't and turned his head to address Joel. "I keep forgetting to ask. How did it go at your cousin's wedding last week?"

Joel settled the box in his arms. "Since you ask, it was a disaster. My aunt's terrified of spiders, eh, and one crawled over the head table when the best man was giving his speech. She screamed, jumped up, the table went crashing over, the bride's dress got splattered with red wine and she burst into tears and wouldn't speak to her mom."

Ethan winced, no sign of amusement showing. "Ouch. I'm sorry. I know how much work your cousin put into making the day perfect."

Andy's smile faded. He'd been about to laugh, ask if anyone had uploaded the footage to YouTube yet, but Ethan's empathy with a woman he'd probably never met shamed him to silence.

"It worked out in the end." Joel cleared his throat. "I kind of came to the rescue with the dress."

"How?"

Ethan was genuinely interested, Andy could tell. He stood, cut out of the conversation, excitement draining.

"And put the box down. It looks heavy."

"I'll take it." Andy all but snatched it off Joel. "You two finish chatting."

"Sunshine Boy's not smiling today," he heard Joel remark when he walked away, but Ethan's answer was lost since Andy was muttering curses under his breath, all directed at himself.

That had been as smooth as sandpaper. He had to get a grip on his emotions or accept working with a man he was fucking was impossible.

He filled the dishwasher with the glasses, making sure they didn't touch, then set it going. He had a list of jobs to complete, but none of them were difficult. He'd picked up on the routine fairly easily after the wobbly start, motivated by the need to impress Ethan.

Now he had a different goal—keeping his relationship separate from his job—but the motivation hadn't changed.

"You didn't sleep well?" Ethan walked into the room, and closed the door behind him with a soft click. "Why was that?"

"I slept okay."

"So why lie to Joel?"

"Telling him I was spacing out daydreaming about you wouldn't have gone down so well."

"Ah." Ethan arched his eyebrow. "It's not going down too well with me either. Focus, Andrew. I won't be happy if I have to address this matter again."

"Is that you flirting or do you mean it?" Andy asked.

"I mean it. You fuck up at work and you face the consequences any employee would—no more, no less."

Consequences. Between them, that word was heavy with meaning. Ethan was playing him under the front of being all business and that was fucking cheating.

"So what do I get for daydreaming, huh?"

"You got a reminder it's not what we pay you for. It's done. Now—"

"Then why follow me in here?" Andy persisted. He wasn't sure what admission he wanted to get out of Ethan, but it didn't stop him pushing.

"One reason you might have had a bad night's sleep is if you were in pain. That's down to me and I wanted to check in with you."

Caught off guard, Andy floundered for a moment then touched his nipple. "It's rubbing against my shirt, but I iced it and that helped. And my ass is, well, it's bruised, but nothing I can't handle. I don't sit at work often anyway."

"Wish I could see it." Ethan took a step forward, expression warm, then grimaced. "Okay, I'm breaking my not-at-work rule. Get on with what you were doing."

"When can I see you again?" He tried not to sound desperate or embarrassingly needy. Truth was, when he wasn't with Ethan, something went missing from the world, a color he'd never noticed until it was gone.

"I want to see your place," Ethan said unexpectedly. "When's a good time?"

Totally thrown by the request, Andy gaped at him until Ethan cleared his throat meaningfully. "Huh? Uh, anytime." Andy tugged at his earlobe. "You know our schedules better than me. What works?"

Ethan screwed up his face in thought, visions of spreadsheets dancing in his head, most likely. "Let's see. Not today. Tomorrow morning at ten?"

Andy nodded, mind blank after Ethan left the room. Ethan seeing how he lived was too terrifying a thought to contemplate. He'd described his place as small, cheap and cheerful, two-thirds truth, one-third flat-out lie. He'd missed out the leaking tap in the kitchen that released a gurgle followed by a splat of water at teeth-grindingly erratic intervals and the faint smell of damp.

And would Henry be there? He didn't want those two meeting. Henry had a shy person's habit of blurting out disastrously frank comments at times and Ethan's age might prompt one. He spent the next ten minutes in a fruitless attempt to remember Henry's schedule before giving in and texting him. He didn't bother adding a reason for his question.

Henry would be in class. Good. Now he had to figure out how to clean the place without raising suspicions or staying up until the small hours with the risk of oversleeping.

* * * *

Henry left at eight, looking presentable for once. Mahito was definitely a good influence. True, Henry's sweater was mud-colored, but his new jeans clung to his ass and Mahito had dragged him into a salon for the threatened haircut. Turned out he had strong opinions on self-improvement through the wonders of product.

Ethan and Mahito had a lot in common.

Andy didn't like lying to Henry, even by omission, and keeping quiet about Ethan definitely qualified. The chances of Henry mentioning Ethan's and Andy's relationship to anyone who could drop them in it at work were remote, but when it came to protecting Ethan's job, Andy wasn't prepared to take risks. Secrecy in a good cause was no sin.

When Henry left, Andy threw himself into cleaning. He'd tackled his bedroom the night before, covering the noise by claiming he was looking for something important. All his clothes were hanging up, folded into drawers or in the laundry hamper. He ran the vacuum cleaner around, washed the dishes, put on a pot of coffee and showered, taking particular care. If sex followed the inspection, he wanted to be Ethan-ready.

By the time Ethan knocked on the door, he'd reached the point of despair. He looked great according to his mirror, but no matter what he did to the place, it wasn't close to acceptable on any level. Short of gutting it and starting over, it never would be.

"Hi." Ethan walked in and paused a few feet past the door. He wasn't looking around the room, though. He fixed his gaze on Andy. Smiling, he pushed Andy's hair back off his face. "Still damp. You're clean?"

That was shorthand for asking if he'd douched. "Yes, sir."

Ethan's expression softened as if the respectful answer had struck the right note. Sometimes it made him shoot Andy a wary or impatient look, treating it like a bad habit instead of Andy's attempt to emphasize the nature of their relationship. He stepped closer, taking Andy into his arms for a kiss. It was unexpected and for a moment, Andy stiffened with surprise, but Ethan didn't allow him space to pull back or the option of refusal. With a sigh of acceptance, Andy returned the kiss, eyes closed, nerves settling.

"That's better," Ethan said when he'd ended the kiss. "I thought you were about to pass out. Now you're smiling."

"I've been tidying for *hours*. It's still a mess, but I did try." He gestured at the kitchen area. "There's coffee."

"Later. I didn't come here to inspect the place, you know."

"You didn't?" That left him obscurely disappointed. So he was scrutinized head to toe but his place got no more than a glance after all his work?

"More to get a feel for this side of you," Ethan continued. "You said you were disorganized. Is that something I can help with?"

Andy ran his hands through his hair, strands clinging to his fingers, ruining the style he'd created with a comb but not caring much. The actor in him craved the physical expression of his emotions. If they came over as larger-than-life when his audience was a foot away, it was too ingrained a habit to break. "God, I don't know! Where would you even begin?"

Ethan did look around then, as if he'd been waiting for permission. "A tidy environment is a good starting point. If you're organizing paperwork surrounded by chaos, you've made your job that much harder."

"Okay." Andy darted forward and scooped up a pile of magazines and free newspapers off the coffee table. He'd stacked them neatly without going one step further and trashing them. "These can go in the recycling bin." He spun around clutching them to his chest. "Sorry. Should've moved them before. They've been there so long I kinda stopped seeing them. Part of the furniture. Except they're on top of the furniture. Though things that go on top of furniture still count as furniture — or are they accessories?"

Ethan took the papers from him and put them back on the table. "Even for you, the babbling's excessive. Relax. This place looks ten times nicer than my student digs did and it's messy in places, yes, but it smells clean and that's the important part."

Guiltily aware of how long it had been since the toilet had received more attention than a squirt of bowl cleaner from him, he flushed. "Uh, that's mostly Henry. He's got this thing about germs. Not OCD about it, but man does he like to scrub stuff."

"A man after my own heart," Ethan said. "Okay, I've seen in here —"

"Doesn't take long, does it?"

"And that's an interruption." Ethan raised his eyebrows when Andy sighed out a long, relieved breath. "Well, now. Look at you calming down. Why does breaking a rule settle you?"

Honesty with Ethan had become a habit. "I do it a lot. I'm used to it. And I love how you punish me for it."

Ethan rolled his eyes, but he was grinning. "You've guaranteed you'll have to earn your next spanking by being well-behaved. Nice going."

"What? That isn't fair! You like spanking me as much as I like getting one."

Ethan nodded. "Is that an added incentive? Not wanting to deprive me of something I get off on?"

"Yeah, I guess." Andy took a deep breath. "So what do I get for interrupting you?"

Pointing down, Ethan said, "Six push-ups. Proper ones. Take it slowly."

Ethan made him repeat any push-ups where he didn't go low enough or hold the position for long enough, making the total closer to ten than six. When he got to his feet, a sweet ache throbbed through his balls, his mood mellow.

"Your bedroom. Show me your filing system." Ethan's mouth twitched. "That's not a euphemism."

"Funny. Calling it a filing system might be exaggerating a bit..." Ethan's enquiring look coaxed more out of him. "It's stuff in drawers and a cardboard box. Lots of my bills are paperless and I've set up online banking, but..."

"Good." Ethan's approval warmed him. "Show me."

Forty minutes later, after Ethan had dumped everything on the bed for sorting through, Andy was faced with a stack of paper in need of shredding and a second, much smaller stack that needed filing.

"We're going shopping," Ethan announced. "Office supplies to give you a way to organize this, plus a small shredder for the confidential papers. Oh, and I want to set you up with a fitness monitor. It tracks your calorie intake, the amount of exercise you do, heart rate, all sorts of stuff. I'll be able to access the data."

"We can't go back to the sex shop instead?" Andy groaned. "What am I talking about? This *is* your version of a sex shop!"

"Nonsense," Ethan said, but his cheeks pinked up.

Busted.

"And monitoring my heartbeat? Jesus, Ethan! Way to micromanage. Do you plan to tell me when to go to bed too?"

Ethan narrowed his eyes. "Don't put ideas into my head."

"Hey! No!"

"A week. Total obedience and a strict routine."

"You said it could just be the sex—" Horrifying how much he wanted this.

"And you said I could take it all." Ethan was close enough that touching Andy's erection required moving his hand a few inches, no more. "You love the idea. Why will you happily admit to being turned on by a discipline spanking but not by this?"

"Spanking's normal in a kinky way and this isn't," Andy mumbled, wishing Ethan's hand was still on him. "Wanting you to take charge of me... I'm not a helpless baby or a total screw-up, you know."

"No. I wouldn't be attracted to you if you were. You're independent, self-sufficient and tougher than you realize, but you're also disorganized, give into temptation without fighting it and you have a lot of bad habits."

"Wow. Don't sugarcoat it."

"Then don't lie to me about what you want. You're not fooling me." Ethan sighed. "You want the pain and the hot sex. I can do that. Maybe not enough pain for you, but so far what you can take, I can dish out. But that's not enough for me and I made that plain at the start."

"Got to eat my meat before I get dessert?"

"It's all dessert. You need to adjust the way you see it."

"So we come back here with sticky labels and a shredder and I'm supposed to get a hard-on from it? Not going to happen."

"Let me see your fridge before we go," Ethan said, ignoring Andy's pout. "I think we'll drop by the supermarket too."

"You're *not* buying my food," Andy protested. "That's a red, right there."

"I'm not buying anything you'll get to eat." Ethan opened the fridge. "Let's see… Yeah, okay. We'll need the supermarket."

"No food," Andrew repeated.

Ethan only threw him an amused look.

* * * *

"When you said I wouldn't get to eat it, I hope you meant it."

Ethan pulled a face. "Now you're being gross." He brushed his fingers over the plug of ginger embedded in Andy's ass, then gripped and twisted it, sending fresh heat sizzling through him. "It comes out — eventually — and goes in the trash. If it's uncomfortable, you could talk less, file faster."

"Sadist."

"Sweetheart," Ethan replied, eyes twinkling. "Let me see you sort the credit card statements by date."

"I could toss them out. I've gone paperless now."

"You need to keep them for tax purposes. We've already destroyed the old statements."

Shredding in the nude, on his knees, the small machine in front of him, with Ethan slapping his ass for every complaint had seemed like the ultimate in humiliation. That changed when Ethan finished whittling the ginger plug. He'd read about figging and always wondered how hot ginger could be when ginger cookies tasted sweet. Now he knew.

"Is this because I said filing was boring or that you were weird for getting off on it?"

Twist. Jiggle. Burn.

"Let's go with both."

Andy turned to Ethan, sitting close by on a wooden kitchen chair. Sweat beaded his forehead and his dick tingled fiercely. Ethan had cleaned the ginger juice off his fingers by wiping them on Andy's cock. He was keenly aware of every place Ethan had touched. "Let me apologize? Please."

"You're forgiven. No need."

"I don't feel forgiven." Andy shuffled forward on his knees. "I feel punished." He flickered his eyelashes, shamelessly flirting. "Repentant."

"Horny." Ethan had taken his shoes off so the push of his foot against Andy's erection didn't hurt, but it didn't do anything to relieve the swelling either. "I sympathize."

"Let me suck you." He was hungry for it. Ethan kept him on short rations when it came to sex, so it was all he thought about when they were together. "Please, sir."

"Credit card statements."

Andy groaned and got back to it until he heard the hiss of a zipper. He jerked his head around, fast enough to leave him dizzy. Ethan had his cock out, a stiff jut of flesh he worked slowly.

"That isn't fair."

"Life isn't fair. I, on the other hand, am completely fair and reasonable. I gave you a job to do. Now I'm providing an incentive. Finish before I come and you get to blow me."

Andy gave Ethan's cock an appraising glance. Ethan's grip was light, but he knew from personal experience treating a cock like a wet T-shirt in need of wringing out wasn't the only way to get off. He'd made a bet with himself once that he could climax using a single finger. Add in some lurid fantasies and it had taken a few minutes longer than usual, but he'd got there. Ethan seemed like a guy who knew his hot spots.

So. Time to sort and file. Three years of monthly statements. He'd break it down. Sort first by year, then by month. They were mixed up, as if he'd shuffled them, but he could do it.

He'd completed stage one when Ethan moaned, the sound erotic enough to make him fumble his grip on the sheaf of paper.

"Slow down," Andy said through gritted teeth. "I'm almost there."

"Could say the same thing." Ethan's voice was stifled. "Seeing you on your hands and knees, wiggling that hot ass at me—"

He'd almost forgotten the ginger plug in his determination to get his mouth on Ethan's cock. The reminder of how hot his ass was didn't help, but he hurried. Jesus, whose idea was it to have twelve months in a year?

He finished, stacked them neatly and thrust them into the hanging folder, already labelled with a sticky tag, yellow for credit card statements.

Ethan was cheating now, hand blurring as he jerked off. No way. No fucking way. Andy had two paper cuts and dust choked his lungs. He deserved this and he was going to get it. He closed the gap between them, knocked Ethan's hand away and growled, a genuine primal growl. "Mine."

"The hell it is." Ethan took hold of Andy by the hair—one day he was going to get a buzz cut to foil that particular habit—and prevented him from reaching his target. "Let's try again, eh?"

Andy whimpered with frustration. "Please. I finished the filing. Want to suck you."

"Even if you don't get to come?"

Andy closed his eyes, blocking out the view of a darkly flushed cock, the head slicked, waiting for his tongue to make it wetter. "You'd enjoy that?"

"Thinking about it's almost enough to send me over."

Andy nodded jerkily and opened his eyes. "I won't come. I want it to be good for you." It wasn't lip service to Ethan's kinks. He meant it. If knowing he was suffering spiced Ethan's climax, kept him riding the high for longer, it was what Andy wanted too. It wouldn't be Ethan alone who relished the idea. Given a choice, Andy would've come every chance he got but he'd learned that waiting made his climax more intense.

Without replying, Ethan drew Andy's head down until it was an inch or two away from his erection. "Only your tongue. When I shoot, I want to see it over your face, dripping off your lips."

"Fuck." He had to pause to breathe deeply before extending his tongue, the picture Ethan painted melting his resolve. Ethan wrapped his hand around the base of his cock, holding it still for Andy to lap at. It wasn't enough. He wanted to choke on Ethan's cock, feel it fuck his mouth, shape his lips, but he was learning to wait. That would be what Ethan wanted eventually and until then, he'd do it Ethan's way.

And he got what he wanted for a moment or two at the end. Ethan, voice thick with passion told him to open wide and he thrust up into Andy's mouth a handful of times before pulling back when his climax hit.

The warm splatter rained down and he swayed back, tilting his head when Ethan finally let go of his hair, showing Ethan his streaked face and the adoration in his eyes.

Ethan drew his fingers across Andy's mouth then pushed them inside. Spunk coated them, but Andy held still, waiting, waiting…

"Suck them clean."

Yes, sir.

Chapter Seventeen

Good work. I'll have to plan a reward for tonight.

Andy read Ethan's text, grinning widely. He'd jogged to work through a spring morning vibrant with warmth, past smiling faces and planters decked out with a rainbow of flowers. Vancouver had woken from a dreary winter and was ready to celebrate.

After two months under Ethan's firm hand, so was Andy. The text had followed Ethan's daily check of his exercise monitor stats and he knew he was doing well. Eating better, exercising more, sleeping a full eight hours — mostly. Life was good. And his agent had come through with a promising audition for a TV show. His character died after three episodes, but it was a fantasy show and from Andy's experience as a viewer, the writers could always bring back a character who struck the right note. He didn't mind playing a ghost or filming a flashback.

He'd aced the first round of auditions and was on the shortlist of four. The next audition would put him in a scene with one of the main characters, checking his chemistry with her. Ethan had been agreeable to swapping shifts around to accommodate his interviews, telling Andy he'd do the same for anyone. Andy didn't doubt it. Special treatment for boyfriends wasn't Ethan's style. If anything, he followed up a romantic interlude by being a hard ass at work the next day, compensating for any moment of weakness.

"You look happy."

"Huh? Oh hi, Niall." Andy plucked at his damp T-shirt, clinging to his chest. "That glow is sweat. Going to hit the showers and change." His shift didn't start for thirty minutes so there was no rush. Time management was another skill Ethan had drummed into him, often literally, the beat of his hand against Andy's butt reinforcing his lecture on a minute late being as unacceptable as thirty. Which was *so* not true, but Andy hadn't been inclined to argue when his ass was about to spontaneously combust.

"Before you disappear, can I ask you something?"

Andy curbed his impatience. Niall bugged him so fucking much. He was in his late twenties, but seemed younger, the childish pout of his mouth and a tendency to blush hotly doing nothing to lend him maturity. He worked part-time, so their paths didn't cross often, but the crush he had on Andy hadn't faded. He dogged Andy's steps, laughing at even the mildest jokes if Andy made them and somehow managing to make his break and Andy's coincide.

"Sure."

Running his hands through his hair, inexpertly dyed blond, Niall said on a rush, "You're an actor, right? Well, I have tickets to Bard on the Beach. The season doesn't start until June, but I thought we could go? Together? Like on a date?"

The plays, performed under canvas at Vanier Park, were something Andy enjoyed. He and Ethan didn't go out often together, but he'd set his heart on taking Ethan to at least one performance. If they kept it cool, anyone who saw them would assume they were there as friends, no more. To have Niall intrude on his plans jarred him, but aware he was being a jerk, he forced a smile.

"Love going there, but I'm kind of seeing someone. Sorry."

Niall's lips drooped, his disappointment plain. "Really? Since when?"

"Oh, a while now. A few months or so."

"Who is it?"

And, yeah, that wasn't nosy *at all*.

"A guy I met at a club one night. We hit it off and you know how it goes." He shrugged, hoping it expressed volumes then he edged sideways, but Niall blocked the way.

"What's his name?"

"Jesus, Niall, why the third degree?"

Scarlet-faced, jaw set, Niall said, "I don't think he exists. You're the kind of person who talks about his boyfriends and you've never mentioned one all the time you've been here. You're lying! You don't want to date me and you don't have the balls to say so. Well, guess what, Mr. I'm-too-Good-for-Anyone—"

"Hey!" Shocked by Niall's vehemence, Andy stepped back, tangling his feet in the process and falling. Pain shot up his arm from his wrist, and he gasped, drawing it to him and cursing himself for breaking his fall that way instead of landing on his ass and absorbing the impact.

"That wasn't my fault!"

Giving Niall an exasperated look, Andy tried to rise. "I never said it was. Are you going to help me up or what?"

Niall looked undecided, but he hooked his hand under Andy's arm and hauled him to his feet.

"Thanks," Andy said, heavy on the sarcasm, light on the gratitude. The fall was down to his clumsiness but that didn't absolve Niall of all responsibility. "Now on top of a shower I need to ice my wrist so I'll be late. Thanks bunches."

Niall held onto his arm, clinging like a hair on the tongue. "I'm sorry about saying that. You were being mean and I got upset."

"Grow up." Andy was in too much discomfort for tact. "I mean it. Act your age."

"Like this?" Niall lunged forward, pinning Andy's arms to his side and kissing him full on the mouth, jabbing his tongue between Andy's lips. It was repulsive and Andy struggled to free himself, good mood ruined, wrist throbbing violently.

"What the hell is going on here?" Ethan asked, voice icy.

Released so abruptly he staggered, Andy's first act was to wipe his mouth with his uninjured hand. That gave Niall time to speak first.

"Relax. It was only a kiss, boss, and our shifts don't start for twenty minutes."

It didn't occur to Andy to explain himself in case Ethan misread the situation. Ethan was incapable of that level of stupidity and his gaze was on Andy's wrist, not his face.

"How badly is it hurt?"

"Not broken. Sprained, I think. I'll ice it."

"Now," Ethan said. "Then get it strapped up and take something to bring down the swelling."

"Yes, sir."

"I'll go with you." Niall stepped closer. Whether his eagerness was born of a desire to escape Ethan's frosty stare or the misguided belief Andy had welcomed the kiss, Andy neither knew nor cared.

"No, thanks." Andy marveled at his self-restraint. He glanced at Ethan. "I need to shower before I strap it up."

He saw Ethan weighing up the need for first aid against the impossibility of Andy serving customers reeking of sweat. "Make it fast. I'll cover for you until you're ready but don't assume that means you can take your time."

"Got it."

Ethan couldn't do or say anything beyond showing the normal concern of an employer with an injured employee, but he didn't look happy with the situation. Andy was an actor and facial expressions were part of his trade. Even closed-off, Ethan radiated worry and annoyance.

"And this will need entering into the accident book, so before anyone goes anywhere, tell me how it happened."

Andy winced. "It's nothing to do with health or safety. I stepped back, caught my foot and down I went. No biggie."

"Yes, that's exactly what happened," Niall chimed in, a shade too fast to be believable.

Ethan's smile was nasty as fuck. "I'm sure it is." He pinned Niall with an icicle of a look. "Do me a favor and restrain your romantic impulses at work."

"Oh, we will," Niall said, blinking rapidly. "Won't we, Andy?"

Choked with fury Andy spluttered an ineffectual, "What? No! I mean, yeah, but we're not—"

"Save it," Ethan said shortly and stalked off.

"Whew." Niall mimed wiping the sweat off his forehead, a theatrical gesture that would've annoyed Andy no matter who did it. "That could've been worse. He's not so bad if you know how to handle him. Butter him up and he loves it. He thinks he's this tough guy, but—"

"Shut the fuck up," Andy said through his teeth. "Or I go after him and lodge a formal complaint about you."

"What?" Niall gave an uncertain giggle. "For one kiss? Are you kidding me?"

"No. And it was a kiss I didn't want at a sucky time. Or did you miss the part where I fell on my ass and hurt my wrist?"

"You mean my timing was off?" Niall nodded slowly. "Right. *Right.* Got it."

"Wrong, totally wrong." Andy wasn't leaving with this unresolved. "I'm not interested in you. I'm not attracted to you, and I'm in a relationship. So give me some space, huh?"

The stricken look on Niall's face was a good sign the message had finally sunk in but Andy felt like shit when he walked away.

There had to have been a better way to handle the situation but he was damned if he knew what it was. And God, did his wrist ever hurt. He wiggled it experimentally and had to stand still for a moment to ward off a wave of dizziness. His audition was in three days and if he got the part, they'd start shooting next week. A role that called for him to have a wrist in full working order for a fight scene and to rescue the heroine from a burning building. He'd been congratulating himself on building his upper body strength enough it would be a breeze. If the sprain were serious, he'd have trouble rescuing a kitten.

* * * *

"I'll kick his ass from the lobby to the loading area."

"Calm down," Andy said. Ethan losing it was an awesome sight in the true meaning of the word. He could watch him pacing around from couch to kitchen counter for hours.

"If he's screwed up your chances—and where the fuck does he get off kissing you?"

"You know that was all him, right?"

"Do I *look* stupid to you?" Ethan's scathing glare warmed him through and through.

"And my wrist hurts, but it's not too swollen."

"Wait until tomorrow."

"Gee, thanks. Where were you when they handed out optimism? Lining up for an extra helping of gloom and despondency?"

Ethan opened his mouth to reply then came to a dead halt. "I'm sorry. Not helping, huh?"

Andy got up from the couch and gave him a one-armed hug. "Love you getting snarly on his sorry ass, even if he isn't here to see it, but honestly, you've got to pity him."

"Give me one good reason why."

"He wants someone who's well and truly taken?"

"Not recently." Ethan returned the hug carefully. "And it will be a while before I can change that."

"We can fuck," Andy protested. "It's a mild sprain. Tying me to the bed is out, but sex isn't. Use your imagination."

"Hmm." Ethan found the precise place on Andy's neck where a kiss made him shiver and went to town. "No. Later, maybe. I want to take you out to dinner."

"We never go out."

Ethan released him. "No. And we've been playing peek-a-boo with your friends for weeks. I hate it. Neither of us has ever been in the closet but this feels close to it. I'm happy with you. We fit better than I'd ever hoped. I'm sick of pretending I'm single and only being part of your sex life."

"You're all over my life. You've never met Henry, but he knows all about you—not your name, not where you work, not the kink—"

"So he knows I'm a gay man and that's it?"

"No!" Andy shook his head hard and fast enough he risked whiplash. "He knows you've got me to clean up my act in every sense of the word. That you listen to me read lines, push me to get better. If I'm a jigsaw puzzle, you're the first guy who's ever gone to the trouble of sorting out the pieces, doing the border, giving me limits, making sense of the whole picture. I know what I am because of you. I see what I can be and yeah, the acting might not be an option, but if it isn't, I have the hotel and I like it there. Love working with you. For you." He ran out of breath to fuel his words. With a rehearsed speech he knew when to pause, inhale, exhale, how to increase the tempo and layer subtle emphasis when needed. When he spoke off the cuff, it was less easy.

"Andrew…" Ethan looked lost, the severe lines of his face softened by bewilderment as if this was news to him, and it couldn't be. Every step he'd taken, Ethan had guided. And sure, he'd fought it. Ethan had ordered him to go alcohol-free for two weeks and reduce his coffee intake. On the night before an early shift, bedtime was no later than midnight. They were rules he'd have resented as a teenager, let alone a grown man, but when he looked in the mirror these days, he was clear-eyed and alert. He'd stopped drinking out of habit and when he did, he set a limit. He hadn't thrown up since meeting Ethan, or woken up with a sickening lurch wondering what the hell he'd done the night before. He knew.

It wasn't a dramatic change, but a slow shaping of his life until it matched his ideal. Him, not Ethan. Ethan's demands were minimal and they both got off on the waxing, the regular haircuts, and Andy's submission between the sheets. It was Andy who had demanded Ethan take charge elsewhere and punish his failures.

Guess he *was* a masochist, because Ethan's consequences could get inventively sadistic. Being punished for skipping on flossing by having his hands laced together by the stuff, palm to palm, the thin, pale green string not tight enough to dig in, but strong enough to hold him had left him cursing, sweating. Ethan had kept him bound for an hour, doing everything for him, from feeding him bites of breakfast to brushing his hair. Thank God he'd taken a piss before Ethan discovered his dental negligence.

He'd hated that hour. Fought Ethan's consequence as if it was a dragon in need of slaying, but toward the end of the hour, a certain peace had crept in, like fog off the ocean, barely visible at first, then thick as a blanket. He'd submitted via a different route, not the direct path of being over Ethan's knee and spanked tearful and contrite, but an inner journey that left him where he'd begun, but changed.

"Ethan lost for words. New look for you."

"Yeah." Ethan rubbed the back of his head. "You surprise me at times. I think I know you, then you do or say something and I'm left floundering."

"Is that good? Tell me it is."

"It's just you."

"Okay then." Andy perched on the arm of the couch. "So I put in for a transfer and we go public?"

"I'm not sure it's that easy."

"Why not?"

"No vacancies," Ethan said. "Oh, summer jobs, yes, but they won't come to half what you're making now." He joined Andy on the couch, looking up at him. "Unless you take your rent out of the equation and move in with me."

"Huh? How would that help? This place is way more expensive than mine. Oh. You mean rent-free. Yeah, not going to happen."

Ethan spread his hands wide. "Why not? It's big enough for us both and you could contribute on a pro rata basis. I'm not trying to strip away your independence. I'm being practical and yeah, selfish. I want to see more of you and the way our shifts are, living together would take us from a few hours a week to a few days."

"And if we split up, I'm left homeless!" That wasn't the main reason. He owed Ethan enough. They were equal partners in this, always had been. Living on Ethan's charity, in Ethan's space, constrained by Ethan's rigid standards and rules, didn't appeal. Spending more time with Ethan did, but as a guest, not a lodger, sponging off his boyfriend.

"Why do you assume we'll split up?"

"This is still new." Andy gestured vaguely. "You, me, being in a relationship. It's new and it's kinda fragile. I don't trust it yet. I love it. Love you and hey, look at that. I said it. And I do. But I wake up every day wondering if it'll be the last we have. I'm not so much of a work in progress now, am I? I still screw up, but not often. You fixed me —"

"You weren't broken."

"Yeah, true, but if I was a guitar, I needed tuning."

"And you think once I've tuned you, I won't want to make sweet, sweet music with you?"

Andy rolled his eyes, grinning. Ethan being heavily sarcastic amused him. "More like power chords. And I think the drums are your instrument. You sure get off on beating out a rhythm on my ass."

"I do. Every morning could start with one. It would put me in a good mood, I'm sure."

"Oh God, don't *say* things like that." Andy blew air up over his face to cool off. "Love the idea, but to quote Monty Python, after the spanking, the oral sex. We'd be late to work every day."

"I promise we wouldn't be," Ethan retorted. "Never mind. I'm not pushing you into something you don't want to do. We'll figure it out."

"If I click at the audition and it leads to more parts, it won't matter."

"That's a nice idea, but I helped you file your taxes. You don't make enough from acting to live on."

"No, but I could. It's possible. People do." Andy swallowed, hurt choking him. "You mean I'm not good enough to be one of them, is that it?"

"I'm not a competent judge. I've heard you read lines, seen your audition tapes. You seem good at what you do, but you're one of thousands out there. Making it big is as much luck as talent and hard work, and that's out of your hands."

"Yeah." Dispirited, Andy slid off the arm of the couch and settled beside Ethan, stretching out his legs and using Ethan's lap for a footrest. "You're the only piece of luck I've ever had."

"I'm touched."

"Let's fuck," Andy said abruptly. "You wanted to earlier and we got distracted. Take my mind off everything." He shifted restlessly. "No, more than that. Do stuff to me, Ethan. Nice and nasty stuff. Please? Today started great then it fell to pieces. Glue them back together. Hurt me."

A month ago, he wouldn't have been able to ask, tongue-tied by the feeling he was imposing on Ethan, but not now. Ethan's newly found delight in crafting pain for Andy to spin into pleasure made it a shared gift, not a chore.

Ethan pursed his lips speculatively, deep in thought for a minute. He slapped on a poker face when he planned a scene, but Andy couldn't look away even when staring taught him nothing. "You said no bondage, but I can tie you without involving your wrist, if that's okay?"

"Yeah." Intrigued, already aroused, Andy nodded. "Go for it."

"Strip and get a dining chair. Put it in the middle of the room and sit on it."

Ethan had modified the standing order of being naked in the loft with the onset of warmer weather. Sitting out on the small balcony watching the boats go by was something they enjoyed and it made more sense for Andy to undress only when Ethan had plans for him. Once though, he'd knelt naked beside Ethan's chair late at night, shivering from excitement and the cool breeze off the water. Ethan hadn't fucked him out there, hadn't done more than stroke his hair, but Andy, knees cushioned by a folded blanket, a leather cock ring his only adornment, had been on the cusp of a climax the whole time, taken there by Ethan's vivid description of what he planned to do to Andy once they were inside.

Now with the wood of the chair warming against his skin, he waited for Ethan, anticipation quickening his breath until he forced his breathing to regulate, his body to relax.

Ethan cuffed his ankles to the chair legs and his uninjured hand to the arm of the chair using wide Velcro straps. Two more pinned his knees wide. "Put your left hand where it'll be comfortable, but nowhere that blocks my access to your cock."

"If I put it like the other, you could use the strap on my forearm. Might be safer that way."

"If it's not, tell me."

"Sure." Ethan tightened his lips in a warning and Andy amended it to a sincere, "Yes, sir."

Strapped down, immobile, he waited, tracking Ethan's movements when he rummaged in a cupboard in the bedroom overhead. Ethan had used some of his purchases from the sex shop, and tucked others away for a future date. Not knowing what lay in store was a thrill for Andy. When Ethan returned carrying the posture collar and the spiked pinwheel, it was a letdown. Andy kept his disappointment off his face, pasting on a pleased smile for a second. The pinwheel, they'd never got around to. The collar he'd tried on once, declared he felt like an accident victim, and Ethan had removed it a few moments later. To see it now puzzled him. Hell, his position in the chair was a cryptic crossword by itself. He'd expected a spanking or a flogging with supple strands of leather proving their ability to make him howl. Strapped to a chair, his ass protected, what was there for Ethan to do?

"The collar will restrict your view to a certain extent." Ethan fastened it around Andy's neck. "I'd use a blindfold, but I want to see your eyes and I want you to see me."

Watching Ethan's face, rapt, intent, was a huge turn-on in a scene. Being deprived of the view was too, in a twisted way, but tonight Andy needed the connection between them strong and no blindfold helped with that.

The six-inch collar forced his chin up and he wondered how much he'd be able to see of Ethan after all.

"You don't seem to like this, Andrew. Not that it matters, since I do." No softness in Ethan's voice now. Authoritative, chilled steel.

Andy responded to it with a surge of need, longing to please Ethan and hear a word or two of approval.

"You'll be wearing it more often. Naked, on your knees, staring up at me."

The carrot and the stick. Andy loved kneeling and Ethan so rarely permitted it. "Yes, sir."

"This ring on it might be useful." Ethan lifted it with a fingertip then let it fall, the small impact reverberating through Andy's taut throat. "I could chain you to a drawer handle while I prep dinner. Throw you scraps."

Jesus. Would he do that? Andy moaned, caught between shock and a sweet-sour ache of lust.

"But I should focus on what I have right here. You want pain? Let's see what we can do about delivering some."

Andy sucked in his breath when Ethan ran the pinwheel over his left nipple, the pressure light. The average Wartenberg wheel had twenty-one teeth, Ethan had told him, a medical instrument particularly suited for sensation play. When he'd picked it up, he'd gone for one with pointed, not rounded ends to the teeth. Would he regret that choice soon?

"If I break the skin, I'll stop."

"No." He couldn't shake his head, but he put force behind the word. "Yeah, it's a limit, but not for this. If I bleed a little, it's okay. No shirtless scenes in the audition."

"I'll decide that. And I won't leave marks where they'll show."

"Yes, sir," Andy murmured, ceding control over every drop of blood to Ethan, trusting him.

After that, the teeth bit deeper, leaving hot, prickling trails over his chest and stomach, arms and once, his face. It tickled, sometimes it tingled, but it wasn't the intense, mind-wiping pain he craved and Ethan had to know that. Still, he was hard. Being the subject of Ethan's attention always had that effect on him.

Without warning, Ethan ran the wheel along the stalk of Andy's cock and over its head. He used less force, but the location made Andy cry out, startled, fighting the straps holding his legs splayed.

Ethan hissed a warning, his displeasure plain, "No. You hold still for this. For me."

"Yes, sir." Andy tensed, waiting, but the wheel tortured his inner thighs next, deep, scoring runs. He couldn't see, couldn't tell if his skin was damp with sweat or dotted with scarlet beads, swelling and bursting. "Am I— Is there blood yet?"

"You need to trust me." Ethan sounded so fucking stern at times. "Asking questions when you hold all the information shows you don't."

"I do! I—"

"It doesn't hurt enough? Isn't what you want? "

"Yes," Andy whispered, ashamed and breaking a rule right there.

"It's not about what *you* want," Ethan said, reminding him of the basics like a coach telling an athlete how to stretch. "I give or take or withhold. You accept that. It's not complicated."

Andy didn't reply. Ethan punished his silence with a squeeze to his balls that had his ass levitating. "Jesus! Yes! I get it. I get it, sir."

"Hmm." More quick, light runs along his cock, the sensation building, layer after layer of it until even the gentlest of passes provoked a moan. Then Ethan bore down harder and Andy squirmed, panting, no way of shrinking back or shielding himself, open and vulnerable to the vicious dig and scrape of the points.

He pictured his cock, dotted with red, welted and swollen, and shaped his safe word without vocalizing it. Not yet. He could take this and he trusted Ethan. He did.

"Now you're ready." Ethan stood and walked to the kitchen, out of Andy's line of sight then back in it. He was holding a knife.

Every muscle in his body locked tight. Knife. He couldn't move. Ethan could gut him like a fish and there was nothing he could do.

Then the absurdity hit him, a cool wash of relief. This was Ethan. And he trusted him. Loved him, believed in him, and trusted him. Ethan could be holding a freaking chainsaw and he'd feel the same.

Ethan smiled at him, untroubled, relaxed, and picked up a lemon from the fruit bowl, tossing it high before catching it and placing it on a chopping board. Andy couldn't see what he did with it after that, but he heard the drip of juice when Ethan hand-squeezed the fruit. Ethan left the knife and board on the counter and walked back, a small bowl in one hand, a new pastry brush in the other. He set them down and picked up Andy's discarded T-shirt, balling part of it up and using it to gag Andy.

"You'll want to scream, but I've got the neighbors to consider."

The cotton filled his mouth, drying it. He could push it out easily if needed, but instead he bit down on it, bracing himself for what was to come.

Ethan dipped the brush in the juice. "Time to play."

His brain shorted out when Ethan swept the soaked brush over the crown of his cock, rivulets of juice running down the sides, over abraded skin. The pain was pure, hot and searing, and screaming didn't help a lot but he did it anyway, grinding his teeth against the fabric gag when he stopped. The fabric was damp, saturated with the sound of his agony.

Ethan painted his skin with juice, the instant of coolness when the liquid met skin lost a second later in the burn. Wetness on his face. Tears. Ethan noticed them when they fell, standing and bending over to lick them away, the warmth of his tongue as painful as the next brushstroke. Everything hurt now.

He heard the sound he made, grunts, smothered by the gag, moans that echoed in his head, endlessly ricocheting, never escaping. The brush kept returning, always wet, always demanding more from him, more pain, more screams, his surrender. Between one stroke and the next, he gave in, accepting he was suffering and the end of it lay not in his stifled, wordless pleas, but with Ethan's decision.

You, you, he wanted to say. *You decide. You. I want it that way. It is that way.*

Ethan had to know he'd won. He pulled the T-shirt from Andy's mouth and tipped the last drops of juice into the empty space, the tart, acidic trickle exploding against his dry tongue, saliva springing into his mouth, rain on the desert sand.

He swallowed, gulped, wailed, and Ethan went to his knees and took Andy's tortured, stinging cock deep.

The soft, wet lap of his tongue erased the pain, but it was the pain that'd cleansed his thoughts, wiping away the grime of the day, the petty annoyances and the larger worries.

He came, filling Ethan's mouth, giving Ethan the proof of his pleasure to taste, sharing it with him.

Did he trust Ethan? Easiest question to answer ever. It was yes, even before he found out he hadn't bled at all.

Chapter Eighteen

"It's your birthday next week," Ethan said when Andy opened the car door to get out after a warm kiss from Ethan.

They'd spent the day hiking in Mount Seymour Park, finding small patches of snow in shadowed corners, spring flowers studding the fresh green grass like scattered confetti. Andy's legs ached and he was sure he had burned the back of his neck, but the view from the summit of Dog Mountain had been worth it, the city laid out at their feet in one direction, distant, cloud-wreathed mountain peaks challenging them when they turned another way.

He closed the door again. They were parked in the small lot around the corner from Andy's place. Ethan hadn't bought a ticket, but he guessed they were safe to have a short conversation at least. "Yeah. Looking forward to my birthday spanking."

"Traditionalist." Ethan raised his eyebrows. "Besides that, is there anything you'd like to do?"

"Actually, yes. Two things."

"I'm listening."

"First one is a night out with my friends—dancing, drinking, catching up." He saw them all, but not as much, and he didn't want to lose them from his life.

"Your birthday's on Friday, so that should work. Maybe we can do something the following night then?"

"Huh? No!" Andy grabbed Ethan's hand. "Not me and them and you off somewhere else. You there, with me, meeting them. And Henry and Mahito too, though they don't get on that well with my crowd, but it's my birthday and I want everyone there."

"Demanding tonight, aren't you?"

"It's time. I'm sick of being mysterious about you. Why the hell are we hiding? We're not doing anything wrong. I've told my parents about you and they're thrilled I've met someone I'm serious about. Well, okay, that's a slight exaggeration when it comes to my dad. He doesn't get thrilled about anything except hockey, but he said he was pleased for me."

"Okay," Ethan said cautiously. "A night out. Alcohol. You dancing, me watching you dance. I can do that."

"You're dancing with me. End of story."

"Consequences. Be prepared for many. Like trampled toes."

"Bring 'em on."

"Oh, I will. So what's the second?"

Andy chewed his lip. "Uh, it's work-related and it might not be possible, or at least not right away, but—"

"Spit it out."

"I want to see one of the Elements rooms," Andy blurted out. "Any of them, I don't mind which."

"Ah."

"The hotel's so fucking fancy, but I'm used to that now. Those rooms, though, they're spectacular. I've seen photos, but it's not the same. I'll never be able to afford a night in one, but I want to walk around and pretend. Five minutes, that's all. I wouldn't tell anyone, I swear. Could I?" He trailed off, reading his answer in the regret filling Ethan's eyes.

"They're booked solid throughout the summer, sweetheart. And they have a late checkout so housekeeping has a short window to work in. The guest leaves and it's like a racing car in the pits. They swarm over the suite, getting it perfect again and when they leave, the next person in there is a guest. You'd mark up the carpet. They vacuum it in stripes, finish at the door, so there's not a single footprint visible."

"Fine. I get it." Andy shrugged, irritated with himself for feeling so crushed, face heating as it did when he'd made a fool of himself. "Only an idea. No biggie."

"If I could—"

"I *get* it, okay? When I'm rich and famous, I'll rent all four for a week and sleep in a different one every night."

Ethan didn't reply. The audition had gone great—or so he'd thought—but his agent had called the next day to say the part had gone to someone else. Not his finest hour as he'd raged about favoritism and unfairness, harping on about his grievances until Ethan had given up on showing his sympathy in words and moved to action. Being hauled across Ethan's knee, jeans pulled down, ass bared, and getting the mother of all spankings hadn't seemed like kindness at first, but when he dissolved into tears he could blame on smarting flesh, not his hurt pride, he was grateful.

With a surly goodbye, Ethan made him repeat without the pout, Andy got out of the car, hitching his backpack onto one shoulder. Hot bath, cold beer, watch a movie, then go to bed made up his to-do list for the evening. He could've had those at Ethan's, and these days he spent more nights there than at home, but he wanted to see Henry, who was currently on vacation, semester over. They'd missed each other for five straight days and he wanted to catch up.

Throwing off his bad mood, he made his way home, acutely aware of his sore feet. His hiking boots were old enough to be comfortable and not rub, but even so, each step reminded him of the thousands he'd taken during the hike on slippery rocks and muddy, sometimes icy ground. It was late May, but winter still lingered in the mountains.

"Andy! Hey, wait up!"

Niall appeared beside him, out of breath and flushed. "Thought it was you. Saw you getting out of that car. Where've you been?"

Always with the questions nudging into intrusive. "Hiking."

"By yourself? It's not safe, you know. Always hike with a buddy. Did you? Go with someone? The guy in the car, maybe?"

Shit, would Niall know Ethan's car when he saw it? Best not to ask. "Yes, and now I'm going home, so I'll see you around, okay?"

Niall's face fell. "Don't be like that. We're good, aren't we? I never seem to see you around at work."

I avoid you, that's why. "Yeah, guess it's the way our shifts are."

"Yeah, you're right. Ethan makes sure of it."

"Huh?" Andy rubbed the back of his neck, stopping when the friction made the sunburned skin smart.

"Well, he arranges them, yeah, but I seriously doubt he's deliberately—"

Niall clicked his tongue impatiently. "Of course he is. He's been on my case since that time you tripped and hurt your wrist, like he blames me for it when I didn't do anything."

Not touching that one. Curbing his irritation, Andy said, "Take it up with him if you think there's a problem."

"Well, he's not going to admit he's keeping us apart, is he?"

"No," Andy agreed, wondering if Ethan *was* doing that. Ethan didn't play favorites, but he might consider it for the good of the team. Part of Andy wanted special treatment and liked the idea of Ethan protecting him, so he didn't plan to complain either way. Anything that gave him less Niall in his life got his vote. "Mainly because he's not. Look, I'm shattered and I stink. See you around." He managed two steps before Niall was back in his face. "Niall, you're in my way."

"I don't want that." Niall didn't look scary-stalker guy now, but vulnerable. "I want us to be friends."

"Yeah? I get the feeling you're looking for more and I'm not interested. I don't know you that well and I don't—we don't—click."

"You don't like me."

"I don't *dis*like you," Andy said, lying without shame. "But you come on a little strong, to be honest."

"So there's no chance of hanging out with you, or going back to your place for a coffee?"

Too tired to let him down easily, Andy asked, "What would be the point? Not interested in you as a friend or a boyfriend. I know that's harsh, but it's the truth."

He braced himself for anger or a scene, but Niall bit his lip, then he nodded sharply as if he'd reached a decision and stepped aside. "In that case, have a nice life and fuck you very much, asshole."

"Oh yeah, not passive aggressive at *all*," Andy muttered, walking on. His feet hurt, he'd parted from Ethan under less than ideal circumstances, and now he'd been cast as the bad guy in Niall's personal soap opera. Great.

* * * *

He was still ticked off when he emerged from his bath in a cloud of steam. Discovering his nose had caught the sun too didn't help.

"You look like a clown," Henry said through a mouthful of noodles drenched in soy. "Ever heard of sunblock?"

"I was slathered in the stuff."

"If you mean the bottle that was in the bathroom, it was three years old. It expires, you know."

"Whatever." Grabbing a second beer, Andy settled next to Henry on the couch. "What's new?"

"I'm taking Mahito to meet my mom soon." Henry pushed up his glasses, a shy smile showing. "He can drive and we're renting a car for the weekend."

Pleased, Andy raised his bottle in a toast. "Yeah? That's awesome, man. Tell me when, huh? I want to send her something. Does she like flowers? Candy?"

"You don't have to do that."

"I want to." A thought occurred to him. "You won't be away for my birthday, will you?"

"No," Henry assured him. "It's arranged for the weekend after that."

"Cool, because we're going out. Everyone. The Crew, you and Mahito and my boyfriend. Uh, that would be Ethan."

"Ethan. *The* Ethan?"

"The one and only."

Henry widened his eyes. "He's the guy you've been seeing? The man of mystery? Color me…not surprised at all."

The hell? Andy smacked Henry's arm. "You guessed?"

Henry nodded, grinning broadly. "You wouldn't stop talking about him, then you did, which was all kinds of suspicious. You're a persistent kind of guy. Shutting up meant you'd hooked him. And once, I…uh…came home and you and he were in your room and…um. You said his name. More of a whimper, really."

"You heard us having sex?" Andy burst out laughing, refusing to feel even a trace of embarrassment. "Guess that evens the score for when I walked in on you."

Henry winced. "Mahito refuses to have sex here after that."

"You were the ones getting freaky in the open. Don't blame me."

"Changing the subject now," Henry said firmly. "So what's he like? Is he why you've started tidying up? Are we talking actual good influence here?"

"He's…he's Ethan. And yes. He's got this way of making me want to live up to his expectations and he's a fan of everything having a place and floors you could eat off." Remembering Ethan's plan to feed him scraps, he flushed hotly, rolling the beer bottle against his cheeks to cool them, but Henry seemed oblivious.

"I'd like to meet him." He tilted his head. "Is it weird working with him?"

"Only a little. No one knows at work yet, so we have to keep it strictly business, but even if they did, he's so focused on his job, I don't think he'd be any different."

The conversation drifted after that, the two of them swapping news, squabbling over what movie to watch, and eventually deciding not to bother. Andy drifted off to sleep, body aching but in a better place emotionally. He had the morning off, so he didn't bother setting the alarm. These days, Ethan-trained, he woke early by himself, but if he needed more sleep, he'd take it.

* * * *

The insistent jangle of his phone's ringtone woke him. With a sleepy curse, he grabbed it from the nightstand.

"H'lo."

"It's Ethan."

Andy yawned. Ethan was at work, so phone sex wasn't likely. He scratched his balls idly, the heavy weight of his morning wood tempting him to play with it while he had Ethan's voice in his ear. "Morning off."

"I'm aware of that. Could you come in anyway? As soon as possible. There's a situation here involving you."

Something about the guarded tone sent a frisson of alarm through him, dispelling the last shreds of sleep from his brain. Situation? It didn't take a genius to work out what that was. Management had found out about his relationship with Ethan. Had to be. Shit on a fucking stick.

In case anyone was listening in, he made his reply crisply professional and by the book. "Yes, boss. On my way."

"Thank you. When you arrive, go to the manager's office, please."

"Yes, boss," Andy repeated, the hollow sensation in his stomach unrelated to hunger.

He skipped a shower and got dressed into his work suit. Food consisted of a few gulps of orange juice and a cinnamon bagel eaten on the way. He was outside the manager's office thirty-two minutes after the phone call, palms damp, waiting to be announced.

Charlotte Dawes was in her mid-fifties, as devoted to the hotel as Ethan from all accounts, and implacable when it came to any misdemeanor affecting the guests. Her parents owned a luxury hotel in Jamaica but she'd chosen to move to Canada and make a name for herself without trading on her background. Andy had never exchanged words with her, though she'd passed him in the hallway once or twice and smiled in an abstract way. Gray streaked her short, dark hair, lending her an air of authority she didn't need. Andy guessed even when she was younger, a hard stare from those cool brown eyes would've had most people clearing their throats and stammering excuses.

Walking into her office, a quietly beautiful space in keeping with the hotel without being extravagantly lush, Andy slipped into the refuge of pretending he was playing a character. A confident, assured man accustomed to sitting in a sinfully comfortable deep leather chair.

Ethan stood by the window, looking out at the water, his back rigid. Oh yeah. It was bad.

"Thank you for coming in at such short notice, Mr. Naylor."

The confident, assured man had the perfect reply, but Andrew found himself croaking, "No problem" in a strangled voice.

God, what was *wrong* with him? He'd done nothing wrong. Nothing.

"I'll cut to the chase. An employee has alleged a relationship exists between you and Mr. Mason and as a result you've received preferential treatment and other employees have been, well, the word used was 'persecuted', but that's a little dramatic for my taste."

Finding strength and a normal voice in his anger, Andy said, "And by employee, you mean Niall Brent, right?"

She placed her elbows on the arms of her chair and brought her fingertips together, tapping them lightly. An emerald ring caught the light, a winking green flash. "Interesting question. What makes you think he's the source of the complaint?"

"He was waiting for me outside my place last night, trying to get me to agree to a date. I turned him down. *Again*. I guess this is his way of getting back at me, but it's bull—I mean, it's, uh, groundless."

"Is it? All of it?"

Crunch time. Without looking at Ethan—still staring out of the window anyway and no use what-so-fucking-ever—Andy stepped up to the metaphorical plate and swung his bat.

"It's true we're dating. Not true about the special treatment. Ethan treats me like everyone else. He rides my ass, making sure I get everything right and if I screw up, I hear about it. The only time he moved my shift around was for an audition I had to go to and he asked who wanted to cover it and had three volunteers, so no one minded."

Charlotte nodded. "I see. And are you aware of the guideline concerning work relationships?"

"Yes. And I can see why it's there, but—"

"But it doesn't apply to you?"

"Charlotte." Ethan sounded unutterably weary. "He's young. Romantic. Of course he doesn't think it applies to him. I'm the one who should've known better."

"It's frowned on, not forbidden," Andy said. "We didn't do anything wrong."

"Then why was it a secret?" When neither replied, Charlotte raised her eyebrows. "No answer? Then tell me when it began. Is it how you got the job?"

"No!" Andy leaned forward. "The first time I met Ethan was at the interview and there was nothing between us for weeks. Five or six weeks. And when it started, we weren't sure how long it would last and when it didn't stop, we were going to tell people and see if I could transfer, but there aren't any openings right now, so we...we—"

"Continued to hide a relationship that should never have begun, but once it did should've been disclosed immediately," Charlotte finished.

"What exactly am I accused of?" Ethan asked, swinging around. "Did Niall provide anything concrete or was it all vague hints?"

"He thinks you arranged his shifts so they didn't overlap with Mr. Naylor's out of possessive jealousy." Charlotte's voice was tinder-dry. "Apparently, you're worried he'll take Mr. Naylor away from you. Let me say I don't believe that. His motivations were pretty clear and he's done himself no favors."

"Well, then," Andy began.

Charlotte cut him off, "I can't permit you to work together. It's detrimental to team morale now that it's out in the open."

"My team—"

Ethan got no further than Andy. Charlotte sure was fond of interrupting people. "Will tell you they don't mind. They'll probably even mean it in the moment, but how long before something happens that has them whispering behind your backs? No. This ends."

"You can't stop us seeing each other!" Andy said.

Lips tightening with impatience, she shook her head. "Of course not. But I can terminate your employment, Mr. Naylor."

"On what grounds?" Ethan demanded.

"The unsatisfactory reports littering his record."

"He had a rocky start, but he's doing fine now." Ethan folded his arms across his chest. "This isn't fair, Charlotte. You're assuming problems that haven't occurred yet are inevitable."

She shrugged, her thin shoulders rising in an elegantly expressive gesture. "Or I'm making sure they never happen by letting an employee go who's vocal about his ambitions to be an actor and less so about his commitment to his job here."

"I like it here." Andy surprised himself by how much he meant it. "I like being part of what we do."

"And if you were offered a part, you'd leave us in the lurch without hesitation." Charlotte addressed Ethan directly, "Let's pretend he's in the kitchen dating the chef and you don't know him. If this was your decision not mine, what would you do?"

Reluctantly, his gaze flicking to Andy, Ethan gave the only answer he could and still be Ethan. "I'd split them up. If that wasn't possible I'd fire the one less useful to the hotel."

She clapped, silent pats of her hands. "Exactly right."

"You're firing me?" He'd known things would get sticky when people found out, but he'd expected a lecture on not sucking face at work, no more. "That's not fair! We haven't done anything wrong. Never. We've kept work and personal stuff separate. If that twisted little —"

"Andrew." Ethan silenced him with a word. "This situation began to unravel the first time we — This was inevitable."

"So I get punished for it and it's business as usual for you?" Andy demanded.

"You want me to make a grand gesture? Resign in protest? Say if you go, I go too?"

Yes. "No." Andy glared at Ethan "That would be pointless."

"I agree," Charlotte said.

"So do I," Ethan replied. "But I'm doing it anyway unless you find a way to fix this, Charlotte. If I'm essential, as you told me at my last appraisal, you'll want to at least try."

"I won't be blackmailed or manipulated."

"I'm doing neither. I'm asking you to do your job. Hotel manager. We're part of your staff. Manage us."

"I think I have all the information I need from you." She gestured at the door. "You're excused. Both of you leave. I'll cover for you today, Ethan."

"What does that mean?" Ethan asked, tapping out a restless beat with his foot until he visibly caught himself doing it and stopped.

"I need to pursue this without you here. I'm not sure I can phrase it any more clearly than that. When I'm ready to make a final decision, I'll let you know."

Andy stood, unsurprised to discover he was shaky on his feet. Adrenaline rush. "Whatever you decide, don't take Ethan's job away. He loves it here. It's part of his life."

"So are you," Ethan said.

In that moment, no one else existed for Andy but Ethan. The connection between them, forged at their first meeting, frayed by arguments, strengthened by shared pain and passion, became unbreakable. If they'd been alone, he'd have dropped to his knees and taken the consequences, but all he could do was tilt up his chin, symbolically offering his lips and throat. Ethan noticed the gesture if the soft hiss of his breath was an indicator, but Charlotte seemed oblivious. Nerves steadying enough that he could walk without stumbling, Andy followed Ethan out of the door.

Charlotte's office was on the fiftieth floor, a long way up, a long way down. "That was rough," Andy said, after realizing Ethan wasn't going to speak, only stride along the hallway to the elevator.

"That was—" Ethan sucked in a deep breath. "Never mind."

The elevator arrived after one stab of the button from Ethan, as if it knew who'd summoned it, and they stepped inside.

"So what do you want to do now?" Andy asked, stomach lurching, ears popping, when the elevator sank. "We've got the day free now."

"At the risk of sounding melodramatic, I'd prefer to be alone."

"What?" Andy grabbed Ethan's arm when the doors opened. "Don't shut me out. We need to talk about this."

"Nothing to say and I'd be terrible company."

"Then let me put you in a better mood."

"Sex isn't the cure-all you think it is."

"Doesn't hurt," Andy said. "It'll pass the time until it's not too early to get drunk."

Ethan stared at him, face blank, then he smiled slowly, amusement dispelling the blank look in his eyes. "It's never too early for that. Come on then. But if I snap and snarl, don't say I didn't warn you."

Chapter Nineteen

Ethan's place was pristine, but it seemed quiet, as if it knew the two of them shouldn't have been there. After brewing a pot of coffee, they sat on the couch.

"Want to talk about it?" Andy offered. "Discuss creative ways to make Niall pay for being a slimy, sneaky, scum-sucking weasel?"

"He doesn't deal with rejection well. It's a certain fact."

"I never gave him any encouragement. It was a crush and he had no fucking right to take it out on us." Andy took a large gulp of coffee then choked when he discovered it was too hot to swallow. He dribbled it back into the mug, sticking out his tongue to cool it. "Ow."

"If he saw you now, his infatuation would die a swift death. Here." Ethan passed him a clean tissue from his pocket and Andy mopped up.

"Thanks." Andy raised his eyebrows. "So what would it take to turn you off?"

"Cheating on me."

"Never would. What else?"

"That's about it. When it comes to you as my boyfriend, I find I'm amazingly tolerant of your flaws."

"What flaws?" Andy shook his head. "No, forget that. Tolerant? You spanked my ass raw last weekend for leaving wet towels in the bathroom. Bent me over the sink and whaled on me."

"Slight exaggeration. A couple of hard swats that barely left a mark."

The truth lay somewhere between their versions, but the spanking and the sex that had followed—Ethan fucking him with a focused ferocity that had left Andy wobbly-legged and blissful—had been a great start to the day. He loved being fucked in front of a mirror, able to watch Ethan in the moments when his eyes weren't screwed shut concentrating on how good it was to have a thick, hard cock rammed into him at the precise angle needed to reduce him to a whimpering mess.

"I love you," Andy said.

"For spanking you? You're welcome."

"You never say it back." Andy swallowed. "Do you? Or am I rushing it?"

"You rush a lot of things, but love isn't something you can schedule or plan for. It happens when it happens and that's all there is to it."

"Still not answering my question."

"When did you know you were in love with me?"

"*Another* question? Jesus. Um, not on sight. That was lust. I was another version of Niall, minus the vindictive asshole behavior. I think it became more than that when you showed me how to slice the lemons your way instead of firing me. Then it built. No one defining moment. It got to the point where if someone asked me if I loved you, there'd only be one answer and that was yes."

Ethan leaned in and kissed him, as if he couldn't help himself, cupping Andy's cheek. "Thank you. I never get anything but the truth from you. I can't tell you how much I appreciate it."

"Your turn."

"For me, it was a moment. Yes, I wanted you from minute one. I don't think that's a surprise. You were so—" Ethan screwed up his face. "You were like a vase out of place on a shelf. I wanted to fix you. I wanted to get my hands on you and guide you—"

"That's what we're calling a spanking these days, huh?"

"If you keep interrupting me, I'll show you exactly how it works."

"You can. Right now if you want. Take it out on my ass and make me feel better too."

"I know I can. But it's my call, remember?"

"Yes, sir," Andy said, but it lacked the zing and sizzle today with everything hanging over them.

"But I wasn't attracted enough to make a move, not with the complication of us working together. I almost wished you'd leave, get an acting job, so I could put you out of my head, or look you up and see if you were still interested. Then you did something and I saw you in a different way. Less a fantasy, a hot man to fuck and spank and control, but a person, a—a nice person." Ethan rubbed the back of his neck. "I'm not as good at this as you."

'You're doing fine," Andy assured him, intrigued. "What did I do that put the hearts and flowers in your eyes?"

"You gave your pizza to that homeless guy." Andy gaped at Ethan, the memory surfacing, but the significance escaping him. "I'd walked past him and he'd asked me what he asked you, I guess. Except I had nothing, so I told him I'd be back and went into a sub shop. I was waiting in line, watching him out of the window, and I saw you go by, stop, walk on and I judged the hell out of you for a moment. Then you ran back and I saw your face, how horror-struck you looked, and I saw you give him the pizza."

"And you followed me."

"After I'd delivered the sub, yes."

"Wow." Andy contemplated Ethan's revelation. "That's something else. Fate. We were fated to be together."

"If you like."

"You still haven't said it." Andy met Ethan's gaze without artifice or pleading. "I love you, Ethan."

"I love you too."

The silence hung between them, shimmering with possibilities. Andy wanted to gather them like fruit off a tree, store them for later, glut himself on the ripest now. Love couldn't cast him in the perfect role or smooth away every difficulty in life, but it meant he wasn't alone in facing those difficulties and neither was Ethan. They had each other's backs.

"Now can we get drunk?" Ethan asked.

Andy grinned. "Spank me first?"

"Can't spank you drunk, it's true, but I don't want to spank you sober either." Ethan drew his finger across Andy's lips. "Want you."

"I'm right here."

"So you are." Ethan got to his feet, then held out his hand. "Come to bed."

Ethan was capable of a quick fuck, but those weren't the ones Andy enjoyed the most. It was times like this, when Ethan set aside hours to spend fucking him, that resonated the most. His submission became Ethan's sole focus. Intimidating at first, it was now addictive. Even with the worries of the day clouding his emotions, Andy couldn't hold back a grin.

* * * *

It wasn't until he was riding Ethan with slow rocks of his hips, pinching his nipples, tormenting himself on Ethan's orders, for Ethan's pleasure, that Andy let the events of the morning truly register. His rhythm faltered, his hands dropping away from hot, throbbing flesh.

"I didn't tell you to stop." Ethan propped himself up on his elbows then tilted his head, eyes narrowing. "You okay?"

"Not so much," Andy admitted. "Shit, I got fired. And you—God, call her. Call her and tell her you didn't mean it. It's stupid for us *both* to lose our jobs."

"I'm not having this conversation when my cock's buried in your ass," Ethan said. "And I'm not removing it from there until I come. I'm in a bad enough mood without that."

Andy clutched Ethan's arms. "Don't pull out! I want to come too. I'll shut up, I swear. Maybe change position?"

"No." Ethan's voice was inflexible as steel. "Ride me. Twist your nipples."

"They hurt," he whined, wondering at himself. They did, but no more than he could bear and he loved being on top but not in charge, moving as directed, Ethan's control never wavering until those last gloriously frantic moments when everything was forgotten in the rush of pleasure. Why was he pushing Ethan, annoying him with disobedience when this was supposed to make them feel better? Stupid question. He knew why. He wanted Ethan to push back. Release the roiling misery in a physical way for both of them.

He wanted the fucking spanking he'd asked for.

"Good."

"There's no need to be an asshole about it. How about I twist your fucking—"

He got that far, reaching out to grab Ethan's nipples, when Ethan flipped them over, still joined, cock to ass.

"Stop pushing me," Ethan growled. "I don't like it."

"Then punish me for it, *sir*." Andy stared up at cold gray eyes. "It's my fault. All of it. I didn't deal with Niall the right way. I've ruined things for you at work, no matter how this goes down. Spoiled your perfect record so you're not the ideal employee, but the guy who couldn't keep his hands off a hot piece of ass." He drew in a breath, shouting the words, using volume as emphasis, biting off each syllable. "And now I'm fucking up the sex by not doing what I'm told. So punish me, dammit. Hurt me. Clamp my nipples until breathing on them makes me scream. Make me cry. Make me fucking sob my heart out for you." His breath caught and he swallowed, whispering the next words, "Let me give you that much at least."

There wasn't an ounce of tenderness in Ethan's expression. "You'll give me everything I want to take, Andrew. Not what you choose to give. If I want your tears, do you think I need to leave bruises to get them? Do you?"

"No, sir." He knew it was true. His cheeks were already wet with hot, angry tears.

Ethan captured his wrists and pinned them to the bed, hurting him, the pressure of his strong fingers unyielding. He withdrew until the tip of his cock, no more was in Andy's ass, then plunged forward, impaling him, repeating it over and over, a slow, relentless fuck with Andy welcoming each thrust with a gasp, a moan, an anguished, grateful, sobbed out 'sir'.

With his climax imminent, ass clenching around the solid length forcing it wide, Andy lost all sense of self. He was here for Ethan to fuck. He didn't need to be anything else, think about anything else. It was simple. It was easy. He found refuge in his purpose.

Then Ethan pulled out, an abrupt desertion, leaving his hole empty.

"You don't get to come today," Ethan said harshly. "And no sneaking away to jerk off in the shower. I'll cuff your hands behind you if I have to."

Andy shook his head, bewildered, resentful. "Not today," he pleaded. "Fuck, Ethan, any other time, yeah, but not today. I need this. Please."

"And I needed you to obey me today more than ever, but you haven't."

Understanding dawned. Andy brushed his fingers over his nipples, tender but no more than that. He'd been playing with them, going easy on himself. "I'm sorry."

"When has that ever saved you from a consequence?"

He waited for anger. Found none. Ethan was right. He'd agreed to let Ethan call the shots. It was the basis of their relationship and he'd put cracks in it at a time when it needed to be rock-solid. It was Ethan's kink not his and he'd gone along with it to get Ethan without understanding why Ethan needed it.

Fish or cut bait.

"It hasn't. It shouldn't. You don't need to cuff me unless you want to. I won't touch myself without permission, sir."

The surprise flickering in Ethan's eyes told its own story. He'd expected arguments, a gentle nagging until he changed his mind, not capitulation. God, he'd been a sucky boyfriend to Ethan in some ways. He could've discussed his reservations with Ethan, worked out compromises when they were dressed and not horny instead of manipulating events during sex when they were on edge and emotionally worked up.

Saying that to Ethan gave him a nice, dirty low-down tingle. He had this idea that to keep Ethan interested, he couldn't be a pushover. Maybe that wasn't the case.

"Do you like it when I challenge you? Do you get a kick out of...uh...conquering me or something?"

Ethan widened his eyes. "No. It's exhausting and I start to worry you're not happy with the way things are between us."

"You wouldn't get bored of me being some kind of perfectly obedient bed-slut?"

"Bed-slut?" Ethan repeated incredulously. "What the hell kind of word is that? But no, I'd love it. If I thought it was remotely possible for you to be perfect and obedient, anyway."

"Hey! I could be!"

"Prove it." Ethan rolled to his back. He peeled the condom off then snagged a handful of tissues from the box beside the bed. "Ride me until I come and twist your nipples—hard. I want to see you suffer, Andrew. Watch you force yourself to keep going. I could do it myself and hurt you more, but I want you to do it for me."

Heart hammering, cock rigid with need, Andy said, "That's kind of twisted." And he loved it.

Ethan nodded. "Thank you. Get a condom out and put it on me."

"Yes, sir."

"And let's make one thing clear. You screw up again today and I'll send you home. That'll be the consequence. But if you stay, you're as good as fucking gold, understand me?"

"Yes, sir."

"And no matter how good you are, no matter how many times I come in or on you, you won't be rewarded with an orgasm."

"I get that." Andy put the condom on Ethan's cock, sheathing it snugly. "I don't deserve it."

Ethan slapped his flank sharply. "That's not your call to make. It's mine. And it's not a question of deserving it or earning it. It's down to whether I choose to let you. Today, I don't. I want to see how you perform when your only goal is pleasing me."

"But I'm still not your sub?" Andy asked wryly. "I think the lines are blurring, sir."

"I think I told you to ride me." Ethan tossed him the lube. "You'll need some more of that. Turn around so I can see you with three fingers crammed into your hole."

Weak with lust and love, Andy caught the bottle. "God, I love you so fucking much when you're like this."

"I'm always like this," Ethan said.

"Starting to see that," Andy muttered, slicking his fingers.

He put on a show for Ethan, adding a finger at a time, when he could have pushed all three in at once. Ethan brushed his knuckles over the inner curve of

Andy's ass, the light touch making him shiver. "Remember those clothespins I used on you?"

The memory carried such emotional weight that Andy didn't dwell on it often. Too precious to be worn thin with use. "Yeah. Blew my mind."

"It was intense." Ethan touched the tip of a finger to Andy's hole. "Room for another finger?"

Four was a lot. Fingers weren't as easy to take as cocks or dildos. Sharp nails and the irregular bump of bones made them a challenge. Ethan kept his nails short and smooth, though, and so did Andy these days.

"I think so."

Slowly, more to prolong the experience than concern for Andy's comfort, he guessed, Ethan inserted a lube-slicked finger into Andy's crowded hole. It stretched him, nerve endings sparking as the shape their fingers made put pressure in different places. Finding a rhythm, they moved in unison until Andy was panting, sweat damp on his forehead.

"Ready for my cock?"

"Always."

He said it fervently enough to get a chuckle from Ethan. "I wish I could take advantage of that willingness more often."

"Anytime, sir. I mean it. You want me, call and I'll come running, I, *uhn* —" The loss of the fingers in his ass, Ethan withdrawing his and tugging Andy's free too, brought a choked groan from him.

"Duly noted. Stay facing that way and get on my cock."

The angle was awkward, but the smooth thickness filling him was perfect. Andy rose and sank, adjusting to the fullness. "Fast or slow, sir?"

"Surprise me. Be inventive."

An order like that didn't free Andy to do whatever the hell he liked. Ethan meant exactly that. Thrown, panicking, he gave a few half-hearted bounces, unsure of a way to make a straightforward act interesting. He couldn't even lean over and kiss Ethan or play with his nipples.

Ethan slapped his ass hard. "You can do better than that. So much better."

Another slap, this time to the opposite cheek. Ethan was using both hands but that didn't mean one ass cheek was getting a lighter spanking. Slap. Slap. The scorch on his butt aroused Andy, but that didn't solve his problem. In fact, it distracted him to the point where he was barely moving at all, soaking up those punishing slaps, cock jerking in time.

"I told you to ride me." Ethan sounded annoyed, rare when they were in bed.

Swallowing, forcing his mind away from the spreading glow in his ass, Andy leaned forward, back arched up. He slid his hands down Ethan's legs, caressing them, careful to keep Ethan's cock inside him. Cocks were flexible to a certain extent but this position meant Ethan's was angled away from his body already.

Pain was his hot button, not Ethan's—experiencing it, anyway. He straightened, a graceful movement, languorous as he could make it, then reached down with both hands to fondle Ethan's balls. Tempted to touch his own cock on the way, but he resisted.

He handled his balls with rough tugs when he jerked off, but it wasn't an option here. He didn't want it to be. He fucking worshipped this cock, these balls. The lube bottle was close by. He picked it up and squeezed a generous amount into his palm, warming it between his hands before returning to his task.

"Better." Ethan rested his hands on Andy's hips. "But you're not moving." A sharply struck blow landed on Andy's ass, driving Ethan's message home.

Move. Right. Rolling Ethan's balls inside the slippery cradle of his hands, Andy fucked himself slowly on Ethan's cock, thigh muscles burning at the pace he'd set.

Surprise factor. Right. He paused, lifting as far as he could without losing Ethan's cock.

"Love this, just the head in me, God, so good." He squeezed the outer ring of muscle, trapping the tip of Ethan's cock in place, then relaxed and let another inch slide inside. "But I know what it feels like when you're balls deep in me and don't ever make me choose."

Down a fraction, more, hold, then drop... Behind him, he heard Ethan's breath quicken and smiled, delighted.

"I dream about your cock in me. Mouth or ass, hell, even my hand, I don't care." He wished he dared let his hands rove lower. How would Ethan react to a finger slid gently into his ass?

"That explains some of your mistakes at work."

Stung, Andy twisted around to glare at Ethan. "Hey! I don't think about you that way when I'm at work."

Ethan raised his eyebrows. "Really?"

Huffing, unable to lie, Andy swung around, avoiding Ethan's skeptical, amused eyes. "It doesn't affect what I do," he muttered. "And I don't want to think about work now."

"Neither do I." Ethan grabbed Andy's hips. "Enough. Hands crossed behind you."

Relieved to have Ethan resume control, Andy obeyed and let Ethan set the pace for a few minutes, moving with Ethan's guidance. He discovered Ethan preferred steady to fast or torturously slow. He approved, not that it mattered what he thought. It kept them on the edge without pushing them too close.

After a while, Ethan stopped. "The angle's not working for me. Off."

Andy risked one final plunge down, punished for it with a flurry of slaps. He rose, with a groan of loss, and cast an apologetic glance over his shoulder.

"If you think wide eyes and a quivering lip have an effect, you're mistaken."

"I didn't mean to—"

Ethan scowled. "You knew exactly what you were doing."

Aware lying was a cardinal sin in Ethan's eyes on any day, let alone one this fraught, Andy's penitence was instant and genuine. "Yeah, I did. I'm sorry."

"I said I'd send you home if you screwed up."

Aghast, Andy shook his head. "Don't. Please. That wasn't—it was a mistake."

"The lie was deliberate."

That inflexible tone made him shudder with lust sometimes, but this wasn't one of them. "I'll go if it's what you want. No nagging, I won't even beg you to let me stay. But you didn't come."

"I can take care of that myself."

"For God's sake, I'm *right here*." Andy moderated his voice. "Sir—Ethan. You're wound tight and pissed, and I didn't make it better the way I wanted to, but you can use me to get off before you kick me out. I can't promise I won't get something out of it, but it would be for you, not me. I'd *try* not to enjoy it."

Ethan looked at him for a long moment, impassive, stern, then smiled ruefully. "Come here, you aggravating brat."

Being kissed before being put across Ethan's knee for a brief spanking was like winning the lottery twice running. Of course, Ethan altering a consequence was a sign the world was ending, but he'd enjoy the reprieve and worry about the apocalypse later.

Spanking over, Ethan drew Andy's hand to his erection. "Touch me before I suit up again. Want to feel your hands on me."

"Only my hands?"

"For now."

Andy nodded. Ethan knelt back on his heels and Andy crouched lower. The spanking had cleaned the slate but it didn't hurt to emphasize his contrition. He mapped the curve of the crown, the shape of the shaft. He went lower, fondling Ethan's balls, still slick with lube. The musky smell of Ethan's skin teased him with every breath. He wanted to taste what he touched. Hungry for Ethan's cock.

As if he'd read Andy's longing, Ethan tangled his fingers in Andy's hair. "Now I want your mouth. No hands."

Andy flattened himself on the bed, arms folded beneath him. The submissiveness of the position excited him and losing the use of his hands added a new dimension to a familiar act. He prided himself on giving good head — no, great head — but Ethan's cock, wet from licking, kept slipping from his mouth.

Frustrated, he glanced up.

Ethan met his gaze. "Need some help?"

"Yes, sir." He hated admitting it, but Ethan's expression warmed as if he'd passed a test, instead of failing.

Ethan gripped his dick at the base and used his hold on Andy's hair to tilt Andy's head back at an angle painful enough to draw a murmur from him. Ethan eased back an inch, raising his eyebrows, and Andy, unable to nod, smiled instead.

Ethan drew the damp head of his cock over Andy's face, painting him on forehead, eyelids, cheeks and neck, until he ached to taste it. He smelled the musk of Ethan's cock and the dark, secret scent of his balls, arousing him like the slow rub of Ethan's cock against his face.

He found that dreamy, quiet space again, pushed deeper, not jolted out of it, when Ethan slapped Andy's cheek with the side of his cock.

Throat a taut bow, he moaned, gasping out strangled words, "Yeah. Oh God, yeah."

Ethan struck him again, the weight of his cock slamming against Andy's parted lips. The dull blow left his lips stinging, hot and swollen. He passed his tongue over them and tried to capture a fleeting taste of Ethan's cock.

"Want something?" Ethan asked. "Like my dick down your throat?"

Without waiting for Andy to reply, Ethan pushed Andy's head forward then jerked it back. "Guess that's a yes, but you can do more than that. Anything I give you to lick, you do it."

Dazed with lust, Andy let himself be pushed to his back, two pillows under his head. Let Ethan straddle his face and grind his balls against Andy's mouth to be lapped at frantically. He was smothered by musky hot flesh, probing the tight furl of Ethan's hole with his tongue, existing to do and be done to.

When Ethan groaned and pulled away, he knew he'd done well. "Promised you my dick to suck, but I'm too close to coming to do that and fuck you."

Andy couldn't reply at first. His throat ached, sparks shattering the darkness when he closed his eyes. Spunk swelled his balls, held back by an effort of will.

"I'm not going anywhere." His voice shook. "Do what you want now then fuck me later."

He saw the struggle on Ethan's face, but they were too keyed up to prolong this. With a bitten-off groan, Ethan slid his cock between Andy's lips, thrusting deep at once, forcing Andy to breathe between the fast, forceful strokes.

The thick vein along the underside of Ethan's cock pulsed and he waited for the taste, the heat, but after the first surging spurt, Ethan withdrew, hand on his cock, directing the next spurts over Andy's lips.

Instinctively, Andy darted out his tongue but Ethan beat him to it, sealing their lips together in a messy, slick kiss.

The eroticism of the act was one stimulus too many. Hating to disappoint Ethan, aware a climax was forbidden, Andy twisted his head to the side, desperation sharpening his voice. "Gonna come!"

"Yeah," Ethan said, lips glistening, eyes bright. He closed his hand around the leap and jerk of Andy's cock. "I've changed my mind. You are."

Ethan tore at the throbbing nipple with his teeth, targeting it one final time, completing the circuit, and Andy came screaming Ethan's name, body locked in a quivering, ecstatic rush of pleasure.

* * * *

Waking with Ethan's hand wrapped around his cock was like stepping from one dream to another. Andy sighed, eyes still closed, and concentrated on keeping still. His instincts drove him to fuck the tight tunnel of

Ethan's palm and curled fingers but that qualified as taking more than Ethan offered. Big no-no. So he lay unmoving, only the stifled gasps he gave when Ethan's teasing fingers made silence impossible, betraying his desire.

"You're very well-behaved when you've just woken up," Ethan said into his ear, moving closer so his erection rode the cleft of Andy's ass. "I could get used to this."

"Me, too," Andy murmured back. "Waking up on my own isn't this much fun."

"No? But I bet you do this to yourself most mornings, hmm?"

"If I'm not running late and these days, I'm usually not."

Ethan released his grip. "Show me." He captured Andy's hand and drew it down. "Your hand on mine. Exactly how you'd do it."

"Oh God. Can I move now? Please?"

Ethan bit his shoulder sending a sweet jolt of pain through him. "Sure. Pretend I'm not here."

"Not possible."

That got him a chuckle. Cautiously at first, he began, guiding Ethan's hand over his shaft, sometimes dragging it over his balls, rolling them roughly. It wasn't an ideal angle or a practical way to jerk off but it was arousing as hell and romantic too.

After a while, Ethan pulled his hand out and shifted position, rolling Andy to his back and kneeling between his legs.

"Time to fly solo." Ethan grinned, taking hold of his erection. "Race you."

"What do I get when I win?" Andy asked, hand flying.

"Who says you get anything?"

"It's a race. There's a winner. Winners win stuff. It's why they're — uhn — why they're winners."

"I'll spank you until your ass is hot enough to fry eggs. But you won't win."

"Are you kidding — ?" Andy rolled his eyes, then watched the creamy spurts jet out, landing on his stomach, dripping over Ethan's hand. "You cheated."

"That's a serious accusation. And hands off." Ethan slapped Andy's wrist. "Time's up. You snooze, you lose."

"I can't finish?" Andy wailed, the lessons in submission he thought he'd learned by heart slipping away. "Please, sir!"

"You're forbidden to touch yourself. Hands behind your head."

Trying not to pout, Andy did as he was told, but he couldn't resist protesting. "It's unhealthy all this frustration. My balls are confused. Stop, start, yes, no."

"Poor things," Ethan said with a noticeable lack of sincerity. "Do you want a blow job or not?"

"What? Really?" Andy beamed at him. "I love you."

"Cupboard love. Or whatever the equivalent is for sex, not food."

"No, it's —"

"Button it. It puts me off."

Funny how it was okay for Ethan to interrupt *him*, Andy thought, but forgivingly since Ethan was licking his balls with strong, thorough laps.

A blow job from the man you loved bought a lot of forgiveness for trivial bad habits.

* * * *

They breakfasted by the water, sunlight bedazzling the blue waves, the cloudless sky a rich blue. The small restaurant was busy but their coffee cups were never left empty and the food was worth waiting for. A waiter brought them tart pink grapefruit juice, and French toast made with buttery brioche stuffed with juicy raspberries, drizzled with maple syrup and buried under a cloud of whipped cream infused with orange zest.

"Pick a boat we can sail on around the world." Andy gestured at the harbor with a laden fork.

"I get seasick," Ethan confessed. "Love the ocean, but only from the shore."

"You're kidding me!"

"Nope. We had a family vacation on Cape Breton once and went whale watching. I was fine for the first ten minutes, then the captain opened up the engine and we skipped over the water like a stone." Ethan mimed it, hand rising then slapping the table. "Bam, bam, bam. Banged my elbow against the side and thought I'd fractured it. Then we got to the whales and he turned the engine off. Three seconds later, the boat wallowed, lurching from side to side. There were a lot of whales, but all I remember is dragging a little girl away from the bucket so I could throw up in it. Not my finest hour."

Andy was laughing so much he had to finish Ethan's juice and his to calm down. "That's hilarious. How old were you?"

"Ten. Now stop laughing."

"Can't."

"Try."

Andy gave one last snicker and sobered up. "Sorry. I—" His phone beeped and he pulled it out. "Hang on. Let me see if it's urgent." He read the text and blew out an aggravated breath. "It's from Gary, asking if we can do my birthday drinks on the Saturday instead. He's been speaking to people and Friday doesn't work for anyone. What the hell?"

"Is it a problem?" Ethan asked. "We can spread the celebration out over the weekend and you and I can do something on the actual day."

Andy brightened. "Yeah? That would be kind of cool, I guess." He grimaced. "Unless we're both unemployed by then and there's nothing to celebrate."

"It'll still be your birthday."

"True." Andy speared the last raspberry on his plate and ate it. "I'm so full. This isn't diet food."

"It won't hurt you once in a while." Ethan picked up the bill. "I'll pay this and meet you by the car."

"I can get it."

"My treat," Ethan said firmly. He did let Andy pay for some things, but more often than not Andy was left shoving his wallet back in his pocket. That was something they needed to discuss but not now. Too much hung over them to focus on the details of their relationship.

Ethan was a while returning and Andy wandered to the path bordering the shore, searching idly for interesting pebbles without any luck. Hearing his name called, he jogged back to the car.

"I'm here. Where to now?"

"Charlotte called." Ethan's voice was flat and cool. "She wants to see us in an hour."

"Shit." Andy swallowed, genuinely afraid he was about to lose his breakfast. "Ethan, don't let her fire you!"

"She has no grounds to fire either of us."

"Doesn't matter. If she wants us gone, we're history."

Ethan drew him in for a hug, a seagull swooping around their heads squawking mournfully. Andy hoped it wasn't an omen. "Legally, we could fight it, but—"

"But working there after that would suck," Andy finished, then yelped when Ethan slapped his ass. "I know. I interrupted."

"I'm going to think of something to break you of that habit," Ethan said darkly. "It's getting worse."

"Yes, sir." Andy rested his forehead on Ethan's shoulder, breathing in the scent of warm, clean Ethan, nerves and stomach settling. "I'm in a rush. Want to get to the end of the sentence too soon."

"If you did that on stage, you'd be in trouble." Ethan chuckled. "Poor Juliet would ask, 'Romeo, Romeo, wherefore art thou—?' and you'd chime in 'Romeo' and piss her off so much she'd marry Paris."

"She'd get to live if she did."

"True." Ethan stroked the back of Andy's head. "Come on. Let's go home. I want to change into a suit for this."

Home. The word conjured up an image of Ethan's place now. Like falling in love with the man, that shift had been gradual. If Ethan asked him to move in, Andy thought he'd agree now. He wouldn't be leaving Henry in the lurch. Mahito was making noises about having plenty of room for Henry at his place.

Something to consider.

On the way to the hotel, Ethan wearing a charcoal gray suit, a pale gray shirt, and a deep purple tie, Andy texted Henry about the plans for his birthday, getting a reply within minutes agreeing to the date change. That done, he stared out of the window, people-watching, mind blank.

Instead of going through the staff door, Ethan led him through the lobby. "We can get to Charlotte's office this way and I don't want to talk to anyone."

"I wouldn't mind talking to Niall," Andy said. "With my fists."

"Calm down, tiger."

"Well, okay, I wouldn't punch him, but it's a tempting idea."

"Can't argue with that."

It was odd being in the hotel as neither staff nor guest. Andy had the sensation of being invisible, yet targeted by gaze. He half-expected a security guard to challenge them, though common sense told him that was unlikely.

Outside Charlotte's office, his nerves returned, but he had Ethan with him now and that helped. Ethan was a solid presence, his annoyance simmering but cloaked in an icy calm. It must be killing him to be in this position and guilt threaded through Andy's panic. Reminding himself Ethan was in favor of their relationship, Andy followed Ethan into the office.

Charlotte was dressed in a dark red suit that sent the same message as Ethan's—*I'm strong. I'm powerful. Don't fuck with me.*

She greeted them with a half-smile and waved them into two chairs in front of her desk. "Thank you for coming in. I'll keep this brief. I've completed my investigation into this situation and I'm happy to say that other than the original complainant, I can find no one else who feels your relationship affects your work adversely or has a negative impact on their jobs and working conditions."

"I see," Ethan said neutrally.

"I'm still not happy about the two of you working together."

Why the hell not? trembled on Andy's lips but remained unspoken. He'd been told to keep quiet by Ethan and that was one order he'd obey. He didn't trust himself not to screw things up.

"Understandable," Ethan agreed.

"But I have no grounds—or desire—to terminate your employment. In your case, Ethan, I'd fight tooth and nail to keep you. You're a valued employee." She gave Andy a look that qualified as apologetic in the loosest sense of the word. "That's no reflection on your performance. Ethan's exceptional."

Andy found his voice, "You don't need to tell me."

Charlotte grinned. An honest-to-God grin. "I'm sure. Now what I propose is this. There's nowhere to move Andy, but there is an opening for you, Ethan. John retires in three months. How would you feel about taking over as deputy hotel manager, reporting directly to me?"

Andy had been at the hotel long enough to grasp the significance. Deputy Manager? That was a huge promotion.

"There are other people more qualified than me." Cracks appeared in Ethan's composure. "I won't deny I'd welcome the challenge, but—"

Apparently, no one had given Charlotte the memo about not interrupting Ethan. "And that's it in a nutshell. You see it as a challenge. An opportunity, not a pay rise. That's the kind of person I want to work with. You can think it over." Her gaze drew Andy in. "Talk it over, too, of course. There's no rush to give me an answer. Until then, since everyone seems fine with the current situation, it can continue. If you decide not to take the position, we'll need to discuss it further."

Ethan's glance at her was wryly amused. Andy wasn't surprised. If Charlotte wanted Ethan working with her, she'd applied the subtlest of pressures to push him into place. Not blackmail, no, but a glint of steel showing.

"I'll give you an answer in the next few days," Ethan said.

"Good." She passed him a folder. "The contract and relevant details are in there for you to look over. Now I suggest you both get back to work. There's been enough time wasted on this nonsense."

"What about Niall?" Andy asked, blurting out the words against his better judgment.

"He decided his future lies elsewhere," Charlotte said blandly. "Under the circumstances, I waived the need for him to serve out his notice. You'll be shorthanded, Ethan, but I'm sure you'll manage."

"Count on it." Ethan stood, tucking the folder under his arm, then extending his hand to Charlotte, who shook it briskly.

Andy didn't offer his hand. He was about as relevant to this conversation as roller skates on a duck.

Chapter Twenty

"Give me a clue where we're going so I know how to dress." Andy studied his closet as if he had a wide range of options, which he didn't.

"Wear anything." Ethan poked Andy's bed. "This mattress sags. Doesn't it make your back ache?"

Andy took out a pair of jeans with holes in strategic places even he didn't dare wear out clubbing after one of the holes had ripped a crucial inch too much. "I'm used to it. These?"

"Only if you plan on eating dinner standing up after I've fucked you raw. And you won't have to suffer it much longer."

A pleasant tingle went through him at the reminder he was moving in with Ethan next weekend and the promise of rough sex. He was so easy when it came to Ethan. Total pushover. "I could wear them next time we stay in."

"Excellent idea." Ethan pursed his lips. "It's surreal talking to you like this five minutes after assuring your parents I've got your best interests at heart."

Andy hid a snicker with a cough. He'd had to drag Ethan over to his laptop where his parents were waiting on Skype to meet him, but once face to face with them, Ethan had done and said enough to make a great impression. "I think they know I have sex. They don't like to think about it, but they know."

"Change the subject."

"Sir, yes, sir." He snapped off a salute, grinning when Ethan gave him a hard stare. "Can't get mad at me on my birthday."

"I have a long memory."

Andy finished dressing, still curious about Ethan's plans. A meal out, followed by lots of sex sounded fine to him, but Ethan had refused to share any details at all, telling Andy he'd be by for him at three. Three was too late for lunch and too early for dinner or a show. Being told to wear what he wanted made it unlikely Ethan had an outdoor activity planned.

"You're too good at keeping secrets," he complained. "A hint? One?"

"How about no, none?"

Andy pouted, partially mollified by the kiss he got on his lips and the slap delivered to his ass. "Fine. I'll let you surprise me."

"Somehow I thought you would, since you don't have a choice in the matter."

They drove through the city, discussing Andy's impending move and Ethan's promotion, which he'd accepted after making Charlotte wait a few days. Ethan said it was to give him time to read over his contract, but Andy suspected a power play. Not his business. The atmosphere at work had settled down after the shock of learning Ethan would be leaving the department. Andy had been blamed, but in a good-natured way, and Amanda was returning from maternity leave to take Ethan's place, which pleased everyone.

And now it was his birthday and Andy refused to let anything dim the dazzle.

Pulling up at the staff parking lot for the hotel came close. "What're we doing here?" He groaned. "Don't tell me you forgot something vitally important that needs signing?"

"No."

"If it's a surprise party, I wasn't joking when I said I hated them. I do. I hate them."

"I heard you the first time you ranted and you know I'd never do that to you."

"So why are we here?"

"I need to pick up your gift. I left it in my office."

"Oh!" Relaxing, Andy settled back. "Well, you don't need me."

"Yes, I do. Out. Come on."

Once in his office, Ethan rummaged around in his desk then took out an envelope. "Happy Birthday, Andrew."

Andy took the envelope from him. It was too heavy to contain paper. He saw the edges of a card. A gift card? Not imaginative, but maybe Ethan wasn't used to buying for a boyfriend. He ripped open the envelope and drew out a room key, glinting gold.

"I don't—what is this?"

Ethan checked his watch. "From now until noon tomorrow, we're booked into one of the Elements. Air, to be precise. We can go out later if you like, or we can stay there until they kick us out. Your choice."

Stunned, incredulous, Andy glanced at the key, then Ethan. "But they were booked! You said—"

"It wasn't a lie," Ethan told him. "They were. And one of the suites was booked for one night by me."

Andy launched himself at Ethan. "You're the best fucking boyfriend in the world. Seriously." He kissed Ethan exuberantly. "And the Air suite? If I'd had to choose, it would've been that one."

"Good to know." Ethan kissed him, a teasing flirt of a kiss. "Ready?"

"We can go in there?"

"Yeah. I checked us in, took care of everything. And Henry packed a bag for you earlier, so you've got something to change into and a toothbrush."

"You let Henry pack for me? Have you seen him?"

"He was choosing from your wardrobe, so how wrong could he go?"

"Good point." A thought occurred to him. "Is this why everyone was too busy to party with me today?"

"I might have called around and asked them to shift it to tomorrow," Ethan admitted. "I couldn't get the room—any of them—tomorrow. This was a sudden cancellation and I snapped it up."

"Hey, I'm not complaining," Andy assured him. "Not one little bit. Except…"

"What is it?"

"I know how much those suites cost. We're talking crazy amounts of money."

"Staff discount," Ethan said succinctly. "Don't worry about it."

For some people, that might've taken the gloss off. For Andy, it was a relief to know Ethan hadn't blown a couple of weeks' wages on a bed for the night.

The private elevator opened directly into the lobby of the suite with another door to open after that.

"Normally we'd get taken up here and shown around, offered all kinds of amenities, but I wanted to show them to you myself." Ethan inserted the key, then opened the huge double doors with a push. "Partly because I plan on getting you naked soon too."

"Holy shit." Andy stood on the threshold, taking in the view. "I can't do it. Suppose I break something? Or spill a drink?"

"Someone once brought their vintage Triumph up here and changed the oil a few feet from where you're standing. Another guest let four puppies with the runs loose in the place. Trust me, even if we do spill a drink or two, no one will mind. Not that I plan on it." Ethan took his hand. "Come in. It's yours. Happy Birthday."

"It's ours," Andy corrected him, allowing himself to be towed forward and the doors closed behind him. "This is… It's spectacular."

The photographs in the brochure were carefully angled to hint at the room's luxuries, not reveal them, he realized. He'd known the color scheme was blue, white, and silver and a huge fireplace dominated one wall, set into a crystal surround that ran from floor to ceiling, glittering in the sunlight. He hadn't known the bed was suspended in midair. Okay, it was an illusion, but when he first looked up, that was his initial impression. The space was huge, split into two floors, much like Ethan's loft in a way. The bedroom was open, reached by two staircases leading up from the sitting area curved until they met to form a balcony and made out of translucent material shot through with silver. The bed rested on a floor of the same substance, easily a foot thick, but ethereal, swirled through with white and silver, as if a cloud supported the furniture.

The sheets and quilt were white, with seven cushions arranged against the pillows. They were the colors of the rainbow but muted, washed to a bare hint of the shades, playfully elegant.

Andy stood and looked around. "There's a piano. There's a freaking piano in here."

"Do you play?"

"No."

"Pity."

He kept looking—floor-to-ceiling windows opening onto emptiness and a spectacular view of the mountains, sky blue drapes remotely controlled and pale gray carpet so lush and thick he wanted to walk on it barefoot and feel it yield under his feet. Chairs, tables, lamps scattered around so anyone wanting to sit by the fire or look out of the window could do so in comfort.

"The TV's hidden behind the mirror," Ethan told him, gesturing at a wall. "Gaming system, music, anything you can think of. Room service, of course, but, yeah, we get some freebies too."

He kicked off his shoes, Andy following suit, and they went to a table supporting a huge arrangement of flowers. Andy recognized irises and the pungent peppery sweetness of freesias, but the rest were new to him. Beside the flowers was a bowl of chocolates shaped like fruits, tiny strawberries and cherries, oranges, pears...

"They're hand-painted with white chocolate colored by fruit juices." Ethan picked up a lemon, eyes twinkling. "I won't ask you to slice this one."

Andy let Ethan pop it into his mouth and bit in. Soft centers were his favorite but they were sometimes cloyingly sweet. This was tart and refreshing—the cool center, liquid velvet. He made a sound so close to orgasmic he blushed.

"And champagne." Ethan twisted the bottle in the ice bucket toward him to read the label. "Nice."

"Did you see the shape of the ice?" Andy picked up a piece. "Stars!"

"Details," Ethan said. "It's all about the details."

Andy shook his head. "I'm overwhelmed. I'm freaking out here."

"Nope. Not allowed." Ethan tapped Andy's chin. "You're in your home, for today and tomorrow at least. Run around. Bounce on the bed. Take a bath."

"Can I do any of those naked?"

"I'd definitely advise it when it comes to the bath."

Andy stripped off his jacket. His shirt. Unzipped, peeled off, then discarded until he was naked, Ethan watching him, a familiar hunger darkening his eyes.

"Don't feel so freaked out now."

"Good," Ethan said softly.

Andy went over to the windows, crossing acres of thick carpet to get to them. Standing with his breath clouding the glass, the distant mountains called to him.

"I feel as if I could step forward and take off."

"Yeah. I was glad you said heights didn't bother you when we were in the mountains."

"I don't think I could jump out of a plane, but this is incredible."

"I'm enjoying the view." The caress his ass received made it clear Ethan wasn't looking out of the window. He leaned against Ethan's chest, his cock, rising and filling, less from arousal than pure delight. He wanted Ethan to stroke that hardness. Instead, he got the cool touch of metal when Ethan took out a cock ring and slid it into place.

"What the hell?"

"Today's your day. Ask me to take it off and I will, but if it stays on, we play the way we always do."

"By your rules."

"Yes."

"When have I ever had a problem with that?" Andy turned in the circle of Ethan's arms. "I love you like this. Love *you*." He kissed Ethan then slid to his knees, needing the comfort of submission. He wrapped his arms around Ethan's legs, holding on, face pressed against Ethan's groin, breathing in the scent of his clothing and the overlay of aroused male. "Trust you."

Ethan's only answer was a light downward tug on Andy's hair. He clasped the back of Andy's neck, then squeezed it. "Ready for your birthday spanking?"

"Yes, sir."

"So you're twenty-five. That's not many. We'll have to spread them out."

Five by the fireplace, his ass pointed at the leaping flames, on his hands and knees, Ethan turning his left cheek scarlet with a series of slaps. Five more in the sybaritic bathroom, again on his left cheek, standing, facing his reflection in a long mirror, hands behind his head, legs spread, watching his face twist, hearing his soft gasps. Another handful braced against the table with the hospitality gifts, his mouth crammed full of chocolate he was forbidden to swallow until Ethan finished decorating his right cheek. Five more on the stairs leading up to the bedroom, delivered as he walked with Ethan behind him, urging him on.

"Over my knee for the last ones," Ethan said. "Kneel on the bed. I want to see you there."

Andy positioned himself, knees spread, arms behind him. He was already floating without the illusion the bedroom provided, the spanking making him feel at home here. He watched Ethan undress, glorying in the sight of the lean, wiry body. Ethan flexed his right hand and Andy shivered with expectation.

Once over Ethan's knee, eyes closed, he could've been anywhere. It didn't matter. All he cared about was the slow beat of flesh on flesh when Ethan delivered the final five slaps plus one to grow on that drew a groan from him. It was so fucking perfect that last slap— hard and loud and strong—and he was all those things too.

Cock ring removed, they watched the sunset paint the mountains with rose and shadow, as they drank champagne mixed with freshly squeezed orange juice, the pulp sieved out because Andy hated getting shreds of it in his teeth. He learned a guest could be specific with room service and they didn't bat an eye—or mind when told to leave their delivery outside the door because when it arrived, Andy was tied hand and foot, a glass dildo deep in his ass, Ethan's cock filling his mouth.

They spent hours making love without reaching a climax. Ethan didn't come either, pulling out, bringing them back from the edge over and over. They ate, more room service delivered promptly, announced with the most discreet of taps on the door, and they soaked in a hot tub on the glassed-in balcony. Watched a movie with a bowl of fluffy, buttery, salted popcorn drizzled with caramel between them and never stopped touching, kissing, fucking.

Andy went from begging to come to begging for this to never end. Arousal suffused every cell of his body, a spark of desire lit in a thousand places. Ethan hurt him in delicious new ways, bringing out clamps and a flogger from his overnight bag, and finally, when Andy's skin was striped red from shoulders to calves, tingling, alive with sensation, he murmured, "Time. I'm going to drain your balls. Get every last drop out of you."

Past speech, supine on the bed, Andy nodded. He expected his ass to be filled again, crammed with Ethan's fingers, rounded and stretched by his cock, but Ethan slid his hands under Andy's ass, raised it and bent his head.

Ethan licked the hot, bruised, used skin with infinite care, tracing the shape of Andy's hole with the tip of his tongue then pushing deep inside. Forbidden to come for hours, Andy hesitated, body conditioned to pull back from the edge, not step over, but Ethan gave him no choice.

With a wail, torn apart by the intensity of the climax rolling over him, Andy surrendered, losing himself in pleasure, but never losing his connection with Ethan. Ethan moved, capturing the head of Andy's cock in his mouth, prolonging the orgasm with flicks of his tongue until he'd swallowed the last drop.

It was a while before Andy could speak, his throat aching as if he'd screamed, his breathing ragged. "Ethan."

"Right here."

"That was incredible."

Ethan kissed the hollow of his hip. "I'm not done with you yet."

"Can't take any more."

"You will," Ethan said. "You'll take everything I give you."

Andy groaned, heartbeat quickening when his body responded to the dark promise. When Ethan told him something in that tone of voice, he'd learned to believe it.

Ethan slid a finger deep into Andy's hole then added another, and desire Andy had thought slaked demanded more. "Well?"

"Yes. Yes, Ethan." Andy moaned, fucking himself on two fingers, then three, eyes closed, exhaustion forgotten. "God, please. Anything you want. Need you. Love you. Love you so fucking much."

Ethan replaced fingers with his cock. "Love you too, sweetheart. Still going to make you scream."

* * * *

It was three in the morning. Andy had slept for an hour after a shower, then had been woken by the taste of raspberries when Ethan dripped vodka onto his lips. He licked them clean, smiling muzzily up. "Sir?"

"This is what you'd been drinking that first night."

He nodded. "Do you like it?"

Ethan dipped his fingers into the glass, then held them over Andy's lips to drip. After setting the glass down, he drew his tongue over Andy's mouth. "With you in the mix, yeah."

"If you're planning to fuck me again—"

"I am, but not now. I want to hold you. Come here." Ethan lay beside him and drew him close, caressing skin that still bore the marks of the flogger in places, though most of the stripes had faded. Ethan had whipped him a lot, but lightly. "Enjoying your birthday? Anything you want? Night or day, I can get it for you."

"Got everything I need right here," Andy assured him. He brushed the scars on Ethan's back. He'd touched them a dozen times, knew their shape, but he'd never asked about them after that first time. Now he lingered, kneading the mended flesh. "Does it hurt when I do this?"

"No." Ethan leaned his forehead against Andy's, breath soft against his face. "Are you still curious about them?"

"Little bit," Andy admitted. "You in a bar fight...doesn't seem likely."

"I was stupid. I saw someone my age getting beat up by three guys and tried to help. Big mistake. Turned out he deserved everything he got and more. Drug dealer, who made his money targeting kids on the playground."

Sometimes the world was a scary place filled with monsters. Andy shuddered, needing to show the physical expression of his disgust. "What an *asshole*."

"Yeah. But I only found that out later. So I waded in, got a fist in the face. Like in a movie, I went flying. Lot of glass on the floor, pointy side up, and I landed on it."

"Shit."

"Not a great Friday night, no. Taught me to ask questions before picking sides, though."

As life lessons went, it had flaws. "You don't always have time for that. Sometimes you need to react and trust your instincts. You tried to help someone and I know you'd do it again. It's the way you are."

"Yeah, well, I might take a second look first." Ethan pulled back. "The scars don't bother me if they don't bother you."

There was a lot he could've said, but he settled for a simple, "They don't." Ethan seemed to appreciate the lack of an eloquent speech, if his warm kiss was anything to go by.

Andy hadn't planned to sleep again, but somehow, between one breath and the next, it was morning with Ethan waking him to see the sun rise.

Chapter Twenty-One

Checking out nearly killed him. "I'm spoiled now," he said mournfully, after using the bathroom one last time. No need to slip a freebie bar of soap into Ethan's overnight bag. A full-size set of all the toiletries was provided for him, courtesy of the hotel, and as for the decadent robe, if he wanted it, he could have it. A guest of the Elements didn't need to resort to routine pilfering.

Though Andy guessed if he tried to walk out with one of the *objet d'arts* scattered around, his credit card might take a hit.

"Too good to move in with me now?"

Was that a hint of anxiety showing? Andy shook his head, wandering over to the window for a last, long look at the incomparable view. "This is a fantasy. *Loved* it. God, you have no idea how many photos I took to send to my mom, but your place is home — or it will be when I've given it that lived-in look."

"I wouldn't count on my current indulgent mood lasting long if you do."

"Relax, I'll be—" His phone rang and he broke off to answer it. "H'lo. Oh hi, Paige."

"Want a belated birthday gift?" his agent asked with the seductive purr in her voice that meant she was about to make money.

"Sure." Ethan drifted away, setting the room to rights, tweaking a cushion here, a drape there and giving Andy some privacy.

"You got the part."

"What part? I didn't audition for anything."

"The three-episode part in Hell Falls. They went with Ashton Henderson because, well, I have my own ideas about that, but I have it on good authority the lead wanted you. She said you clicked with her."

"We had good chemistry." Andy liked her. Lexie was a rising star still close enough to the days of obscurity to feel cautious about her future, but secure enough to be generous with a nobody. She'd given him some good advice about career paths and steered him away from the craft services potato salad. "I don't get it. They changed their minds?"

"Not exactly." She drew out the words. "Henderson checked into rehab last night."

"So they went for second best?"

"And you can check *your* ego," Paige said sharply. "This is show business. It's cutthroat, competitive and you need a skin that makes a rhino's look like tissue paper if you're going to make it. Are you in or out?"

"I—" A month ago, the answer would've been simple. Now though... Three episodes meant three weeks off work at least. He didn't have much leave accrued and if he took the role and it led to something else, what then? And if he handed in his notice to play the part and after this came nothing, he'd lost everything.

Ethan appeared in front of him, scowling. No more working with Ethan. Okay, they'd be in different departments soon, but even so. No more being part of a team, a trained, competent team dedicated to the twin goals of happy guests and a smooth-running hotel.

"I don't think I want the part."

He got that far, then Ethan took the phone, stunning him to silence. Who did that? Seriously, who *did* that? "This is Ethan Mason, Andrew's employer. I need him for a moment. Please ignore that last statement. He'll call you back in a few minutes."

"What the hell?" Andy said through his teeth after Ethan ended the call. He snatched back his phone, clutching it in a shaking hand then shoving it into his pocket. "This is my decision, not yours. You can't overrule me, hang up on my agent—"

"Yes, I can." Ethan's calm was absolute, unshaken by Andy's outrage. "You gave me that right. You asked me to take control of your life."

"Not for things like this!"

"No? That's not the way I remember it." Ethan raised his hand then drew it back without touching Andy. "I wanted to be in charge when it came to sex. That was it. You wanted more. More than I wanted to give, but I've always been easily swayed when it comes to you. From day one. And I learned to enjoy it. I've eased back in a lot of areas and you haven't noticed. When you could fly solo, I took a back seat. When was the last time I quizzed you about your food or gave you hell for not exercising? There's no need. You know what you should do now and you handle it."

"You're bored of babysitting me, is that it? The novelty's worn off?"

"No. When it comes to you, I can't see me ever getting tired of being the one you trust to guide you. But don't complain when I take the authority you gave me and exercise it. Why did you turn down a part?"

"It's that three-episode part. I couldn't do it and stay at work and if I leave now, after all the trouble I've caused—"

"People come and go all the time," Ethan said. "Yeah, keeping your job open wouldn't be possible, but if this role doesn't lead to anything else, you get another part-time job until it does. I have contacts in a dozen hotels. I could get you a position with a few calls, no problem at all."

"But I wouldn't be working with you." Andy experienced a wrench of loss again at the thought of it. "Ethan, I like being here. I like what I do. Acting—it's a dream. Sure, I got this part through luck—if some poor guy with a drug habit is a piece of luck—but it's nothing I can count on. I can't trust it and I'm not sure I'm good enough to make it."

Ethan scratched his jaw, the scrape of fingers over smoothly shaved skin creating a whisper of sound. "But you love acting. You said it was what you were. What drove you."

Hearing his words repeated made him realize how pretentious they were. "Maybe you've changed more about me than you thought. That's not who I am now."

Color rose in Ethan's face, hot and vivid. "I don't want to be responsible for killing your dreams, your ambition! God, Andrew, don't put that on me!"

"Why not? You did. But I'm not blaming you for it. I'm grateful."

Ethan shook his head, eyes blank, and backed away. "Take the part," he said, voice harsh. "Take it and see what it's like. This is your big break—"

"It's a small role on a cheesy show that's probably going to get cancelled and my character dies horribly. It's not all that. Here at the hotel, I have something real going on—a future I can rely on." He stepped forward, closer to Ethan, where he wanted to be. "I have you. Ethan. If you can't see I've hit the jackpot right there, you need to look again."

"Take this part. *Please.*" Ethan caught his hand in a painfully tight grip. "I'll arrange it so you can keep your job. Pull strings, call in a favor or two."

"Save them for when you need them," Andy said. "I'm quitting the acting career. My decision, made by me. Accept it."

Ethan released Andy's hand and folded his arms across his chest, drawing himself up, the picture of a determined man. "That's not going to happen."

"I'm not very good at it." A difficult admission, but the truth. "Think about it. At my interview I played the role of an experienced bartender. Did I convince you? Even for a minute?"

Ethan smiled reluctantly. "No."

"Yeah. That's what most people say when I go to auditions. I'm one of thousands out there and I'm mediocre at best."

"I accept it's a competitive field but being offered this part proves you're more than that." Ethan touched Andy's arm, caressing it lightly. "Can't you take this role at least? You won't need to be on set every minute. You could do some shifts and I'd cover for you."

It was tempting, but it would make walking away from that world even harder. "I take the part and I'm hooked again, shoving quarters into a slot machine always thinking a big win's waiting. It's not. Just years of trying to get somewhere and if I did, would I like it? The pressure breaks people."

"It wouldn't break you." Ethan took Andy's hand, this time a loose clasp, stroking Andy's knuckles with his thumb. "I wouldn't let it."

"Why won't you let me do this?" Andy jerked his hand free and scrubbed violently at his hair with a wordless cry of frustration. "I don't get it! I'm being mature and sensible and—"

"You're scared," Ethan said. "Of trying and failing. You worry too much about what people think. If you called your friends, what would they tell you to do?"

Andy snorted. "Take the part. No-brainer. They want to be able to say they know someone famous and they want me to get something I've dreamed about for years."

"Family?"

"The same, I guess. They've always supported me, even though they know it's a risky career."

Ethan nodded, lip caught in his teeth for a moment before he released it. "Everyone in your life who matters wants you to do this and you don't. I'm not saying yours isn't the most important opinion, but I'm saying you need to examine your reasons for walking away before you take that step."

"Gah!" Andy swung away, heading for the windows again. The vastness drew him, reducing his problems in scale. Water, mountains, sky and the swirling wind…and he was behind glass, surrounded by rented luxury with a decision to make.

He waited for Ethan to speak again, persuasive, sensible words to make his path clear, but though he was conscious of Ethan's gaze on him, Ethan stayed where he was, giving Andy space and silence.

"You've seen me fail so many times," Andy said. "Sometimes I wonder if you get off on me being someone you can help."

"In a way, but if you think I'd be happy for you to stay a failure, dependent on me, you're wrong."

"If I do this and nothing comes of it but a shitload of online criticism, fans hating me, reviewers saying I suck—"

"Some will. You know that."

"It will hurt." His voice was reduced to a whisper. "Ethan, it will hurt worse than anything."

"More than being plagued by what ifs and maybes a few years down the road?" Ethan joined him by the window and slung his arm around Andy's shoulders. "Failing hurts. Not trying doesn't avoid the pain. It's another form of failing."

"Listen to us being philosophical first thing in the morning." Andy gave a choke of laughter that turned into a sob. "Let's not make a habit of it, huh?"

"Sounds like a plan." Ethan tightened his arm. "Let me give you this, Andrew. I can't make it risk-free because, yeah, you might suck, but I can make sure you have a job waiting for you and I'm sure as hell not going anywhere."

"Promise?" Andy turned away from the view and found a different comfort close to hand in Ethan's cool gray eyes. "If I do this, I can't do it solo."

"You can, but you won't have to." Ethan patted Andy's ass over the bulge his phone made. "Make the call. We have to check out."

Paige answered after one ring, puzzled by the delay in accepting what she viewed as a windfall, but not inclined to scold. Andy suspected he could get away with a lot for the next few days where his agent was concerned. He arranged to visit later and let the pleasure of having a role soak in. God, he couldn't wait to tell everyone. Not by text. He'd wait until tonight when he could do it face to face and be hugged breathless.

"Time to go," Ethan said, breaking his reverie. "Do I have to drag you out or are you ready to go back to normal?"

"You've taken normal off the table." Andy blew out a breath. "I'm going to be on TV. Shit, that's unreal."

"You won't regret it." It was an order, delivered with flat certainty. Perfect reading of the line even if they knew Ethan couldn't guarantee that. Though he'd convinced Andy that the consequences of not trying would lead to deeper regrets, so maybe he could.

"Yes, sir."

"Are you ever going to stop calling me that?" Ethan asked, smiling at him.

"When it stops turning me on, sure — so probably never." Exuberance rising, dispelling his fears, Andy kissed him, wondering how Ethan still smelled the same even after using the hotel toiletries. "Best birthday ever. Staying here, getting the part — all of it — but I'm looking forward to moving in with you more."

Ethan ran his hand down Andy's back, a slow, possessive sweep. "Is that so?"

Doubt struck him. "If you're sure that's what you want. You're used to having the place to yourself and it might feel crowded with me underfoot messing it up. If you want to wait, I will. There's no rush."

He clamped his mouth shut before he talked his way out of what he wanted so desperately. Ethan's life was perfect, tailored like his suits. In the time they'd been together, Andy had disrupted it on many levels without meaning to. Every consequence flowing from their relationship had been a good one for Andy, but could Ethan say the same? He waited for Ethan's answer, surrounded by waiting silence, conscious of the slow, steady beat of Ethan's heart against his chest. The pause stretched beyond the limits of his patience but he waited.

"It would feel empty without you," Ethan said.

About the Author

Jane Davitt is English, and has been living in Canada with her husband, two children, and two cats, since 1997. Writing and reading are her main occupations but if she ever had any spare time she might spend it gardening, walking, or doing cross stitch.

Jane has been writing since 2005 and wishes she'd started earlier. She is a huge fan of SF, fantasy, erotica, and mystery novels and has a tendency to get addicted to TV shows that get cancelled all too soon.

She owns over 4,000 books, rarely gives any away, but is happy to loan them, and is of the firm opinion that there is no such thing as 'too many books'.

Jane Davitt loves to hear from readers. You can find her contact information, website details and author profile page at http://www.totallybound.com.

Totally Bound Publishing

Home of Erotic Romance